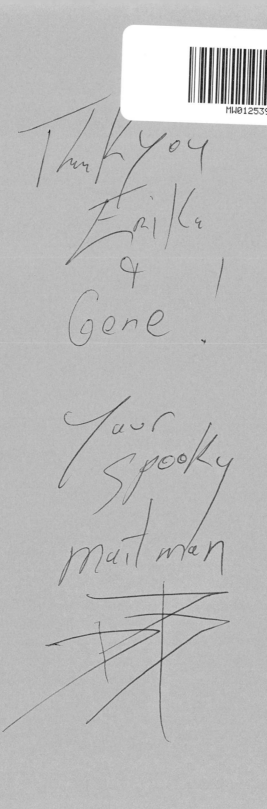

Thnk you
Erika
&
Gene .

Your
Spooky

mail man

REROUTED

RE>ROUTED

DANIEL BRYANT · STORIES

The Porcupine's Quill

Library and Archives Canada Cataloguing in Publication

Title: Rerouted : stories / Daniel Bryant.

Names: Bryant, Daniel, 1963– author.

Description: The "Re" in Rerouted on title page is printed backwards with letters reversed. | Short stories.

Identifiers: Canadiana 2019008295X | ISBN 9780889844216 (softcover)

Classification: LCC PS8603.R93 R47 2019 | DDC C813/.6 — dc23

1   2   3   •   21   20   19

Published by The Porcupine's Quill, 68 Main Street, PO Box 160,
Erin, Ontario NOB 1TO. http://porcupinesquill.ca

Edited by Chandra Wohleber.
Represented in Canada by Canadian Manda.
Trade orders are available from University of Toronto Press.

We acknowledge the support of the Ontario Arts Council and the Canada Council for the Arts for our publishing program. The financial support of the Government of Canada is also gratefully acknowledged.

Canada Council for the Arts   Conseil des arts du Canada

Canada

ONTARIO ARTS COUNCIL
CONSEIL DES ARTS DE L'ONTARIO
an Ontario government agency
un organisme du gouvernement de l'Ontario

Ontario
Ontario Media Development Corporation

CONTENTS

D E A D W A L K

deadwalk: noun. *Postal term: a section of a letter carrier's route where no mail is delivered because (a) the letter carrier has delivered to those houses and businesses earlier in the route, (b) the houses and businesses belong to another letter carrier's route, or (c) there are no houses or businesses. Slang: a systemic failure of the planning process. Repetition without meaning.*

It was hot: thirty-two Celsius with a humidex that made it feel closer to forty. It was a moist, humid hell.

At least tomorrow was Friday.

Joel's blue-and-white-striped polyester shirt clung to his skin like plastic wrap. The bright red double satchel, cinched tightly at the waist and across the chest, was crammed with addressed advertising, unaddressed advertising, magazines, and bills. There were very few letters.

Joel Wozzeck had been working at the post office as a relief carrier for five years, covering routes when someone was on vacation, sick, or on long-term disability. Most of his co-workers at Station Y were much older and planning retirement. Joel was not planning retirement. Joel could retire when he died. Right now, he was focused on retiring his student debt. Five years ago, he had dropped out of university before finishing his PhD, and he still owed a lot of money. The anxiety kept him up at night. Sometimes he had very dark thoughts.

Joel had covered Route L7 the longest. No one owned the route. No one wanted it. Joel didn't want it — although he didn't *not* want it either: the people were nice and the dogs were friendly, but it had a brutal deadwalk of two hundred metres before the last thirty houses.

It was a deadwalk past an abandoned tannery fronted by crumbling stone walls and vaguely offensive smells. It was a deadwalk past a brush-choked corridor of corroded hydro towers and constant electronic thrumming. It was a deadwalk of broken sidewalks and lurking rats. It was …

Rats.

Joel hated rats.

These rats were as bold as raccoons. Occasionally, he might see one or two sitting on their haunches on the sidewalk, watching impassively and waiting for *him* to scurry past.

It was an inversion of the natural order.

Joel looked at his sweat-soaked forearms. Blue veins bulged like wires beneath the skin.

He took a swig from his water bottle and continued walking.

Joel liked to think of himself as a machine: working without incident — no slips, no trips, no falls, no stress leaves, no sick days. Every morning up by four, at the sortation case by five, on the walk by nine. After the burnout of university, he welcomed the unthinking repetition of being a letter carrier. His mind wandered. His body worked. The opposite of graduate school.

Within the first six months, Joel dropped twenty pounds and stopped smoking. To compensate, he drank more. It was all about balance. His girlfriend at the time — ex-girlfriend now — disagreed.

Still, he needed to drop a few more pounds. The last forty were the hardest.

Joel skirted a dead rat that was half in the bushes and half on the sidewalk. Pink rivulets of flesh bloated out from the black fur.

Probably died from the inside out, thought Joel.

Like everything these days, thought Joel.

He walked a little faster.

His iPhone vibrated. He pulled it out of his breast pocket and clumsily swiped the screen a few times. His hands were too sweaty. The screen wavered with the message *Missed call.*

He was expecting a call, or more likely a text, from the ex about Socrates, their blue-eyed cockatoo. It was a custody battle of sorts, except that both wanted the other person to take custody.

Right now, the bird lived with him.

Socrates was a lot of work. Like her philosopher namesake, she was very inquisitive and liked to pick things apart, tearing them down to their essential Forms—a sturdy box of cereal with its enticing image of healthy raw ingredients became sugary shit scattered everywhere.

Unlike her philosopher namesake, the bird talked endlessly without always making sense.

Then again.

Joel put the phone back in his pocket.

The next house was metres away. Joel readied his double bundle of mail, cradling the oversized magazines and pamphlets in the crook of his left arm, and holding the lettermail in his left hand. He reached with his right hand into the satchel for a fistful of flyers. Some houses had a recycle bin beneath the mailbox. A few clever customers put up a sign with the words *Flyers here* and an arrow pointing into the deep blue bins.

It was vaguely funny the first time he saw one of those signs. Now it was simply depressing: all the trees cut down for pizza flyers and real estate ads, and then all the energy to recycle them into more pizza flyers and real estate ads.

#Eternalreturn. #Adnauseum. #Doomed.

'Hi Ms Evelyn,' Joel called out as he walked up the driveway.

Ms Evelyn Wickks glanced up from a tangle of rose bushes lining the walkway. A loose bouquet of vibrant yellow roses lay in a bundle by her feet.

'Hiya honey.' Ms Wickks got up and smoothed the front of her jeans.

Joel thought she must be in her early fifties but could pass for early forties. It looked like she had had a lot of work done around the face and neck. Her hair was bleached blond, laced with streaks of dark honey.

She was wearing a white blouse with no bra.

Sweat seeped into Joel's eyes and streamed past his lips. Burning torment and a salt lick.

Lot's wife.

Lot's lot.

'Any cheques today?' Evelyn's voice rasped. Her hands drifted to her hips.

Joel looked at her hands. The veins popped and threaded between bone and sinew.

Nicotine stained the fingernails.

Joel never saw Evelyn smoke.

'I'm afraid it's mostly junk mail today,' Joel said.

Joel handed over a fistful of flyers and one piece of actual mail. Evelyn always got interesting 'real' mail, usually from abroad. This envelope was covered with a few exotic-looking stamps: palm trees, splayed fruits, mustachioed men, a ziggurat. A couple of stamps were missing. Their empty spaces were saturated with royal blue, unlike the rest of the faded envelope. If Joel had been remotely interested in anything other than finishing the day and getting home, he might have been able to say where the letter came from, but he didn't care and so he couldn't say.

'Better than bills, I suppose.' Evelyn leafed through the glossy admail.

'Cheque's in the mail.' Joel smiled. The jokes were always the same with everybody on every route — always about money — getting it, owing it, wanting it. Recycled wit.

Evelyn was not really listening or even looking at him anymore. She turned the airmail envelope over and brought it closer to her face. She squinted. Joel remembered there was a seal on the back of the envelope. Unusual. It was reddish black with some weird animal figures pressed into the hard wax — nothing he recognized. Most 'wax' seals these days were made of plastic and embossed with a company logo or name. A marketing tool to upscale the pitch.

'Have a nice day.' Joel waved and walked away.

'Yes, sweetie. Have a nice day....' Evelyn's voice trailed off.

Joel strode to the next house, trying to remember if it had a mailbox or a door slot. Mailboxes were the best. Some mailboxes were better than others: the wider the lid, the deeper the trench, the easier the delivery.

Like giving birth, imagined Joel.

Unfortunately, this house had a door slot. He hated door slots. Every letter carrier hated door slots. They were little brass guillotines for your fingers. He creased the mail lengthwise and jammed it through with the palm of his hand.

He stepped back and cut across the lawn.

He was in full march and rhythm — step, swing, push, pull, drop, retreat. Already on the fifth house, he looked back at Evelyn and noticed she was lying face up on the sidewalk, her hands clutching the admail like a paper bouquet.

He hesitated, looked at his bundle of mail, and looked at Evelyn.

Jillian Hampstead twitched her curtains and watched the postman stop in front of her mail slot. The young man—Job, Joel, Joe, Jeff, something like that—looked back down the street while shuffling through white envelopes and brightly coloured flyers. He was stout like a lumberjack, with a shaved head and a bushy, dirt-coloured beard. Today he wore an undersized baseball cap. It perched on his head like a beak. Sweat rimmed the edges.

'Hmmph,' Jillian muttered.

The postman stopped, stepped back, scrambled down the stairs, and disappeared in a flurry of snapping button flaps and Velcro fasteners. Jillian's mail lay scattered on the porch.

'Hmmph,' Jillian muttered again.

The pub was crowded with fellow posties: fat, skinny, male, female, white, black, olive, ochre, blue.

'That walk is cursed,' Matt, the blue one, said cheerfully. He puckered his purple lips and guzzled down half his pint. Foam flecked his red beard. 'I knew Lester Keane, the station supervisor, who did it a long time ago. I tell you, something happened to him on that walk. No one's lasted on it for more than a month. They get all angsty and bugger out.'

Joel nodded and sipped his rum and coke. He was numb. After watching Evelyn's life ebb away on the sidewalk, he needed something stronger than a beer for his afternoon buzz.

'Yeah, I heard. He seems tightly wound,' Joel said.

'Tight ain't the half of it. The story goes, they found him one morning, under his sortation case, stabbing his palm with scissors ... safety scissors, mind you. Apparently, he'd been there all night. He became a supervisor soon after.'

Joel thought about Lester Keane. Lester was in his sixties—spindly, stooped, spittle mouthed—a flesh-and-blood Ichabod Crane.

Good honest work could do that to a person, thought Joel.

A few more letter carriers drifted in, and the noise level amped up. The Quill and Quotidian was *the* hangout for the Brothers and Sisters of Station Y. It was central to most of the routes and a short bus ride away from all the others. News of the death drew everyone today. The dark wood interior jostled with mugs of beer, sweat-stained blue-striped shirts, and bright red satchels. It was late afternoon.

Matt got up and staggered away. Lenora slid in.

'I've been meaning to ask.' Joel lowered his voice and tilted his head slightly toward Lenora. A delicate floral scent hung about her like an aura.

Joel inhaled again.

Joel asked, 'Why is Matt blue? You've been at the station for a long time. I'm embarrassed to ask anyone else, and I certainly don't want to ask him.'

'It's silver poisoning. He grew up downstream from a silver mine in Tennessee. Contaminated ground water, constant exposure—causes blue skin apparently.'

'Really?'

'Yeah, there might be some recessive gene lurking somewhere too. Just don't call him Papa Smurf.' Lenora giggled.

Joel watched Matt sit down with the two Trevors. Both Trevors were over six feet tall, lean, and wore wire-rim glasses. One was white. The other black. So as not to cause confusion, and more importantly, to avoid being labelled racist, everyone referred to them by their sexual orientation. White Trevor was gay, so everyone called him Gay Trevor—behind his back. Black Trevor was straight, so everyone called him Regular Trevor, or sometimes just Trev.

There were quite a few doppelgängers at the station—two Bobs, three Lauras, four Ians, another Joel. Everyone got differentiated according to some peculiar physical or social trait: Bob with the Lazy Eye, Laura with the Big Tits, Lesbian Laura, Tall Laura, Bald Ian, Young Ian, Italian Ian, Funny Joel.

Joel Wozzeck was not Funny Joel. That pissed him off no end.

Gay Trevor and Regular Trevor looked over at Unfunny Joel and nodded. Joel nodded back and raised his glass. The Trevors raised theirs. Joel winked for no particular reason other than to punctuate the exchange with a silent full stop. He returned to looking at his drink.

'Are you gonna book tomorrow off?' Lenora asked. 'It'd be legit. The supervisor won't hold it against you.'

'Nah.' Joel shook his head. 'I'd be stuck in my apartment with the bird, you know ... thinking about my mortality, or maybe its mortality. Best to keep moving ... keep that oxygen pumping through my gills.'

Lenora nodded. 'The wisdom of Shark Week.'

'You can learn a lot from TV.' Joel looked around the room and thought about all his postie friends — all fairly normal in a generic human sense — unremarkable, decent — no Icarus or Daedalus archetypes here. Joel thought about some of his past friends in the humanities department at university. They were ambitious and smart as hell. Joel thought about being ambitious and smart as hell, and that was about as far as he got. It was too much work.

On multiple big-screen TVs in the pub, Joel watched a series of images: the talking heads of sports celebrities, entertainment celebrities, business celebrities. The sound was off. He didn't need to hear them. They were all sociopathic overachievers: Satan's diaspora — challenging God, taking advantage of the status quo, making bags of money.

Joel had wanted to use that angle for his graduate thesis — 'Pop Culture and the Miltonic Universe' — but the prof had just looked at him without saying a word and went back to eating her salad.

Harsh.

If he ever had children, Joel would make sure they were unhappy and insecure so that they would be successful.

It was too late for him.

He blamed his parents.

Joel turned to Lenora. 'You have children?'

'Three girls. Had them way too young and way too fast.' Lenora smiled. 'The youngest, Sam, is in her first year at university studying humanities.'

Joel grimaced. *Been there. Done that. Still got the frosh T-shirt.*

'The other two live close by, have real careers. Sienna is a nurse. Amanda is a teacher. Love 'em. None of 'em married yet. Can't stop worrying about 'em. But not for the marrying part. Just, you know ... mom stuff.'

'Mom stuff.' Joel nodded. The rum and cola were making life pleasant again. Joel watched Lenora talk. She had nice lips. She was older than him by at least a decade but in much better shape.

She laughed a lot. He wondered if she laughed in bed.

Lenora stopped talking and looked at Joel quizzically.

'What? Sorry. I keep thinking about that woman dying.' Joel returned to staring at his glass and the frothy foam cola that lurked at the bottom.

Lenora touched his shoulder. 'Listen, you're welcome to come over to our place for dinner, if you like. My hubby won't mind. I'm sure he'll be glad to talk to a guy for once rather than a bunch of women. Mark's a big baseball fan. I don't mind watching a game now and then, but when he starts talking statistics my eyes glaze over.'

'Sure, I'd like that. I can stat with the best of 'em.' Joel motioned to the barkeep for another rum and coke. 'Just gotta check in on my cockatoo first.'

Joel never liked saying 'cockatoo'. He felt self-conscious, like he was trying to be subliminal. Throw in a few 'let's take that thought in a new direction/nude erection' and he would be 'that guy' at the bar: bad teeth, bad skin, bad intentions. Joel turned to Lenora and smiled. It was a tight, self-conscious smile.

Lenora smiled in return — open, sunny, all lips and teeth.

'Can I bring anything?' Joel asked.

'Just yourself,' she replied.

A few drinks later, Joel stumbled toward the bright brass handle of the front door. He found it easier to navigate the seething crowd if he focused on a shiny fixed object in the distance.

The brass knob was his North Star.

Outside, the humid air embraced him. Within seconds, he was sweaty and uncomfortable. Joel thought he saw Lester Keane on the other side of the road waiting by the bus stop. Joel waved. Lester, or his doppelgänger, did not wave back but continued staring straight at, or perhaps through, Joel.

Joel's apartment was on the southeast corner of the third floor of a brownstone walk-up on Main Street. His bedroom window looked south over a small grey gravel parking lot. His living room window faced east against an unruly maple that blocked the sun during the summer, then thrashed against the window with dead grey limbs for the rest of the year. Joel thought it was an apt metaphor for life. His ex-girlfriend thought it was an apt metaphor for *their* life.

Socrates, the blue-eyed cockatoo, did not care for metaphors. The tree was a tree. In the morning, it cast shadows on the parquet floor and Socrates danced among the twirling black leaves. In the afternoon, Socrates danced at the window in front of the green leaves with the soft sage underside. Not complicated at all.

Sometimes Socrates thought about escaping toward the light outside. The screen was flimsy and the fat bearded one sometimes forgot to close the window all the way, but Socrates was comfortable in her cave. It was a paradise full of cane palms, bromeliads, ficus, and dieffenbachia. It was an all-you-can-eat buffet of crackers and nuts.

The fat bearded one was also fond of crackers and nuts. A little too fond. He would eat six to her one.

The golden mean of gluttony.

Outside in the hallway, Joel fumbled with his keys. The hall reeked of turmeric, galangal, togarashi, and za'atar. The building had an eclectic mix of immigrant families and singleton hipsters. Everyone except Joel punched above their weight when it came to exotic ingredients in the kitchen. Joel was a salt-and-pepper kind of guy — and then again, mostly salt.

'Loveyouloveyou,' Socrates shrieked as Joel pushed open the door.

The hybrid musk of bird shit and rainforest slipstreamed into the hall. Joel gulped and ran to open the living room window.

His neighbours probably hated him — the hipsters because he was harshing their culinary buzz; the immigrants because it reminded them of what they'd left behind, and maybe why.

'Loveyouloveyou.' Socrates shifted from one foot to the other on her wooden perch. Her sulphur-coloured crest fanned back and forth. She cocked her head and fixed him with one of her light blue eyes. Joel was fascinated by the fact that birds saw the world through parallel vision. He imagined that it would be like one of those crazy art house movies where two separate frames play out their narrative on the same screen — but with more coherence.

'Love you too.' Joel unlocked the cage and stepped back into the kitchen, grabbing one cracker for Socrates and a handful for himself. He heard Socrates's wings flap, then the clack, clack, clack of her claws on the parquet flooring.

Socrates could fly but she preferred to walk. It was oddly reassuring to hear her at night, clacking back and forth in the hallway and living room, securing the perimeter before coming into the bedroom to perch at the foot of his bed in her covered sleeping cage.

Joel grew up on a farm (a hobby farm really—his parents were unable to make enough money without day jobs) so he had had many pets: fish, cats, dogs, turtles, sheep, pigs, cows. He appreciated all animals: the chosen companions, the chosen dinner entrees—especially the chosen dinner entrees. He always gave a silent prayer and thank-you to the animal that had given its life so he could sustain his. It wasn't about having dominion over them in the Old Testament sense. It was about a perverse co-dependence.

With Socrates, there was a good chance she would out co-depend him. She was five years old now. Cockatoos, and many other members of the parrot family, lived to eighty or ninety. Joel was twenty-nine, but his family was not known for longevity. A massive stroke took out his dad while he was mucking the stable. He was only fifty-nine, dying with his boots on—face down in the manure.

Joel would prefer to die with his slippers on … maybe with a morphine drip on the go, and definitely surrounded by a few kindred spirits who would miss him—which might include the bird.

Socrates flapped up to the kitchen counter and nudged the tap with her beak. She bent down and gnawed the spout, her little pink tongue darted out and lapped at the drops.

'Loveyouloveyou,' she squawked to Joel, or maybe to the tap. Joel preferred to take it as a personal affirmation of their relationship. During the past year, during the downward spiral of Joel's human relationship, Socrates had picked up a few unflattering words like 'asshole', 'bitch', and the occasional 'dickhead'. Some were Joel's words. Some were the ex's.

Mostly the bird kept to the lexicon of love. She got more treats that way.

'Dickhead.' Socrates whistled.

That would be the ex talking.

* * *

'Well, does your ex have a name?' Lenora asked as she scooped butter chicken from the casserole dish and dumped it onto her plate. Oily brown liquid seeped beneath the densely packed mound of white rice. Chunks of pale chicken flesh remained on top, marooned.

The sight was unnerving, but the smell made Joel salivate.

Meat was murder. Irresistible, delicious murder.

'Does your ex have a name?' Lenora asked again.

'Voldemort?' Lenora's husband offered.

Joel sighed. 'Yeah, I know, you're only hearing one side … my side, but … two sides to every story they say. Sophie … that's her name. I'm sure Sophie could say quite a few non-flattering things about me as well; but she's not here … and I wish she was … truth be told.'

Joel wasn't sure if that statement was exactly 'truth be told'. It sounded good, and he missed Sophie; but, he didn't miss her sharp tongue or her sharp truth. Their relationship had tumbled downhill after he dropped out of university without finishing his PhD.

Finish what you start.

Her words.

His thoughts.

Sophie had finished her PhD summa cum laude in linguistics. She now worked part-time at the university … Starbucks. Life could be harsh for millennials. But at least there was always fresh coffee and the occasional smashed avocado on toast.

Joel looked at Lenora, Mark, and their daughter, Sam. Joel smiled.

'We didn't fall out of love.' Joel shrugged. 'It drop-kicked us over different goalposts.'

'Mr Postman. You gave me the wrong letter!' Jillian Hampstead held out an envelope toward Joel. It was a standard airmail envelope: light blue with red and blue hashmarks along the edges. It looked like it had been through a washing machine. It was faded and tattered. Six stamps were missing, leaving behind dark blue shadows. Six stamps remained — a pale yellow ziggurat, mustachioed men, splayed fruit, palm trees.

It looked exactly like the one he had delivered to Ms Wickks the day before.

Joel studied the elaborate cursive script on the front. It was addressed to Ms Wickks.

Weird. Even letters can have their own doppelgängers.

Joel said, 'Sorry, Mrs Hampstead. I got all mixed up yesterday when I looked over at your neighbour … you know, Ms Wickks … and noticed that she was … kind of dying … on the sidewalk. You are right though, I should've been more careful with your mail. Sorry.'

Joel was the king of passive-aggressive. Another reason why he was now single and would probably remain single for the rest of his life.

Jillian continued holding the letter.

'Sorry,' Joel said again, trying to sound more sincere.

Jillian said, 'Anyway I opened it by mistake, you know, an honest mistake. I just open up whatever comes into my house, don't think about it, you guys should be more careful.'

'No worries. I'll slap a damaged sticker on it and the UMO can RTS it.' UMO stood for 'undeliverable mail office' and RTS was short for 'return to sender'. Joel hated jargon, but it had its uses. It was good for bypassing coherence or meaningful engagement.

Jillian clutched the letter. 'Started reading it. Didn't make much sense. All squiggly wavy lines. Realized it wasn't addressed to me. Still don't make sense.'

'That's okay. Life doesn't make sense.' Joel stifled a yawn. He was tired. Socrates had spent many hours late last night 'securing the perimeter' and being otherwise inconsolable. Her behaviour had probably been triggered by the scent of butter chicken on his breath from dinner at Lenora's house.

Delicious, murderous butter chicken.

Joel's face shimmered between a half smile and a full yawn. 'Anyways, I have to carry on, deliver the rest of the route. You know … neither rain, nor shine, nor misdirected mail.'

'Aren't you gonna read it?' Jillian asked.

Joel shook his head. 'Not allowed to … privacy issues — could be fired.'

'Well, it's mighty queer, you know.' Jillian stepped back into the house and shuffled towards the kitchen.

Joel hesitated, then followed her in.

Jillian's kitchen needed a makeover, or maybe a blowtorch. Joel seated himself at a 'country kitchen' table, probably purchased at some discount department store many years ago. The bumpy spindles on the back of the chair rubbed against every incorrect pressure point along the length of his spine. The fridge and stove, harvest-yellow derelicts from the '70s, featured broken knobs and dented surfaces. The kitchen countertop, off-white Formica with badly pitted chrome edging, was a petri dish of encrusted grime and forgotten sauces.

The walls and the cabinets were painted pink — thawed, cadaverous pink. Contrary to modern decorating theory, it did not have a calming effect.

Above the sink was a large window. It was hazy outside. The hydro towers stretched into the distance and disappeared beneath the horizon. Black hydro cables spread out like spider silk.

The letter addressed to Evelyn Wickks lay open on the table. Joel looked at it. Sentences of tightly wound Cyrillic, slithering Anglo-French, and maybe some Spanish or Italian sprawled across the page. Worse still, odd pictographs and odder symbols popped up in those same sentences.

Most letters are written as an act of communication.

This letter was an act of subterfuge.

'So, about this letter.... What do you want to talk about?' Joel began.

'First a cup of tea.' Jillian picked up various mugs from the countertop and appeared to be looking for a clean one. 'Milk or sugar?'

It was another sweltering day and the last thing Joel wanted was a hot cup of anything.

'A glass of water would be just fine.'

Jillian pretended not to hear.

She dropped two bags into the teapot. 'I've known Eva for a long time, way before she knew me. When she moved into that house twenty years ago, we got to know each other as neighbours. Around that time my husband died. My son passed a few years later.' Jillian fidgeted with a thick gold ring on her finger. 'She was very kind — helped with groceries when I didn't feel much like going out.'

Joel stared at the ring. It looked like a wedding band, but it was on the wrong finger.

Jillian noticed Joel staring. She pulled the gold ring off her middle finger and dropped it onto her ring finger. It looked like a loose, ill-fitting crown. 'When you get old, the world and everything in it gets smaller. Even fingers.'

'Something for me to look forward to then.' Joel pointed at his belly and puffed out his cheeks.

Jillian looked at him oddly.

'Or not.' Joel backtracked the conversation. 'Yes, Eva seemed like a caring person. It was nice of her to help out with the groceries. My mom liked to help out the older folks in our neighbourhood too.'

'I ain't the older one.'

Joel looked at Jillian's deeply wrinkled face and then at a spare set of dentures floating in a glass by the window. He remembered Eva as being smooth-skinned, in shape, and hot — mid-century-modern hot.

Not antique hot.

'You were young at heart?' Joel ventured.

'No, younger in age. Eva was born before the War ... the First World War.'

Joel listened to the kettle boil. It was a high-pitched scream.

Joel walked past the hydro towers and stopped at the wrought-iron gates to the tannery. After spending an hour being talked *at* by Jillian, he was tired, befuddled, and hazily curious about the 'real deal' of the defunct Witten Tannery.

Rust pitted the thick bars of the locked gate. A large ornate capital W dominated the middle. Joel stared at the W. It was essentially two V's that intersected when the gates were closed. The left ascender was flat and symmetrical. The right ascender pitched several inches above the rest of the letter in a flamboyant curved wave. Joel thought it was an oddly bipolar font: business on the left, party on the right — like a good mullet. Behind the gate, the broken and desiccated cobblestone driveway ran twenty yards before disappearing beneath thickets of giant hogweed and dog-strangling vines.

According to Jillian, the tannery had gone out of business seventy-eight years ago when she was a little girl living on a farm nearby. During those seventy-odd years, the town of Sparkham expanded north along the creek, grasping and throttling every patch of forest, meadow, or farmland except for the six-acre blot of the Witten Tannery. It was untouchable. No one had the legal right to sell because several parties claimed to own it, including Evelyn Wickks.

And here was the weird bit: Evelyn Wickks was not her real name.

'Okay, okay,' Joel mumbled to himself. 'It is way weirder than that.'

Joel ambled along the sidewalk for a hundred feet as it paralleled the crumbling stone wall of the tannery. Trees leaned aggressively over the fence. Here and there, gnarled roots had kicked through at the base, tumbling rubble outward. Joel slipped through one of these breaches and picked his way along a slender path in the underbrush.

Also according to Jillian, Evelyn Wickks was really Eva Witten, née Puschat. Jillian knew all about the Wittens and the Puschats. The Wittens owned the tannery and the local feed store. The Puschats were prosperous horse breeders in the next township, emigrating to Canada from Prussia after the First World War and bringing with them a stable of Thoroughbreds for racing. The Puschats were also fixers, doping their equine athletes long before it became an Olympic meme. They were money. Everyone knew money.

In 1933, Eva married Douglas Witten, the eldest son of the Witten family, and left for an extended honeymoon at some hereditary estate along the Amber Coast of the Baltic Sea. The tannery was in financial trouble. There was nothing keeping the newlyweds in Sparkham. Jillian remembered hanging out by the Witten Tannery gates and watching the couple drive by in a horseless carriage. It was exciting. Jillian was thirteen. She forgot all about them until a few decades ago when Eva bought the house a few doors down and moved in. She was single now.

Widowed. Exotic new name. Fabulously tight skin. Time had been good to Evelyn Wickks.

Time had not been good to anyone else.

1933: neither of Joel's parents were born yet.

2011: both of Joel's parents are dead already.

1933: Jillian was a young girl with her whole life ahead of her.

2011: life is over, and Jillian is as good as dead already.

Joel pulled out his iPhone. He wondered if the Puschat clan had a history of genetic good fortune.

— 21 —

'Puschat,' Joel barked into the phone with his best Eastern European accent, which was more Hollywood Russian than anything else.

'Here's what I found,' Siri answered.

A phone-sex website appeared.

Chalk another one up for AI.

Joel put the phone away and did a mental calculation of Evelyn's age.

He felt odd.

Evelyn had frequently touched his arm and moved closer when talking, her breasts inches away from his chest.

Like she was a man-hungry cougar.

Now he wasn't so sure.

Maybe she was nearsighted.

Or hard of hearing.

Or worried about falling down and not getting back up.

Eros and Thanatos in one neat little package.

Joel shuddered. Even now, he felt aroused thinking about her.

Joel stopped. Five feet in front of him, a red-brick wall peeked from behind a living wall of green vines and bushes. Joel skirted to his left until he found an opening — a large wooden door buckled inward, rotted and soft. The cast-iron bindings hung loose, reddened with rust. Beyond the threshold: mostly darkness with occasional sparkles of light.

The darkness smelled of must, tannin, and what Joel imagined was the rot of a thousand cow carcasses. After nearly eighty years, the building was still a bricks-and-mortar biohazard.

Joel knew about tanneries. As an undergrad, he had researched medieval tanning methods for a term paper called *Leather Fetishism in Chaucer's Canterbury Tales: A Post-Structuralist Spank*. He didn't remember the exact point of his paper, but he did remember that the hides were steeped for weeks in dog shit and human piss to loosen unwanted hair and cure the skin so it would not rot or wrinkle.

Modern tanning was a little more sophisticated. It used fancy chemicals like trivalent chromium and glutaraldehyde instead of shit and piss. Different words. Same result.

Joel stepped back a little. Twenty feet to his right was another sturdy brick wall and a marble staircase that crumbled into nothingness beyond the fifth step. Joel realized that he was now inside the building, probably the lobby. The roof was gone, replaced by a canopy of branches and leaves. The floor remained a patchwork of dirt, detritus, and broken bits of marble tile.

Joel took out his iPhone and framed a few arty shots, posting them to his Facebook page. A few moments later, his ex-girlfriend Sophie responded with a 'like' on all of them.

I thought she unfriended me a long time ago.

Joel stared into the screen for a while.

Later that day, Joel found himself wedged between a thick, black oak table and a threadbare upholstered banquette at the Dinnsmore Tavern. A few patrons — mostly older men — stared into their beer or watched wistfully as the young female barkeep scurried about. Somewhere in the world it was happy hour, just not here.

The Dinnsmore was close to Joel's apartment but he rarely drank there. They did not have craft beer or Wi-Fi, and the food was generally appalling except for the wings.

Still, this was the place Albert liked to meet when he found himself in town for a movie shoot.

Joel watched the door.

It pushed inward. A triangle of light pulsed across the welcome mat then vanished.

A short pudge of a man stood in the semi-dark. He seemed to be letting his eyes adjust. Joel waved. The pudge waved back.

'Hey, Joelee!' Albert Blackwater walked over and eased himself into the chair opposite. He pointed at Joel's empty glass where white suds clung to the sides like lace.

'What are we drinking tonight?' Albert asked.

'Labatt Blue, although rumour has it they might have a keg of Molson Golden in the basement, still untapped from the '70s.'

'I told ya this was the place.' Albert laughed. 'No word of a lie, this is old school. Look around.' Albert patted the brown upholstery behind Joel's shoulder. 'Authentic Naugahyde. Made in America. Not some cheap Chinese crap. I'm thinking of partnering up with the owner. Gonna promote the hell out of this place through a fake blog. It'll be hipster central in no time. Just need to install Wi-Fi and put some craft beer on tap.'

Albert tilted his chin up slightly as the waitress walked toward them. 'Hey, Robyn. Another pint of Blue for my friend here, a bottle of Corona for me, two shots of tequila — the good stuff. I think you got a bottle of Patron up there hiding on a top shelf.'

'Sure thing, Mr Blackwater.'

'In a dirty glass.' Albert teased out an exaggerated mid-Atlantic accent: Gary Granite: *Flintstones*, season 1, episode 6. Voiced by Bob Hopkins.

Joel chuckled. Robyn probably wouldn't get the reference, but he did. In first year university, Albert and Joel were roommates in residence. *The Flintstones* was their go-to entertainment when their brains had turned to mush from too much caffeine and too much studying. Albert owned a pirated disc of the show and would slip it in the common room DVD player while firing up a joint. They would smoke and smoke and laugh and laugh … and laugh some more when they found the remote and turned on the TV.

Albert *was* Gary Granite: a caricature of a character.

Gary Granite was based on Cary Grant. British born but American raised in the golden age of Hollywood, Cary Grant had a mid-Atlantic accent. Pure fiction. Cobbled together from what Americans thought the British *should* sound like, but it was an accent that only existed in the choppy waves between the two nations.

Fake and brilliant at the same time.

Albert was fake and brilliant in his own way. No one could figure him out at university. He drove an Alfa Romeo but claimed to be broke. He dropped out midway through the second year of a psych degree and disappeared. Joel didn't hear from him till a few years ago when he came back to town as a line producer for a children's show about magical socks.

Robyn couldn't possibly understand.

'Sure thing, Mr Blackwater,' Robyn repeated, and walked away.

'Good kid. She tried out for a small role in my last project. I knew she wasn't for the part, but I gave her a couple of call-backs. Know what I mean?'

'I don't think she looked at me once the whole time,' Joel observed. 'Not that I'm complaining, but you know. It was like I didn't exist for a moment.'

'You need more self-confidence. It's a trick producers use: think you're important and other people think you're important too. Otherwise, if you're poor, middle-aged, and white you're invisible. It's like a superpower no one wants — unless you're a serial killer.'

'I'm not exactly middle-aged but I'll remember that if I make a career change later in life.'

Albert and Joel watched Robyn return from the backroom with a small stepstool. She climbed on top and stretched towards a dusty bottle of Patron. Her short skirt became shorter.

'What are you working on these days?' Joel asked absently.

'A comedy feature with indie cred and an A-list backing.'

'Really?' Joel sort of knew what that meant.

'I can't tell you the principal actor's name right now.' Albert leaned in and pinched his thumb and forefinger to within an inch of each other. 'But … the guy is this close to being Hollywood's biggest A-lister. His wife — well, ex-wife actually — they only broke up last year — sad story really — anyway, she's a big-time actress in her own right and has agreed to be an executive producer.'

'That must be tough.'

'No kidding, the guy dumped her for a woman half her age and not even a third of his.'

'That can't be good.'

'She'll get over it. Hollywood is all about having brass balls. Think Harvey Weinstein.'

'Maybe Hollywood needs brass vaginas.'

'Shaddup. What does that mean? Pffft.' Albert momentarily scrunched his face into a reasonable facsimile of a lemon-sucking pug, then continued, 'Anyway, this movie is gonna put our guy over the top. Not only is he is writing, producing, and acting in it, he is playing multiple roles, multiple genders, multiple ages, multiple nationalities. He even plays the pet dog. In fact, there ain't any other actors in the show. It's all him, all the time, sucking up the screen like a giant fucking leech — a giant gold-plated-Oscar fuck-sucking leech.'

Albert slapped the table. 'It is gonna be fall-out-of-your-tree fuckin' funny.'

Joel could see the fall-out-of-your-tree bit … not so much the funny.

'Can't wait to see it,' Joel lied.

'I'm wearing two hats: production manager and also line producer — you know … the day-to-day nitty-gritty.' Albert rapidly tapped the table with his thumb. 'I got a part for you — off-camera, but it'll pay.'

Robyn slid the tray of two beers and two tequila shots between them.

'And, my dear Robyn, I will have a part for you. In front of the camera this time. With lines.'

Robyn bounced, jiggled, and gushed.

Joel felt invisible again.

Joel sat on a stone bench outside a McDonald's a few blocks from his apartment, waiting for Sophie. It was neutral territory. Although Joel and Sophie had eaten at this McDonald's frequently in the past, it did not hold strong memories or associations for them. There were hundreds of thousands of McDonald's in the world. To experience the pang of lost love every time one sat at a moulded-plastic banquette, or gazed upon the golden arches, would be impossibly exhausting. The brain and heart could parse a more reasonable sentimental fixation.

So Joel's broken heart lay at the entrance of the Greenwood Perk coffee shop — their go-to destination for Sunday brunch and Friday-night poetry slams. He could never step into that dark hipster realm of boho velvet curtains and reclaimed barn-wood tables again.

A close second was another coffee shop: the Mocha El Grande — where they had hung out together as undergrads, before they became serious.

Unfortunately, it had a dancing neon starfish for its logo, terrible customer service, and bad lattes. Not cool. Not romantic. Not really an option for sentiment or for custody meetings.

Socrates squawked and rattled beneath the large yellow blanket that covered the cage as Sophie pulled into the parking lot in her parents' minivan. It was bright red, like an angry boil.

'Hi Joel.' Sophie rolled down the window. Her ginger hair was tied back in a severe ponytail that made her face more taut than usual — like life was a relentless G-force that no amount of smiling could soften.

Joel slumped off the bench, hoisting the bird and cage with him. 'Hi, Sophie. Wanna pop open the back?'

'No room. My parents have all their golfing gear back there.'

'Oh.' Joel looked at Sophie and waited.

'My parents can't have Socrates — allergies. Sorry.'

'Couldn't you have phoned me with that info before I left?' Joel hefted the cage and mimed an extra fifty pounds to the dead weight.

Socrates squawked.

Sophie said, 'We should talk.'

Joel's stomach tightened, then relaxed. At this point in their unrelationship, talking could mean talking, and not shouting.

But that tight ponytail did scare him.

'Ooo-kay,' Joel said.

Joel sat on the futon in *their* living room. Sophie made tea in *their* kitchen. Although Sophie had moved out more than six months ago, the apartment made more sense with her there. After all, most of the stuff in the apartment they had bought together.

The sound of her moving around in the other room also felt natural — pots banging, cupboards closing, feet scuffing. When Joel was by himself it was the sound of one hand clapping — not much fun and a bit of an intellectual mindfuck.

On the floor, Socrates methodically tore through an empty cereal box and scattered the bits of cardboard beneath the coffee table. Shredding, breaking, picking things apart kept her mind occupied. Busy was easier than happy. In that way, birds weren't much different from humans.

'Chamomile or peppermint?' Sophie called out.

'Wouldn't mind a beer.'

Joel listened to the cupboards creak and close, paper tear, the faucet gush and drip, the kettle boil. Joel was not getting a beer. He opened a bag of salt-and-vinegar chips and started munching.

'So that woman dying?' Sophie called. 'Were you freaked out?'

Sophie entered the room carrying two mugs of herbal tea. The little yellow tea tags twirled like mad whirligigs.

'Yeah. I thought it was a heart attack or something, but she might have actually died of old age — from the inside out.'

'No one really dies from old age — you die from a complication associated with old age, like cancer, or pneumonia, or something.'

'The paramedics seemed to think that everything gave out at once, so I'm going with old age. She was over a hundred, according to a neighbour.'

'Really?'

'Yeah, I thought she was in her fifties, but trying to be in her forties. I mean she was in really, really good shape. Hardly any wrinkles. Slim as ...' Joel grappled with an appropriate metaphor.

Sophie snapped. 'Are you, like, in love with her or something?'

A conversation about another woman was now a conversation about 'another woman'.

'No,' Joel whined.

'Maybe you should ask her out. I didn't realize you had a grandma fetish.'

Sophie plonked down on the leather club chair and glared.

Joel reflexively cowed to one side of the futon loveseat opposite, leaving enough room for Sophie if she felt the need to invade his space. He did not like arguing with Sophie. If he won, he lost. If he lost, he lost. It was a no-win.

And so it begins, thought Joel.

Tears formed at the edges of Sophie's eyes. She sniffled.

Or so it ends? thought Joel.

Sophie scrunched her eyes and the tears rolled. A frantic hand scrabbled over the coffee table knocking over a Kleenex box and scads of scratch-and-win lottery tickets.

Socrates merrily hopped over, tearing at both.

Joel did not move.

* * *

Socrates was surprised that Fatbeard did not screech or jump up to save the lottery tickets from her sharp beak of inquisition. He usually went apeshit when

Socrates got too close to the unscratched ones. It was irrational. The fear of losing a potential winner when they were all really losers.

It was like the Schrödinger's cat paradox, except the cat was always dead.

Socrates did not like cats.

No worries, I will render the squalid messages of depression magic into tiny harmlessness. Socrates shredded the largest one—a grotesquerie of glittery gold dollar signs and mad smiling faces.

Socrates was wise to the evils and empty promises of magic writing. Raised as a baby chick in a mall pet store, she had watched many humans outside her cage desperately scratch those shiny papers, or worse, roll up countless paper coffee cup rims, with the same sad result: crushing disappointment when the secret message was revealed.

That was why Socrates never wrote anything down—even if she could. She would leave that to the foolhardy and those with opposable thumbs.

Redhead blubbered.

Socrates liked her the best. Her voice was always soft and melodious, unless she was talking to Fatbeard; then it got wicked sharp sometimes.

Redhead had rescued Socrates from the mall. Fatbeard wasn't happy at first, but he got in line eventually. Socrates trained him.

Fatbeard stood up. He crossed from Socrates's left field of vision and stumbled into the right frame. The left frame remained static with the futon, the open window, the large green tree. The right frame churned with motion as two heaving bodies pressed beakless faces into each other and fell onto the floor.

Gross. Why can't they bob, dance, and mount from behind like normal animals.

Socrates hopped over to the spilled bag of chips and started crunching. Sex always made her hungry. She would get back to those lottery tickets later.

Joel stared at the ceiling. Sophie slept. Her back was pressed into his side. Her ass was ice cold. It was strangely comforting.

He wondered what it was she had wanted to talk about.

* * *

Saturday morning. Joel sat in Albert's office at Big D'nought Productions on the second floor of a dilapidated warehouse. Another production occupied the main floor and was wrapping out. Joel knew from Albert that a lot of productions rented the cheapest, nastiest digs for offices — basic shitholes. Most of the money was spent on what went on the screen — actors, costumes, things to blow up. Narrative was transcendent. Bricks-and-mortar — not so much.

Producers operated from that principle, one of the few they possessed.

Albert confided to Joel that he had once shot a kids' TV show in a condemned pesticide factory because it was practically free — the cost of a good pair of bolt cutters. The money he saved went toward better special effects and a case of skin cream for the crew.

'Suffering for one's art,' Albert liked to say.

Joel watched as assorted office staff and crew members wandered about clutching coffee, cell phones, and cigarettes, talking and smoking into the air. The walls fluttered with headshots, location photos, storyboards, schedules, script pages, revisions, fast food menus, movie posters. Desks were littered with scads of the same.

It was a paperless society — just not here.

'Joel, buddy!' Albert came out of his office with a flustered young woman and a slouchy young man with a bad haircut. The woman and man went in separate directions as Albert grabbed an impossibly large mushroom-shaped pastry from the office coordinator's desk.

Almond-coloured pastry flaked, fluttered to the floor. Large cube-like crystals studded the top. Chocolate oozed from the puckered bottom.

'Buddy, you gotta try one. One of the P.A.s picked them up from some fancy coffee store — Mocha El Grande, I think — on his way in this morning. One bite and wow….' Albert waved his arms around, channelling his inner Italian.

'No thanks.' Joel patted his belly, channelling his outer bloat.

Joel followed Albert back into his office. It was bare except for a large metal desk, two chairs, a land line, and two laptops. There was no paper.

Here was the paperless future. It was bleak.

Albert flipped open both laptops and started typing at both. 'Don't mind me. There's always some fire to put out and not enough time to do it. Back in the day, we did an MOW in forty shooting days. Now they want it shot, edited, and ready for broadcast in less than twenty. My brain is blasting off in ten different directions to keep on top.'

MOW stood for 'movie of the week'. Joel knew that already. He knew a lot of film slang from listening to Albert and his crazy stories. Joel liked film slang. It was exciting and poetic. Blondes, redheads, juniors, and babies were types of lighting. Sky highs, sidearms, and triple headers were the stands and supports for those lights.

Postal slang was neither exciting nor poetic. It was drab and utilitarian. It was numbers, dashes, and letters cobbled together in unimaginative seriation: the spec number on a piece of equipment, a clause in the Collective Agreement, an acronym with no vowels.

How pathetic is that? thought Joel. *An acronym with no vowels.*

'So, Joel,' Albert began. 'I was thinking you could drive talent on weekends. It would be low-key. We shoot during the week and I like to keep the transport boys and girls off the clock on weekends 'cause of the wicked turnaround and overtime penalties. Your work, and it's hardly work, is to drive the main guy and his ex around town when needed. You get a minivan with all the bells and whistles and free gas. I pay you a hundred bucks for the day if they *don't* need you, and, if they *do* need you, I hand over a fat three hundred cash. Sound good? Fatten up that awesome retirement fund you posties have.'

'Great.' Joel lied. He knew Albert got three hundred dollars a day in cash for personal expenses — no receipts required — when shooting in backwaters like Sparkham. Three hundred was chump change. Joel could hold out for more.

'Just let me run it past Sophie first,' Joel said. 'She gets a little antsy if I'm spending too much time away from her. The weekends are important.'

'Sure thing. Tell her the two fifty each week will help out with groceries.'

'I thought you said three hundred?'

'Two hundred can buy a couple of good quality pillows. Women love pillows. Down filled. Fancy stitching. What's not to like?'

'Okay, okay. You got me for the three hundred,' Joel said.

'I thought you'd see my point.'

* * *

Jillian walked slowly past the Witten Tannery gates. It was late Sunday morning and a bright yellow sun dominated the sky. No clouds, just bleached-blue space.

Beneath a wide-brimmed straw hat, Jillian felt a little of the sun's heat but not enough. Even on the hottest days, Jillian felt chilled.

It was Death breathing down her neck.

A little farther along and the stone wall fell away, leaving enough wiggle room for her to shuffle through. Even with the use of a walking stick, the uneven ground made her woozy. Her ankles hurt. She hobbled over to a tree stump and sat down.

After her husband died, after her son died, Jillian had made peace with Death. If it came, it came. Old age was another matter. She did not like old age. It was lonely. It was undignified. It was the body breaking the shackles of both form and function—not caring which followed what. It was the mind slipping and wandering off into the wilderness.

Jillian looked at the riot of green leaves and grey branches that blocked her way. Pops of small yellow buttercups, white daisies, and purple forget-me-nots clustered along the ground.

Flowers she had loved as a child.

She took a biscuit from her pocket and ate it. She wished she had remembered her thermos of tea. It might be a long day.

Having grown up on a farm she appreciated the order that her parents' industry brought to nature: the neatly planted fields of vegetables, the docile herds of cows, goats, and sheep, the large rectangular pens and pastures closed off with fences. She also appreciated nature beyond the fence. Here on the formerly manicured front lawn of Witten Tannery, nature had crept back in: trees reached, shrubs stretched, brambles and vines climbed. The green crawled with life. Jillian felt energized. It was probably why Eva came back after all those years abroad and refused to have the property developed.

Eva had talked about it as a place of rejuvenation.

Some evenings Jillian had watched Eva set off through the hydro corridor towards the dense bramble and broken buildings of the tannery. Sometimes Eva was accompanied by a man—always someone different, always someone middle-aged and doughy. What she saw in those 'gentleman callers', Jillian never understood. Eva kept herself quite trim and could easily get someone younger looking, or at least in better shape.

Maybe Eva had low self-esteem. Jillian had read about low self-esteem in many women's magazines. The articles were usually short, sandwiched between ads for collagen creams and weight-loss pills.

Or maybe Eva couldn't bring herself to date someone who'd be younger than a grandson. She was well past a hundred after all.

Nobody likes a cradle-robbing bitch.

Jillian remembered that Eva always carried a picnic basket with her when she went on those late-night date walks. It was a good-looking basket: light brown weave with a delightful red gingham fabric poking out from the side of the lid. The basket seemed heavy and the men usually offered to carry it. Eva always refused. Eva was like that. Independent. Everything on her terms.

Bill, Jillian's son, obsessed over that basket. In those last few weeks before he succumbed, while still fighting through the discomfort of chemotherapy, Bill would loiter in the backyard at night, unable to sleep. One of those nights, he watched Eva and another new boyfriend amble through the fields towards the tannery with that basket. Later as the sun rose, Eva returned by herself — the basket just as heavy. Bill argued that the basket should have been lighter — the picnic having been consumed. It wasn't right.

Something rustling in the bushes brought Jillian's attention sharply back to the present.

'Well, hello there. You're a nice kitty.' Jillian leaned forward as a ginger-haired animal emerged.

The animal rubbed up against her shins. The tail thrashed about — excitement, fear, or a combination of both. Cats were always of two minds that way, especially feral ones.

Jillian fumbled for her reading glasses to get a better look.

She got a better look.

She fumbled for her walking stick.

The beast had the face of a rat, but the body was covered in patches of orange and white fur like a calico cat. It might have been an opossum — in a previous life. Its claws were large, designed for slashing and gutting, not foraging for bugs and fruit. The teeth were a mess: small sharp spikes stuck out at odd angles, and two large canines curved down outside black-purple lips.

It was a sabre-toothed nightmare.

Jillian shuddered.

'Well, hello, sugar pie, what brings you here?' Jillian's voice pitched to an exaggerated friendliness as she reached with her free hand into her pocket for another biscuit, hoping to mollify the beast. It lifted its snout and sniffed, the nostrils flaring in odd syncopation. A small white tongue darted out, wrapped around Jillian's middle finger, and pulled at the wedding band.

The ring slipped off easily and fell to the ground. The beast gobbled it up and scampered into the underbrush. Twenty-four carats moiling in the animal's gut.

Jillian spluttered.

Grasping her walking stick, she set off in shaky pursuit. She was not about to let a four-legged animal get the best of her. She was a farm girl after all.

Sunday evening. Another date night on Joel and Sophie's journey back to redemption. The rules were simple: authentic interaction with no spontaneous sex. Sophie's negotiation. Joel agreed. He could wait. Unspontaneous sex was better than no sex at all.

They had already enjoyed dinner, a movie, and a long walk. What more could she ask for? Perhaps a scintillating mystery.

Joel scrolled through his iPhone photos and tapped the shot of Eva Wickks's mysterious letter. The script filled the screen.

'Why didn't you just take the letter and photocopy it?' Sophie squinted at the image on the phone. 'I can barely read this. Some of the words are cut off.'

'It's a federal offence to take someone's mail. I could be fired. Besides, photocopying is so last decade. I like to be cutting edge.'

Joel tried to spin the iPhone in the palm of his hand. The device made a lame half-circle.

'Well, a smartphone is only as smart as the person using it,' Sophie said.

Joel spent a good thirty seconds trying to come up with a clever retort. He couldn't.

'Is it possible to see the actual letter?' Sophie asked.

'Yeah. I'll talk to the old lady tomorrow and see when we can drop by. A bit of excitement in her old age, I bet. Defying the feds!'

'I should go home now.' Sophie stood up from the love seat.

Joel jumped to his feet. 'Yes, I'll walk you to your car.'

Sophie leaned forward. Joel breathed her in as they kissed.

It was a gentle kiss, but Socrates cocked her head and wolf-whistled anyway.

'I had a really good time today. I feel that we are communicating much better now.' Sophie continued to hold Joel's hands.

'Yes, we are communicating much better now.' Joel's mind was cotton. His skin tingled.

Socrates squawked. 'Loveyouloveyou!'

'Loveyouloveyou,' Joel parroted.

A week later, Joel dropped by Albert's production office. The vibe had changed. It was quiet. Everyone looked glum, sour, pissed, or a combination of all three. There seemed to be less paper floating around. It was unnatural.

'Hey, Joel-buddy!' Albert Blackwater boomed as he walked out of the bathroom with his right hand extended.

Joel recoiled slightly. He was not a germophobe — you could not survive being a mail carrier if you were — but the extended hand at that moment seemed more of a biological weapon than a gesture of greeting.

Joel offered a fist bump instead.

Albert accepted.

'So, buddy, glad you could make it here! The two principals are out of town for a bit, but I have some other work you might like! Come into my office!' Albert was using his outdoor voice although Joel was only a foot away.

Joel followed Albert into his office as he closed the door. Albert seemed a little too irrationally cheerful and upbeat, even for a movie producer.

'So, there's been a delay — problems with the script! Otherwise, we are on schedule! We've got the locations locked starting next week! We'll go scout them together today!' Albert continued to shout.

Two of the office P.A.s and an office coordinator studied Joel and Albert through the large windows on either side of Albert's door. Albert smiled and rubbed his chin. His hand slowly moved over his mouth in a faux philosophical pose, pretending to be in deep thought.

The Thinker was in stealth mode.

'Here's the deal,' Albert said softly. 'This debt-ceiling-crisis bullshit south of the border is killing me. The Dems and the Republicans won't talk to each other. Standard and Poor just downgraded the credit rating of the entire US of A for fuck's sake and now everyone in L.A. is panicking. Some key players are pulling out. The principal actor and his ex are back in California trying to shore up funding. It's not looking good, but the show must go on, and it will go on, but it might have to go on with some alternative stimulus package of some sort. Are you in?'

'Uh, sure?' Joel's debt ceiling had blown off long ago. A chance to go full bankruptcy might be a relief.

Joel looked out into the room.

Everyone had returned to their work except for one of the P.A.s wearing a headset. He continued to stare at Albert.

'Why are you so interested in making this movie?' Joel turned his attention back to Albert.

'I got skin in the game.'

'You've put your own money in?'

'Are you crazy? No, I'm banging the waitress at that bar. She's expecting a speaking role now.' Albert stopped to think for a moment. 'But now that you mention it, I kind of have my own money invested — in a roundabout way. And probably it's another good reason to keep the show afloat.'

At Joel's quizzical look, Albert leaned forward. 'It's a bit of trade secret, but I'll tell ya — because we're deep in the shit now.'

Joel's perplexity morphed into panic. He did not want to be 'in the shit' with anyone, especially Albert.

'Because I run the budget and do all the payouts....' Albert leaned back in his chair and resumed speaking, still in a whisper-voice. 'I get an advance for a chunk of the budget — a couple of mil in this case. I take that money and invest in some short-term financial vehicle of sorts, nothing too risky.'

Joel leaned forward and cupped one ear.

Albert whispered louder, sounding like a snake being strangled by a bicycle pump. 'I keep that money working and delay payment to the "below the line" workers until the secondary installments come in — halfway through the shoot — and I then use *that* second installment to pay them off for what should have been paid from the first installment. You follow?'

Joel nodded. He didn't really follow.

Albert leaned forward. He rasped, 'So, by the time the movie finishes and everyone is at each other's throats, the original advance has matured, and I cash out — keeping the interest. It's the magic of compound larceny.'

Joel considered himself an honest man, but honesty wasn't giving him much traction in this world. 'What do you need from me? I could muster up a few thoughts and prayers and that's about it.'

Albert swayed back, forward, side to side.

Was it Albert the snake or Albert the snake charmer that Joel was dealing with now?

'Joel-buddy, you have expert*ise* in how the postal service works. And that expert*ise* will impact the movie *we* are making.' The hissing sibilants were softening into a melodious cant.

Snake … charmer.

'Let me explain,' Albert continued. 'In the movie industry we use a lot of guns.'

'Guns?'

'Hold on, hold on. Not real guns. Prop guns. It's all about the illusion of violence. It's Hollywood. Look, even if we were doing a movie about Mother Teresa, there'd be a shootout and a car chase.' Albert stared deep into Joel's eyes. 'Forget I said guns.'

'Forgetting the guns.'

Albert's voice relaxed into a purr. 'It's all about keeping it real — that whole method-acting schtick that actors are always on about. And we need to keep it real for one of the big scenes near the end where the actor, as himself, shoots his dick off with a vintage snub-nose .38, while taking a selfie with the latest iPhone. Yeah, I know — product placement. It's a bit unethical maybe but what can you do? It's Hollywood.'

'Guns? You're talking about guns again.'

Albert sputtered, 'Not *real* guns. I'm talking about *fake* guns. And only one. If I use the plural, just ignore it. A verbal tic. Anyway, as I was saying, with this one gun, we keep the box of firing mechanisms nearby, so the actor can get all authentic when we shoot that scene. His ex-wife, the executive producer, insists. It's part of his contract.'

'I don't know.'

Albert's voice purred again. 'The emotional response follows the truth of the action. It's the reality of what we do on-screen.'

Joel slowly compressed his lips into a thin single line of skepticism.

Albert licked his lips and changed his tone. 'I can get you a part in my next film — with lines.'

'What do you need from me?'

'I need your advice on how to get the firing mechanisms across the border as soon as possible without drawing attention — so the actor can "make it real". You don't have to touch anything. I'll pay you five grand.'

Joel remained silent. His eyes narrowed.

'You drive a hard bargain — three grand,' Albert chirped.

'Three grand? I thought you said five?' Joel started.

'My final offer ... two grand.'

'Okay, okay. I'll take the five.' Joel knew if he didn't agree fast enough, *he* would be paying Albert.

Albert relaxed and looked past Joel into the office. Albert's smile slowly creased into a grimace. Joel turned around. The P.A. with the Bluetooth headset gave a thumbs-up.

A voice reverberated on Albert's speakerphone.

'Hey Mr Blackwater, I'm still waiting for your lunch order. Remember, you broke off to go to the bathroom.' The P.A. consulted a pink sticky note on his desk. 'I believe we stopped somewhere between a chorizo-chicken burrito and the illegal importation of firearms. Did you want fries with that?'

Albert Blackwater did not blanch or blush.

'Oh wait, I see you've already ordered a side order of embezzlement. No fries then.'

'Sure, I would love fries,' Albert said calmly. 'And I believe you'll need some petty cash for that.'

'Yes, I will. A lot of petty cash.'

Joel watched as the young man unfolded himself from his chair and walked into the room. He wore dark mustard-coloured jeans with a loose-fitting tartan flannel shirt in red and grey with accents of dull yellow. His dyed-black hair was as much art as artifice: short back spiked up like a porcupine's ass, long bangs streaked with purple.

Joel wanted to punch him but didn't know why.

'So, ah ... I'm sorry, your name again?' Albert began as soon as the young man closed the door.

'Benny Tak.' The young man folded his arms and nodded. 'I've been a P.A. on most of your shows for quite a few years now.'

'Um yeah ...' Albert nodded. His eyebrows furrowed. 'Not ringing a bell.'

'Oh my god, I introduced you to Drexel, Rufus, and Digby back in the day. Your little import business wouldn't exist without them — unless you've switched partners. Should I call them up to see? Maybe *they* can help out with your lunch order.'

Albert blanched, blushed, blanched again. He remained uncharacteristically speechless.

Benny Tak nodded. 'You owe me. You keep saying so every time I raise the issue, but you keep forgetting who I am. So I'm going to tell you what I want.'

'Anything but actual money.' Albert spoke like a true producer. The blood returned to his face.

'A speaking role in this movie you're working on.'

'Can't. You gotta be an ACTRA member. How about background instead?'

Benny shook his head. 'Been there. Done that. Did *not* get a crew T-shirt. I'm ready for my close-up — with lines.'

Albert turned to Joel. 'Whadya think? Do I give in to blackmail?'

'Probably a good idea.'

Albert looked at Benny. 'Okay, I get it. You got me, and ... and ... I got you ... a choice between two parts ... that haven't been cast yet: one is "distraught bystander", the other is "injured motorcycle cop". Although that role isn't quite solid yet. It may get a rewrite. But it will be a cop of some sort. Guaranteed. Ya always gotta have a cop in a movie.'

'How many lines for each and what is the degree of authentic emotion involved?'

'The first character has a lot of "Oh my god, oh my gods" with a hefty dollop of panic. The cop character is a little more stoic. Fewer lines but more action. Actually, might do some minor stunt work. Can you drive a motorcycle?'

'No.'

'Then you should do that one.'

'Deal.'

'Deal.' Albert offered his hand.

Benny shook it.

Monday evening. Joel and Sophie sat in Jillian's living room. The Sunday paper lay folded on the coffee table with the crossword page open on top. It was partially finished. Jillian puttered around the kitchen, opening and closing drawers, banging cups, clinking silverware. She was making tea.

At Sophie's insistence, Joel had picked up scones from the bakery.

She had suggested fresh.

He had opted for day-olds.

It was a mistake.

Jillian trilled from the kitchen, 'Delightful to meet you …'

'Thanks, it's great to …' Joel started but was interrupted by Jillian's sing-song voice again.

'Better to eat you!' Jillian was clearly addressing the scones.

Joel looked at Sophie and whispered, 'I'm feeling a little …'

'Hansel and Gretel-ish?' Sophie offered.

'I was just about to say the "Walrus and the Carpenter" but I like your version better.'

It was nice to hear her finish his sentences again.

In the kitchen, cutlery clattered to the floor.

'Are you sure we can't help you, Mrs Hampstead?' Sophie called out.

Jillian hobbled into the living room carrying a pot of tea, three mugs, and a plate of cranberry-lemon scones on a silver tray. 'Don't worry yourselves. I'm old but not helpless. If I don't keep moving, everything's gonna seize up.'

'The wisdom of *Shark Week*.' Joel nodded.

Jillian looked at him quizzically.

'Sorry, an in-joke down at the station. Nothing negative. Just a life observation. Gotta keep pumping oxygen through those gills or you … um … ah.'

'Die? Don't have to sugarcoat it for me, honey. At my age, death is just around the corner. You pick your route wisely.' Jillian changed the topic. 'Anyway, these biscuits look real yummy. Generally, gotta watch what I eat—blood-sugar levels and all that nonsense—but today I'm feeling … spry.'

Jillian looked spry.

In Joel's mind, she was almost spritely—as in fairy-like. She had undergone a subtle transformation since last week. Although Jillian's face and neck were as wrinkly as Joel remembered, her hands and arms were now silky smooth, her blue-veined knuckles now pink and plump, her crepe-paper wrists now white and taut. A walking advertisement for a miracle anti-aging cream that worked—on limited areas of your body.

Jillian's eyes sparkled with an odd energy.

Joel picked up a scone. It crumbled into dust as he ate.

'So, about this letter…. Can we see it?' Sophie asked. 'Joel showed me a photo on his iPhone; unfortunately, parts of the text were cut off. I'd like to see the envelope too if that's okay?'

Jillian seemed a bit taken aback by Sophie's directness but quickly regained her composure. 'Sure, dear—it's on the piano.'

Joel looked over at the piano. It was an upright Baldwin with yellowed ivories and a few sunken black keys. The envelope rested against an open book of sheet music—Maier's *Atalanta Fugiens*. The juxtaposition resonated with Joel, but he did not know why. He would Google it later.

Sophie got up and brought the envelope to the coffee table. She carefully separated the letter from the envelope and spread them both on top of the crossword page.

After a few moments of study: 'The stamps missing on the envelope were probably worth something to a collector. I'd say they were carefully removed.

The remaining stamps are unusual. Ziggurats? Splayed fruit? Mustachioed men? Nothing to indicate the price of the stamp or country of origin. Could be decorative. I don't know. I'm not a philatelist. Joel?'

'I know a stamp when I see one.' Joel shrugged. 'And that's about it.'

Sophie picked up a scone but continued talking. 'The cancellation postmark is incomplete. Most of it must be on the missing stamps. I can make out some partial numbers though … a one and a nine at the beginning … nineteen … the rest is gone … as I said — probably along with the missing stamps.

Sophie bit into the scone. It crumbled into dust. She glared at Joel.

Joel started, 'And that means the envelope would have originally been inducted into the mail stream sometime in the 1900s. Best case scenario: 1999. More than a decade ago. Unusual, but not unheard of. It's called snail mail for a reason.' Joel laughed nervously and avoided Sophie's eyes.

Jillian dipped her scone into her cup of tea. The scone held together for a few seconds before chunking off into marbled bits of white flour, lemon zest, and red berries floating in a sea of tannins and antioxidants.

Jillian looked sad.

Joel had really messed up on the scone order, so he continued talking to distract everyone. 'Of course, if the envelope is really that old, or older, it probably was stuck in a mailbag. We've phased them out mostly. It's all trays and buckets and eventually no more home delivery — but I digress. Last week we got a monotainer of mailbags to sort through and there was a letter stuck in the bottom of one of the bags, date stamped from three years ago. Talk about "oops".'

'Must be that cheque everyone asks about,' Jillian said. Her tone was flat. Joel couldn't tell if she was being sarcastic or serious.

'Moving on.' Sophie placed the envelope to the side and redirected her focus on the letter. 'The text jumps between French, English, German, and Spanish with some weird Latinized Cyrillic stuff going on in between. The writer is multilingual and so I guess Eva must've been multilingual too.'

'She travelled a lot. She had a lot of books in her house — every room had books, books, books,' Jillian offered. 'I've seen them. My son liked to borrow the ones about yoga and meditation. Not for me. I like my monkey mind. Keeps me going.'

Joel interrupted. 'The Latinized Cyrillic stuff? Is that those weird symbols clustered mid-way through?'

'No, those would be ideograms, alchemical symbols, and Nordic runes.'

'The chicken scratch at the end then. What's that?'

'My guess is some version of cuneiform — probably more idiosyncratic than historically accurate. Very few people are knowledgeable about that language. Pretend Sumerian maybe?'

'Wow, a real dog's breakfast. Do you think Eva understood all of it?' Joel asked.

'Probably. Sometimes close siblings or people in deep relationships develop their own way of talking to each other that others don't understand: coded words, subtle cues. Although there are some words that are pretty straightforward — like *fresh scones*.'

Joel squirmed.

Sophie continued, 'Think of how languages develop and evolve in the first place. It's not a straight line … from A to B.'

Sophie paused again and looked at her audience expectantly.

Nothing.

Joel squirmed.

Jillian poked mournfully at her scone soup with a spoon.

Sophie sighed. 'Language, especially written language, is complex. Almost a living organism.'

'Speaking of living organisms.' Joel licked the scone dust from his fingers delicately. 'Who wrote the letter? No legible name on the bottom, just a T and some scribble.'

Jillian took her teaspoon and crushed the scone-bergs against the side of the cup as she spoke. 'Eva had a sister in South America — Tessa — and some relatives still in Germany. She didn't speak much of her husband's side. Fighting over the tannery property I suppose.'

'Tessa it is then.' Joel said. 'You ever meet her?'

'Yes. Out here a couple of years ago. Gave me that sheet music on top of the piano with a cute little book of engravings by the composer — Michael Maier. Dainty stuff. Couldn't play it with my arthritic fingers at first, although now they seemed to have loosened up a bit. Trying to give it a go. In Eva's memory.'

Sophie examined the envelope carefully and looked closely at the broken seal. 'A dorky-looking bird chained to a frog. You'd expect something classy for a wax seal.'

'Maybe this Tessa is a fan of Big Bird and Kermit,' Joel joked, or tried to joke. He was not Funny Joel and never would be.

Jillian slurped her tea.

Sophie drove Joel home. The scent of fresh-mown grass and late-Sunday BBQ wafted through the open windows of the car.

'Sorry about the scones. I thought "day-old" was more of a description than an epitaph.'

'Pastry doesn't age well. You know that. Everything has a shelf life.'

'Wine gets better with age.'

'Wine is a living thing. Even in a bottle. And it still has a shelf life.'

'Sourdough then. The mother lump can live forever under the right conditions. I think there's even some restaurant in Alaska that makes sourdough bread from a starter batch linked genetically to a starter batch in San Francisco linked to a starter batch from the California gold rush of the mid-nineteenth century.'

Joel stopped and looked at Sophie. Years ago, during the honeymoon phase of their relationship, their 'thing' was to engage in frequently moronic arguments tricked out in academic doublespeak. Joel had mastered the art of using 'intersectionality' as a verb, noun, and adverb. Sophie favoured the blunt use of loaded prefixes like 'neo', 'post', and 'trans'.

'Microaggression' was their safe word during role play.

As the relationship uncoupled, the arguments took root in real-life issues. Microaggressions became aggressions. Not fun at all.

Joel blurted. 'Sourdough is the Lazarus of pastries. No, wait ... I stand corrected—sourdough is the Jesus of pastries, summoning life from previously inert substances.'

Sophie chided, 'The bacteria in the mother lump may be genetically similar but it has lived and died a thousand times over. You look upon the ancestors of ancestors. It is the illusion of continuity.'

Joel felt strangely aroused.

'What about the Platonic Forms? The Idea of sourdough?' Joel countered.

'You can never step into the same river twice. The river has changed. You have changed. Ergo, sourdough has a shelf life.' Sophie's eyes flashed.

Sophie pulled over to the side of the road beside the rusted Witten Tannery gates. Joel worried that he might be walking home. It would be a long walk. The Sunday bus service in this part of town was spotty at best and he didn't want to shortcut through the Witten Tannery this late in the day.

Sophie leaned towards him murmuring.

He breathed her in. It was sweet scone dust, lip gloss, and tea tannins.

She bit him hard on the neck.

Socrates watched in horror from her perch as Fatbeard and Redhead barged into the apartment, ripping each other's clothes and mumbling all kinds of crazy, that, if Socrates ever repeated, would get her a firm scolding and banishment to her cage with a towel over top.

Socrates had always thought that the two humans were generally good flock-mates, but now it looked like they were trying to kill each other — wearing as little clothing as possible.

Humans were funny like that. Friends one minute, enemies the next. Consistently inconsistent. Like a raging river.

Luckily Socrates didn't have to endure the pandemonium too long. Fatbeard exhausted himself first and flopped to the side. Redhead seemed disappointed, gamely rubbing the other to provoke another attack.

It didn't work.

'What do you make of that Jillian?' Fatbeard asked while nuzzling Redhead's fleshy bits. 'She's an odd bird.'

Socrates perked right up at the talk of an odd bird. Socrates thought she wouldn't half mind a flock-mate of her own — even an odd one. Socrates hopped closer to the gate of her cage and easily lifted the latch using her beak and claws. She flapped down to the parquet flooring and skedaddled her way closer to the sweaty brutes.

She needed to listen to every detail.

'"Odd bird" is demeaning and sexist. Just call her Jillian,' Redhead said.

'How about odd duck?'

'A bird by any other name.'

'Okay, okay, just plain Jillian.' Fatbeard huffed. 'Anyway, she seemed a little on edge when we started talking about the Witten Tannery and wanting to explore the grounds ourselves. Of course, what would she expect after all that talk about the sabre-toothed opossum, the weird tunnel she chased it into, and the glowing cesspool underground. It's like *Lord of the* frickin' *Rings* for god's sake. It could be my Gandalf moment!'

'More like Bilbo Baggins.'

'Bilbo was in *The Hobbit*. Frodo was in *The Lord of the Rings*.'

'Okay. Frodo then.'

'How could you get Bilbo and Frodo confused? Do I even know you?'

'My brain is used for more important things other than storing useless fanboy ephemera.'

'Useless fanboy ephemera? How many times do I listen to you talk about the difference between lip gloss, lip balm, and lipstick? I still don't get it.'

Socrates bobbed her head. This was the good stuff: inane chatter at squawking high volumes. It seemed that all good flock-mates proved their compatibility using this method. If you did not come to blows, you were a good match.

Socrates would employ the same technique when she found this Jillian Oddbird.

'She needs to call up the municipality and lodge a complaint.' Redhead's voice finally relaxed. 'Get them to fence it off. We should've insisted. Imagine if some kid fell in. It's dangerous.'

'Maybe we should call the municipality ourselves ... although they probably won't take us seriously if we say we heard the information second-hand. It's better that we know what we're talking about — maybe have photo evidence,' Fatbeard suggested.

'You are hard-wired to go, aren't you?'

'I am hard-wired to go.'

Redhead pushed Fatbeard onto his back and straddled his thighs. She seemed intent on crushing his pelvis.

'Photo evidence is crucial,' Fatbeard gasped. 'I … got a lot of "likes" … on that last batch. Think … about the visuals…. Cesspool … tannery tanks … broken-down … machinery. Likes and shares … thoughts and … prayers.'

Redhead leaned forward and pushed her large hanging appendages into Fatbeard's face.

It stopped him from talking.

Redhead talked. 'I think Jillian was insulted with your reaction to her near-death experience. She fell into the cesspool and couldn't swim. Your response was to ask about the lighting.'

Redhead sunk her nails into her flock-mate's shoulders. Tiny rivulets of blood sprung up.

Fatbeard screeched.

Socrates squawked.

Socrates skedaddled back to her cage but stopped at the window. This Jillian Oddbird sounded like an excellent flock-mate. She was out there somewhere. Socrates might have to go into the real world herself to find her if the two humans couldn't get their shit together. She would give them a week.

Socrates looked at the two humans. They were rolling around on the floor, making all kinds of rude noises.

Maybe two weeks.

Tops.

But first she needed to break up the fight. Socrates skedaddled back to the bedroom.

Joel rested on his back as Sophie curled into his side, nestling her head against his chest. The parquet floor was cold and uncomfortable. In the heat of passion, any surface will do. In the quiet of reflection, comfort beckoned.

'Shall we move to the bed?' Joel asked while eyeing Socrates warily. Socrates advanced at ground level, her head thrust forward and cocked sideways, one blue eye unblinking. She was on a mission.

'God, yes. It feels like a bed of nails down here. When was the last time you cleaned the floor?'

'Swiffered this morning,' Joel lied. Socrates was a foot away, bobbing and weaving, her white wings spread out. She might be in mating mode. Soon she would be twerking against his head or trying to regurgitate in his ear.

Birds were funny that way.

Sophie brushed clusters of black and yellow bird seed from her thighs as she got up. Joel rolled to his side and up onto his feet in a graceless manoeuvre designed to distract from his fat belly.

It worked.

Sophie was distracted by his fat ass.

'Jillian is not telling us the full story. I can tell by the way she hesitates every so often,' Joel said. 'She's trying to figure out what she can tell us and what she can't.'

Joel walked into the bedroom and flopped on top of the bed — still naked. Sophie followed, pulling one of Joel's T-shirts down over her head as she walked. She slid under the covers beside him.

Socrates flew up suddenly on to the headboard. Her crest fanned forward. She strutted.

Joel pulled the pulled the pillow close to his ears for protection.

'To recap,' Joel said. 'Jillian goes on a Sunday stroll into the wilds of the abandoned tannery. And believe me, it's wild. I've been there. I showed you the photographs. Nature reclaiming every inch of that place. Almost a forest now. I never got as far as the building that houses the tannery drums though. The smell was unbearable.'

Socrates bobbed her head. 'Jillian, Jillian, Jillian.'

'Funny how birds pick out certain words to repeat,' Joel observed. 'It's almost random.'

'It has a lot to do with the emotional tone of the word, the circumstances, and repetition. It's a feedback loop for them maybe.'

'Why *Jillian*? It's the first new word I've heard her say since you … you've … been … away.' Joel fumbled with the wording. He wanted to say *since you left me*, but it sounded accusatory and would provoke an argument — although their last argument had ended with some spectacular sex.

Sophie smiled dreamily and snuggled into her pillow. 'I miss this bed.'

Joel hoped she was speaking out of mistaken transference.

Joel continued, 'Anyway, Jillian made it all the way through that forest to the tannery drums—despite the stink. Although maybe that's what attracted her. As you get older sometimes it's the bad smells that you can still detect. I mean, even the freshest tannery is going to smell like death.'

Socrates bobbed her head and repeated, 'Death, death, death, Jillian, death, death, death.'

'Socrates is going goth on us.' Joel put his hand out to Socrates and coaxed, 'Step up. Step up.'

Socrates stepped up onto his hand and side-climbed to Joel's shoulder.

Joel addressed Socrates as much as he addressed Sophie. 'According to Jillian.'

'Jillian, Jillian, Jillian,' Socrates squawked.

'Yes, yes. Jillian, Jillian, Jillian. Gosh, what is it with Jillian?' Joel had almost forgotten the obsessive-compulsive component of parrot communication. He would not be able to complete a full thought or sentence without her repetitively screeching random words in his ear.

'I'm going to have to put you back in your cage, so I can think straight.' Joel got up, walked into the living room with Socrates, and put her back in the cage.

'Okay. You be a good birdie now. Daddy is going to have a talk with Mommy.'

'Fatdaddy, fatdaddy,' Socrates squawked.

'I'm big boned.'

'Fat, fat, fat.'

Socrates watched Fatbeard slam the door to the bedroom. Socrates only spoke the truth as she understood it. Maybe she should have said 'Fatbeard' instead of 'Fatdaddy,' but 'Fatbeard' was a hard word to say without vocal cords. It always came out like 'Fatbird.'

And Socrates kept a trim figure.

Socrates looked out the window at the leafy green maple and its bony grey limbs. The forest was out there among the trees. The stink was out there among the forest. Jillian was out there where they all converged. Death too. Whatever that might be.

Socrates would give the humans two weeks tops. Otherwise, she would break out and find her Jillian.

Wednesday, hump day.

Joel waited for his friend Albert at the back of the Dinnsmore Tavern. Occasionally, Robyn gave him a cursory glance to see if his glass of Blue was empty, before going back to restocking the bar. It was three o'clock.

Joel had provided Albert with the necessary information to expedite the package of firing mechanisms through the postal system, without arousing undue suspicion on either side of the border. Joel was nervous. He did not fancy going to jail but he reassured himself that he had only given advice and was not directly responsible for the importation of prohibited items. Still, his beer remained untouched.

The door opened. A swath of light cut into the darkness, then just as quickly disappeared.

'Hey Joel! Fancy meeting you here.' The voice did not belong to Albert. It was high-pitched, scratchy. Smoked vocal cords soaked in whiskey.

'Matt?' Joel panicked.

Matt sat down, removed his postal Tilley hat, and dropped it on the table. 'I didn't expect a youngster like yourself to be drinking here. They ain't got no Wi-Fi.'

'Why aren't you at the Quill?'

'Sometimes I don't feel like socializing or being stared at. Mostly nobody in this bar bothers to look up.'

'Matty!' Robyn swooped in and fussed about the blue man. 'So good to see you! The usual?

'You know it.'

Joel felt invisible again.

After a few minutes of awkward small talk, Joel and Matt settled into staring at their beers and tentatively sipping the contents.

Joel heard a rustling sound behind him.

'Joelee buddy!' Albert appeared out of the darkness and sat down beside his friend. He was about to speak again, then stopped. He stared at Matt.

'Albert, this is Matt. Matt, this is Albert.' Joel gestured between the two. 'Matt works down at the station and Albert is a movie producer.'

'Movie producer? Nice. What movies?' Matt asked.

'A lot of TV movies: disease of the week, heartbreak of the week, pure schmaltz. You know — default viewing when you're all binged out from Netflix.' Albert turned to face Joel but kept glancing at Matt.

'Nice. Anyone famous?'

Joel interrupted, 'Matt, don't badger the guy. He's a friend. I'm sure you get a little tired when people ask you stuff about your job like — "where's my cheque?" and, "how many steps do you take each day?"'

'I never get tired of that 'cause I give a different answer each time.' Matt got up to leave. He turned to Albert and held out his hand. 'Nice meeting you, sir.'

Albert stood up and shook hands, a beat too long. 'I'm gonna ask you something and don't be embarrassed about it. Being in the entertainment business, I have a professional interest in this sort of thing.'

'The colour of my skin?' Matt guessed.

'Yeah, is it really blue?'

'As blue as a grey sky, which means yes.'

'How?'

'Grew up in small-town Tennessee, downstream from a silver mine. Quite a few of us similarly affected. You've heard of Blue Man Group.'

'Seriously?'

'Naw. Just messing with you.'

Joel decided to badger Matt. 'Does the blue colour fade or can it get darker like a tan?'

'I wouldn't know. I take colloidal silver supplements as well. Antibacterial and antiviral. Never had a sick day in my life.'

'No kidding,' Albert said. 'Some of my antivaxxer friends in L.A. would be into it I suspect, but they'd need to bleach their skin to hide the blues. Any other side effects?'

'Well, according to my alternative health practitioner there is no such thing as a side effect. It's all part of the holistic journey to self healing. That's why I only got one kidney now.'

Joel gave Matt the stare, hoping he would take the hint and leave.

'So, Matt, you free Friday afternoon?' Albert asked. 'I have a quick package pickup at Customs. No major problems. A box of widgets.'

'Is that a good idea?' Joel asked, switching his stare from Matt to Albert. 'Involving more people? That's a lot of moving parts.'

'It's a great idea. It's called diffused responsibility — Psych 101,' Albert said.

'Anyway.' Albert turned to Matt and said: 'I need someone to pick up a package at Customs and deliver it to a friend. It's a fun surprise gift. We'll set it up like it's part of a normal postal delivery. Wear your uniform and drive an official truck. I'll give you a hundred bucks.'

'A hundred bucks.' Matt pulled at his red beard.

'Fifty bucks,' Albert said.

Matt shook his head. 'No, I'm thinking more in the line of two hundred.'

'Two hundred?'

'Okay, three hundred and that's my final offer. If I'm walking into a Canada Customs office instead of you, then whatever's in that package is not something I should know about. Now I suspect the worst so let's make it … four hundred, plus whatever the duty and tax charge — in cash.'

'Deal.'

'Deal.' Matt shook Albert's hand firmly. 'What name are you using for the pickup?'

'Johnny … Wozzeck.' Albert mumbled the last name, but Joel heard it.

'Where's it going?' Matt asked.

'Working on that. Looking for a local address where no one is home right now, maybe something vacant or under construction. I'll have the … um … birthday boy pick it up later. He is gonna be so surprised. Oh, also the … um … birthday … drop site should be low traffic and secluded. No nosy neighbours. Any suggestions anyone?'

Joel shook his head. He was not going to give any more advice.

'I know,' Matt offered. 'There's that abandoned tannery out by the hydro corridor. Spooky place. No houses opposite or beside it. One big dead zone. Joel knows it. He delivers in that area.'

Joel wished he was invisible.

* * *

Late Friday afternoon at Station Y.

The letter carriers drifted in, bundling up missorts, off-loading letter trays, tidying up their sortation cases, handing in their route keys. Even though it was the weekend, no one was in a good mood. During the morning mini-meeting Lester informed everyone that the station was up for a restructure in a few months and then would 'go live' with the new 'postal transformation' system after completion. The end of home delivery was nigh. Fewer routes and fewer workers. Joel probably did not have enough seniority to survive the bloodletting. Worse: if he still had a job he would be rebranded as a Delivery Agent instead of a letter carrier or mail person.

Delivery Agent.

Who the fuck came up with that one?

A high-paid bureaucrat with a James Bond fetish?

Joel looked around for Matt. Matt's satchel was hanging on the sortation case, but his route keys hadn't been handed in yet. He was probably on his way to do Albert's errand with one of the spare step vans. Joel felt queasy. Matt would be picking up a package with Joel's name on it, and knowing Albert's lack of imagination, probably Joel's address on it as well.

Joel tapped on the supervisor's door.

'Hey, Les, can I have a quick word with you?' Joel asked.

'Sure.'

'You know I do Route L7, right?'

'Of course, any problems?'

'Yes.'

'Oh.' Lester's jaw tightened a little.

Joel closed the door and sat down in the chair opposite Lester.

They stared at each other for a moment.

'Well?' Lester asked.

'Long story short: There is something odd going on at the abandoned tannery. I understand you … uh … encountered some issues a long time ago while doing that route. Any thoughts?'

'Not really. The deadwalk past the tannery *is* inconvenient, but it has been

— 53 —

factored into the overall time value of your day. All routes are created equal, but some are more equal than others.'

It was typical management doublespeak, but the *Animal Farm* allusion was a nice touch.

Joel tried for blunt. 'Okay. I'll phrase it like this: Eva Wickks owned the tannery and she was ridiculously old and ridiculously hot looking when she died. Maybe more than a hundred years old but still boneworthy. Yeah, I said it … boneworthy. Anyway, Jillian Hampstead, her long-time neighbour — slightly younger than a hundred but looking every millisecond — is now snooping around the property. Jillian is getting younger by the day. Soon she'll be Jill running up that hill and I'll be the Jack tumbling after. I give it a week or two tops.'

Lester sighed.

'Yes?' Joel prodded.

Lester bowed his head. 'I knew Eva, too well perhaps. She was a beauty.'

'And?'

'It's not what you think. Okay, maybe it is. Anyway, we had our moment and then it ended. That's why I left.'

'Wow. So are we talking *The Postman Always Rings Twice* kind of territory, because I am all ears.'

'No. More like the postman can't bring himself to ring even once, so he just stands there with the package in his hands.'

'Umm, I think we're talking about two different movies. Did you break it off? Did she break it off?'

'I broke down in fear.'

'Fear of rejection?'

'No, pure fear.'

'Really?' Joel leaned back in his chair and clasped his hands together, referencing the posture of the archetypal therapist.

Lester continued, 'Eva kept pressuring me to go on these romantic picnics all the time.'

'Too much intensity so early in a relationship can overwhelm a person.' Joel nodded sagaciously. 'We're talking about fear of commitment then?'

'No, pure fear. Those romantic picnics were supposed to be late at night, under certain phases of the moon, and in the abandoned Witten Tannery.'

'Did you talk about it in a judgment-free manner? It sounds like she was really about ready to open up about her needs and desires, could've been a breakthrough moment.'

Lester ignored him. 'I kept putting her off for quite some time, but then she started dressing more provocatively: pointy Wonderbras, tight polyester pant-suits, coral-pink lipstick. I was going out of my mind.'

Lester was of a different generation.

'I couldn't take it anymore,' Lester shouted.

'*You* had the breakthrough moment. Excellent.'

'One night I showed up at her place with flowers and a bottle of wine. She hadn't flirted with me that day, so I was worried. Before I could knock at the door, I heard her giggling and a male voice coming from the kitchen.'

'You could hear that from the front door?'

'No, the kitchen window was at the back. I had to walk down the side of the house.'

'Did they see you?'

'Not really, I was crouched down the whole time.'

Lester was telling a very sanitized version of the narrative.

'Go on,' Joel said.

'I was not the only man in Eva's life. I was heartbroken and a little jealous.'

'How long did you stay there?'

'An hour I think.'

'Why?'

'I was going to confront the man.'

'It took you that long to work up the nerve?'

'No, the sex went on forever. I even had time for a quick smoke out front, for God's sake. Is there no decency in this world?'

'Apparently not. Go on.'

'They left through the back door and headed into the hydro corridor, towards the Witten Tannery. It was very dark except for a sliver of moon. Waxing or waning I can never get that straight. Anyway, I followed. Eva was carrying a picnic basket. The man — some schleppy middle-aged loser — carried nothing. I would have offered to carry that picnic basket.'

'You are obviously the greater gentleman — and not a schleppy middle-aged loser like that other guy.'

Lester continued, 'They were giggling and laughing and making small talk all the way. I think he might have been related to the family that originally owned the tannery. Some distant cousin of her ex-husband or something. Anyway, the man kept grabbing her butt. She didn't seem to mind. I lost them when we got onto the Witten property proper. It's such a maze of broken walls and wild bush. As I said, it was pretty dark. Eva knew her way around no problem though. I eventually had to follow the sounds.'

'Sounds?'

'At first it sounded like gibberish or maybe French. It became somewhat sing-songy at one point. Just Eva. Couldn't hear the guy. I followed the singing to an opening in the ground — a tunnel that popped out thirty yards from one of the crumbling buildings. I had to hunch down a bit to enter. It was a steep grade. Broken bricks, grabbing vines. The smell was terrible. It was like, uh....'

'A thousand buttholes?'

'Yeah. Exactly. You haven't been there, have you?'

'No; however, I know my way around a metaphor — studied English at university. Minored in psychology as well I might add. Continue.'

'So, Eva's voice pulled me in. It was beautiful. I couldn't resist it.'

'A siren's song.'

'Siren? You run away from a siren or pull over if you're driving.' Lester looked at Joel like he was an idiot, then continued. 'After a few yards, I noticed the plants were glowing — yellowish green. I also noticed the walls were stone and curved up and arched across the ceiling like some medieval dungeon. Eventually the tunnel led to an opening the size of a hockey rink. I could see a couple of shimmering pools and some large wooden drums on their sides — as big as T-Rexes, going right past the ceiling to another floor. Still underground though.'

'Where was Eva?'

Lester stalled. 'Weren't you gonna tell me about her neighbour? Jillian. I remember her. What's her connection to the tannery?'

'She's been going there recently, and her skin is looking better. And it's not just the fresh air. What about Eva? Did you see her down there?'

'Yes.'

'And?'

'Eva was bent over her guy and beating his brains out with a large silver candlestick — I mean literally.'

'Is there any other way?'

'At one point, it looked like she was trying to scrape the brains into one of the shimmery pools. Eventually she pushed the entire body into the water and jumped in herself. She was totally naked. She had a fine figure.' Lester's eyes misted up. 'I waited for her to come back out, but I left after a half hour. It was two in the morning already and I had to be at my sortation case in a few hours. By that point, I wasn't sure I saw what I thought I saw.'

'And you didn't report anything to the police?'

'The place stank. The chemicals could've messed with my mind. Besides, I thought I might have a chance with her still, without the getting-murdered bit.'

'What about the dead guy?'

'I read the news to see if anyone was reported missing.'

'And?'

'Nothing right away. A few weeks later, there was a short article near the crossword section about a man who went out for a bag of milk that same day and never came back. He had been married for thirty years. Could've been a runner. Anyways, none of my business.'

'I'm surprised you haven't made zone manager.' Joel shook his head. 'I think I need to bid on another walk.'

Lenora banged on the door and stepped in without waiting for an invite. 'Hey, Matt just texted me. He's been trying to get through to you for the past couple of minutes. Your phone is on voicemail.'

'Did he say what he wanted?'

'Yeah, he's tied up at Customs. Needs you to talk to the supervisor there.'

Lester pulled the landline towards him and pressed a few buttons. 'All right, my work day isn't over yet, obviously, so have a nice weekend and we'll see you Monday.'

Joel waited at the Witten Tannery gates.

Lenora had dropped him off on her way home a half hour ago. Their conversation had been a little flirty, though Joel wasn't sure what he had said exactly. He was distracted, furiously texting Sophie at the same time. Joel looked at his texts. According to the predictive interpretation of his mad finger dash, he wanted Sophie to meet him at the witty tanning salon and perhaps discover the fountain of YouTube together.

And now Joel waited.

He closed his eyes. The humidity had broken so the sun felt good against his skin for the first time in weeks.

The sound of an overburdened four-cylinder engine approached from the left.

Joel opened his eyes expecting to see Sophie's red minivan. Instead, a blue minivan approached the gates and rolled to a stop. The occupant remained inside for a full minute before getting out and walking over to the pillars. It was the P.A. from Albert's office. He groused around the bushes for a few moments, one hand parting the greenery, the other hand holding the purple bangs out of his eyes.

Joel wanted to smack him.

Benny's clothes were a mixture of preppy incoherence and boho insanity: yellow collared shirt neatly pressed, lambswool sweater jauntily draped around his neck, brown velvet jodhpurs, forest-green silk sash tying it all together.

Joel didn't want to smack him. He wanted to punch him — maybe knock a few teeth out. Joel was surprised by his murderous impulse. Fashion could do that to a person.

'Hey dude,' Benny called out. 'Did you drop off a package here? I've been expecting one.'

'No *dude*. I did not.' Joel used the sarcastic pronunciation of *dude*.

Benny stared at Joel. It was obvious that he did not recognize him.

'So ... Benny, you live here?' Joel asked. 'Nice place. I love open concept architecture.'

'No, I ... hey, how do you know my name?'

Joel stretched his arms like he was slipping off a cloak of invisibility. 'We met at Albert's office last week. I'm his friend — Joel.'

'Oh yeah, sorry. The postie uniform threw me off....'

A sudden loud snap from the forest interrupted the conversation.

Benny turned around and peered into the green.

Joel saw it too. A dark shadow moving between patches of light. It made deep grunting sounds as it thrashed towards them.

Benny sprinted past Joel to the van.

Joel had two options: fight or flight. His bladder chose the latter.

'Hey Joel!' The shadow extracted itself from the brambles, the blue-and-white postal shirt ripped, the blue skin scratched and bloody. It was Matt.

Matt pulled at some burrs embedded in his beard. 'Jeez, how do you deliver to this place? I walked for a long time looking for a mailbox and couldn't find one. I gave up and put the package by some door. There was no building behind it, just a door leaning against a tree. I'm done. Lost my watch in there too.'

Matt looked at the blue van. 'What happened to the step van that I was driving before?'

Joel looked over at the van. Benny was hunched forward in the passenger seat — hammering his iPhone with furious thumb jabs. Occasionally, he would glance up at Joel and Matt, then scowl.

'That's a good question. That van belongs to a production assistant who's here to pick up a package, probably the one you delivered to the broken door.'

'Dang.'

'Hey Benny.' Joel walked over to the van and tapped on the window. 'We know where your package is.'

The window rolled down.

'What? Oh yeah. Great. I'm texting Albert now.'

For a few moments Matt eyed his surroundings suspiciously. 'I'm sure I parked the step van in front of some pillars.'

'There's another set of pillars on the other side of the property. No fancy gate though.'

Ben rolled up the windows and got out of the van. 'Albert wants me to go in and fetch the package. And he wants the blue dude to help.'

Matt balked.

'"Play or no pay." Albert's words.'

In the distance, Joel heard the whine of another overburdened four-cylinder engine.

'If you wait a bit, Sophie and I will tag along,' Joel said. 'We're big fans of urban spelunking.'

Joel didn't say: *We're bigger fans of murder mysteries.*

'Gotta look out for each other,' Joel added.

Joel didn't add: *And maybe a few fresh body parts.*

Joel suspected Jillian was falling into the same madness as Eva. On his route today, she had been waiting for him with a come-hither look. Her skin was radiant. The wrinkles were gone.

He was afraid.

And a little turned on.

Sophie pulled into the driveway and stopped. Joel studied her as she meticulously applied the hand brake, unbuckled her seat belt, checked her reflection in the rear-view mirror. He wondered if Sophie would ever succumb to that Witten darkness. She seemed more content these days with their rejuvenated relationship. Then again, she had talked about Botox earlier this morning, ultimately reassured when he immediately scoffed at her need for it.

Injecting dead things under your skin for the sake of beauty seemed somewhat counterintuitive.

'Hey hon.' Sophie kissed him on the lips.

Joel loved that feeling. He lingered too long.

'Joelee,' Sophie admonished, and pulled away. She smiled.

'You got that text about Lester's history with this tannery?' Joel didn't feel like sharing the details of that history with Matt or Ben, so he employed his Kabuki eyebrow skills to indicate that there was an important subtext to his words.

Sophie replied, 'A fascinating history. As I mentioned in our earlier conversation, shouldn't we be talking to … *the professionals* … about it?' Sophie opted for a more subtle use of pause and inflection. Her face remained impassive.

'Yeah, but it happened so long ago that I don't trust the … *professionals* to take it seriously. Worse, if you report it, they tend to think that you're the one who should be charged with … professional misconduct.'

Matt chirped. 'Wow, these professionals sound like dicks. I'm glad I'm not a professional.'

Ben pulled a couple of machetes out from the back of the van. 'All right, let's go. I'm paid on a flat, anything past ten hours and I'm making less than minimum wage.'

'Where'd you get the machetes?'

'Props department. I got a bunch of guns too. I'd offer you one but they're not much use … without a firing mechanism.' Ben winked.

Joel did not wink back; however, his left eye tremoured.

'Sophie, this must be the tunnel Lester was talking about.' Joel pointed to a large berm that snaked out from underneath a crumbled building, its mouth agape in front of them. 'Maybe we should all go in and check this place out, while we're standing here — together as a group.' Joel's voice trembled.

Sophie knew the reason for his fear. The others did not.

'I don't know,' Matt answered. 'We still haven't found that door where I left the package at.'

'I agree with Matt,' Benny said. 'Let's just find the package and get the hell out of here. My boss is freaking. He's texting me every twenty seconds for another update.'

Sophie was already well into the tunnel by the time Benny finished talking. Joel could only follow. The other two remained at the entrance arguing about which direction to go in next to find the package.

'Slow down, Sophie,' Joel hissed. He was afraid to shout, expecting to stumble upon another murder scene or disturb the ghosts of crimes past. Sophie did not slow down. It was if she was being sucked into the darkness. Joel observed the curving walls of the tunnel and the glowing plants. It was as Lester had noted, except in Joel's mind the prosaic observations of his supervisor were transforming into something oddly poetic: the large grey stones bricked in perfect arches were held together with the weight of their own collusion; bio-luminescence creeped about, casting light and shadow, swallowing up truth.

Or something like that. Poetry wasn't Joel's forte.

'Sophie?' Joel called out softly as he stepped into a cavernous room filled with broken tanning drums and shimmering pools of water. Sophie was by one of the smaller pools.

'Check this out.' Sophie nudged a broken chunk of metal into the pool with her foot. The chunk, the size of a scone, skimmed across the surface for a few feet, then slowly melted, spreading slowly across the surface like butter on a warm skillet.

'That's sort of like a pool of mercury but with extra melty powers. Do you think that's the pool that Eva used?' Joel asked.

'I don't know. Maybe.' Sophie moved to a slightly larger pool and dropped a chunk of metal in. The water splashed up into her face. Sophie screeched and tried to rub the moisture off with her hands, instead it spread into a very fine film across her face and eyelids.

'You know this doesn't feel half bad.' Sophie started patting it dry.

The liquid glowed as it hardened into a silver mask.

'Oh my god! Sophie!' Joel tried to peel it off, but Sophie knocked his hand away.

Her lips hardened into a sexy half smile.

Joel heard Matt and Benny running down the tunnel towards them, but his attention turned to the small pool.

Air bubbles popped to the surface. Small waves undulated to the edges. Each disturbance carried snatches of soft singing. A female voice amplified within the liquid.

The singing stopped.

Matt and Benny stumbled into the cavern as the surface frothed. Joel grabbed Sophie by the hand and guided her back towards the tunnel.

'Lordy, there's something bobbing up,' Matt shouted.

A body floated to the surface. Coral lips, alabaster cheeks. Breasts and pelvis thrust up to the dark.

Joel screamed.

Sophie screamed and whirled around in blind terror.

Matt screamed and edged towards the exit.

Benny screamed and angled his iPhone for a selfie with the body clearly visible in the background.

'Jeezus, can't a lady get some privacy around here without a bunch of gawkers barging in?' the body said.

'Jillian?' Joel recognized the voice but not the body.

'Who wants to know?' The body floated to the edge of the pool and climbed out.

Jillian was Venus on a clamshell, but without the coy modesty and proportional body parts. The nipples on her large breasts pointed in different directions while her tiny ass and boney hips seemed to belong to someone else altogether.

'Eyes up here, everyone.' Jillian pointed to her face. 'And while I'm waiting for that to happen could someone get me my clothes from behind that large spindle thingy over there?'

No one moved except Benny, who moved closer to Jillian and continued taking selfies.

'What the hell is going on?' a voice bellowed from the rafters.

Joel looked up and saw Albert picking his way through the top part of the building through broken cogs, splintered beams, rusted latticework. A medium-sized package was clutched under his arm like a football.

'Am I the only one who knows how to get things done around here?' Albert bellowed as he worked his way down, jumping from ledge to ledge with the ease of a mountain goat. 'I had to find these … uh, widgets myself. I have a good mind to — well, hello there.'

Albert stopped in front of Jillian and gawked. 'I don't think we've met.'

'Well, until I get my clothes on, consider we haven't.'

'Of course, young miss.' Albert bowed solicitously to Jillian and hissed at Benny, 'Get this woman some clothes. Even if they're the ones you're wearing.'

Benny fetched Jillian's clothes. Jillian took her time putting them on.

Back at their apartment, Joel gently peeled the mask off Sophie's face, paying special care to her gilded eyelids. As Jillian had suggested, it only required soap, persistence, and a gallon of distilled water.

Sophie's skin glowed.

'Well, what happened? I heard everything, but I couldn't see much.' Sophie rubbed her cheeks and looked in the bathroom mirror. 'Wow, I look ten years younger. The crow's feet are gone. What's in that mask?'

'Don't get any ideas, Soph. I don't want to see you running off with a younger man.'

'Oh, that's sweet. I'd be happy to grow old with you ... as long as I can have smooth skin.'

Joel wondered if he was teetering on the edge of a spontaneous marriage proposal. He pulled back for a moment. 'You heard everything. What did you make of it?'

'You and Matt can scream pretty loud. Louder than me I think. Although you could hear a pin drop when that woman started talking. She's the old lady from your route? Jillian. I recognized her voice.'

'Yes, Jillian.'

'Naked, I gather. Was she swimming somewhere in the grotto? Bizarre. She wasn't in that same pool that splashed up in my face, was she?'

'No, another one.' Joel was reluctant to give away too much information. Beauty secrets were secrets for a reason. He remembered studying the life of Countess Báthory, a sixteenth-century Hungarian noblewoman who bathed in the blood of virgins to keep the wrinkles at bay. Not a practice you'd want to encourage with your future wife ... or anyone really.

'Who was that other guy?' Sophie asked. 'All flirty and bossy at the same time. Sounded like a real asshole.'

'That would've been Albert.'

'Your old friend from university? I'm glad you never introduced us back in the day. I would've slapped his sexist face back to the '50s and I doubt I could've fallen for you.'

'Why not?'

'Birds of a feather.'

'He was my roomie. Friend by default. Contrary to the popular saying, you don't always get to choose your friends.'

Sophie brightened. 'Is he the one Jillian was beating when we were leaving? I can only hope.'

'No, sadly he wasn't. That would've been Lester. He came in rather quietly at some point towards the end and offered himself up to Jillian.'

'Your supervisor? Wasn't he in love with Eva?'

'Yeah, he never got over her. Maybe he believed Jillian beating his brains out with a blunt metal object would redeem him for not letting Eva do the same. Albert was beside himself with the filmic potential of the unfolding drama. You probably heard him pitch the film to himself, negotiate the rights, and get a lock on the property permits during all the screaming and moaning. That's why you're confused.'

'Unbelievable.'

'Believe it. Hollywood has changed him.'

'Benny and Matt then? What happened to them?'

'Benny left with Albert. Quite happy. He's got enough dirt on Albert to guarantee a decent film career if Albert doesn't kill him first. Obviously, he'll get a role in this abomination, but I overheard them talking about another project coming down the pipe: a boy-band biopic. They want to shoot in Northern Ontario — a lot of tax credits involved. According to Albert, the storyline is pretty fluid right now, but the locations and tax credits are solid.'

'Did Matt get paid at least?'

'Matt might be dead? He fell into one of the pools.'

'And you left him there?'

'He sank pretty fast. He might resurface. We just have to wait, apparently.'

'I heard a baby crying. Was that him when he fell in? He's got some pretty odd vocal mannerisms.'

'That was Jillian crying.'

'Jillian rasps. I doubt she could make that sound if she tried.'

Joel fidgeted. He might have to give up the beauty secret.

'Joel.'

Joel sighed. 'Okay. It's like this. Jillian started bludgeoning my supervisor with an iron bar as we were leaving.'

Joel thought about the times he had fantasized bludgeoning his supervisor with a blunt instrument. His act would've been murder. Hers was consensual: a low-tech suicide.

So unfair.

'Yeah, I got that already,' said Sophie, interrupting his reverie. 'Jillian bashing Lester. Check.'

'Anyway, Lester was taking it rather well, then he started moaning. Matt lost it. He ran in and started fighting with Jillian. She was very strong, pinned him to the ground and started bashing *his* head in with the iron bar. As she split his forehead open, he rolled with her over the edge into the pool. They both sank. I think Matt's high silver content messed with the chemical balance in the waters. Silver is antibacterial and antiviral, you know. The water foamed like crazy for a few minutes. We watched. None of us were about to jump in. Then the singing started after five minutes.'

'Wailing more like it. I heard it. The first round I heard was singing. The second wasn't.'

'Okay, wailing.'

'Banshee wailing.'

'Okay, banshee wailing. So, if I can continue?' Joel did a mock curtsey. 'Eventually, a body rose up — all tiny fists and big lungs. We think it might've be Jillian. White skin and no penis. A baby version of Jillian? It certainly wasn't Matt.'

'You left a baby there?'

'Not exactly. Albert fished her out of the water, mumbling something about contractual obligations.'

'Did Matt surface?'

Joel shook his head. 'He might. Albert promised to send Benny early tomorrow to check. Heck, I'll pop in when I do that part of my route in the afternoon.'

Sophie remained sceptical, but Joel was momentarily distracted by the bird.

Socrates was out of her cage and pacing in front of the open window, occasionally pulling at the pins keeping the screen secured into the frame. It was evening. The sun was setting behind their building, casting long shadows out across the small patch of green and into the parking lot.

Socrates squawked, 'Jillian forest. Jillian forest.'

Joel walked over to the bird and offered his hand.

'Step up. Step up,' Socrates squawked. She scampered up to his wrist.

Joel moved his arm up and down, so Socrates could simulate flight and exercise her wings.

'You know, Socrates, I don't think you want to go out there. The real world is full of terrible people and terrible things. You are much safer here. We'll put the TV on. It'll be Netflix and chill. Not the metaphor. The real deal.'

'I'll make some popcorn,' Sophie added as she walked into the kitchen.

Joel lowered his voice. 'And I will propose to Sophie soon enough. You watch. It's time to start adulting.'

Joel and Sophie squeezed into the love seat with their back to the window. Socrates perched between them. The television clicked on. Joel started scrolling through the choices. They had binged a lot of shows already. Finding something to agree on might be hard.

'Hey, you know that coffee shop near the university that we used to hang out in before we officially started dating?' Joel asked.

'The Mocha El Grande.'

'Yeah, well Albert told me a funny story of how they were shooting a movie out there a while back and — '

'Oh my god.' Sophie spilled popcorn as she spoke. 'I forgot to ask about your supervisor, Lester. Is he dead? Should we call the police?'

'He's pretty messed up, but alive. Jillian's eyesight isn't that good, so she missed more often than she hit. Albert and Benny promised to drop him off at home. They dunked his head in the pool a couple of times before leaving. He looked ready for the lucha libre circuit. That silver mask is pretty awesome.'

Sophie reflexively rubbed her cheek and murmured.

'He'll be at his desk early tomorrow morning as crusty as ever. I'll text you,' Joel assured her, although it seemed she had momentarily drifted off into her own little world.

'Yes, text me … and take a picture of his face. Not that I don't trust you. Just … curious.'

'Sure.' Joel looked at his wrists, noticing a cluster of age spots. It was the beginning of the death spiral. He remembered his face this morning as well while trimming his beard. Thinning lips. Bags under his eyes. Wattle neck. Entropy. The body falling apart as planned. He should fix that. He could fix that.

Sophie reflexively rubbed her cheek and murmured again.

How far would she go? She spent an awful lot on serums and creams already. Those pharmaceutical companies were making a killing.

Murder maybe?

Murder maybe.

'Where's the money?' Drexel stared into the till. The Lady Smoothskin pantyhose covering Drexel's face began to wrinkle. Sweat seeped through taupe nylon pores. He'd been hoping for a quick smash and grab, but it was going south fast. It didn't help that a movie shoot had set up outside his mom's apartment the night before and kept him awake with screechy megaphone demands like 'Action!', 'Cut!' and 'Back to first positions!'

To Drexel, movies were like hamburgers. You didn't want to watch or hear them being made. You just ate them up.

Drexel ripped out the till and slammed it on the counter. There was a clutch of twenties, tens and fives along the middle row. That was it. The nickels, dimes, quarters, loonies and toonies were still wrapped in their sleeves and stacked neatly beside the cash register. More coins sat in two slash-proof bags on the floor.

'Where's the freakin' money?' Drexel said again with a little more force. He did not swear or shout. He did not like swearing or shouting. He could rob people at gunpoint but swearing and shouting were impolite. It was un-Canadian. He had been raised better.

So he talked softly and carried a Glock instead.

Turning towards one of the baristas, Drexel snarled, 'Is that all there freakin' is?'

Keeping the safety on, he pressed the gun into her shoulder.

Stacey looked down at her shoes. The words seemed to catch in her throat. 'Morning float — it's all we have.'

Drexel stared at the girl for a few seconds. She was cute. Thick black hair and a curvy body. The Mocha El Grande uniform did not do her justice. It was like a prison jumpsuit, but in canary yellow instead of orange.

Her face looked drained and she didn't smile much.

Drexel wondered if maybe she hadn't put on enough makeup this morning before coming in to work, or maybe she hadn't got a good night's sleep.

'Hey Rufus, any action you can see outside?' Drexel said without breaking the creepy stare.

'Don't think so.' Rufus tugged at the fishnet stockings covering his face, trying to adjust the thick seam away from his right eye as he struggled with the front door blinds.

Drexel walked over to the front door and peeked through the slats of the blinds himself.

The empty parking lot was dominated by the Mocha El Grande sign: a neon-blue-throated starfish with big eyes and no mouth. It danced like Shiva — four arms wielding blaze-white cups of coffee and sloshing bits of blue light into the darkness. It was five fifty-five in the morning, and the store didn't open till six, but that sign was all fired up and promising caffeinated salvation.

'Is there any way to turn that light off?' Drexel asked.

'No,' a voice squeaked. 'It's on a timer.'

Drexel stalked over to the pastry display case where the other barista, pale and thin, lay stretched out and face down on the tiles. Blood trickled out of the side of the barista's mouth.

Drexel bent down and used the nose of his gun to poke the barista in the side. 'You got cash on you? Or wheels? We ain't leaving till we got something more than a couple hundred bucks. I don't get out of bed for less than a grand.'

The barista on the floor apologized. His swollen lip made speech painful. 'No sir, and again I was not trying to diss you when I said it was odd to rob a business ... before ... it opened for business. It was only an observation.'

'Observe this.' Drexel pressed his foot down on the barista's back.

The barista wheezed.

Drexel eased up on the pressure.

The barista continued, 'In my assistant management training course we call it ... "synergizing the parameters of the cube". You regular folk might know it as "thinking outside the box".'

Drexel pressed his foot down and leaned in. 'How'd you like to be thinking "inside" the box — a coffin box. Cut the management bull crap and think about how I'm gonna walk out of here with more money.'

'Why don't we just cut and run?' Rufus walked over and hefted the two bags of rolled coins from the floor. An inked mermaid rippled along the length of one of Rufus's forearms. A dragon uncoiled down the other. Blue veins popped on white skin. 'We got some serious weight going on here.'

Drexel growled, 'Do I want to be running down the street with a big bag of money like some cartoon bandit?'

Rufus stared blankly through the quarter-inch spaces of the fishnets. The black seam was now over his left eye.

'We're professionals,' Drexel whispered through clenched teeth. Drexel returned his attention to the female barista. Studying her name tag, Drexel tried a more coaxing tone. 'So ... Stacey. How much money you think you can get from your bank machine, or from your co-worker's bank machine?'

Drexel pointed to the barista on the floor.

'Hey, you on the floor. What's your name?' Drexel asked.

'Robert.' The barista's voice was muffled, his lips and nose still crushed against the tile.

'Robert, how much you got in your bank account?' Drexel asked.

Robert slowly turned over on to his side. 'I'm overdrawn. Probably the same as Stacey. Student debt and minimum wage. Sad but true.'

Drexel felt like shouting and swearing.

Rufus walked over to the shelves stacked with expensive coffee paraphernalia. 'We could grab whatever cash and some of this fancy coffee gak. All these chrome coffee mugs got to be worth something. We could sell them or give them to Digby. Cover some of the debt, you know.'

Stacey's eyes widened.

'No names, doofus,' Drexel hissed at Rufus.

'Awright. Ixnay on the amesay.' Rufus winked, one of his eyebrow piercings catching on the fishnet.

Robert raised himself up on one elbow. 'He's got a point — about the coffee peripherals. Even with the employee discount, the mugs cost twenty bucks per unit, and don't get me started on the mobile espresso makers. Three hundred per unit. You could easily cart off a few of those. They're lighter and more efficient than anything else on the market.'

Drexel stepped on Robert and pushed him back into the floor. 'How about we sell this stuff from here? We open the store and sell it all — coffee, snacks, mugs, whatever you got.'

Drexel paced over to the takeout window and glanced outside. Five cars idled within a few meters of the drive-through lane. It was four minutes before opening. In another three hours he had to be in school. He didn't want to be late for class.

'You on the floor,' Drexel barked. 'Get up and open the drive-through.'

Robert dragged himself over to the window, punched his employee number into the register, and slipped on his headset.

'Help! Help! May I help you?' Robert whispered into his mic.

Drexel glared. 'Buddy, no one knows we're open yet. Do something to get their attention — like isn't there some light for the drive-through entrance you can turn on?'

Robert flicked a switch and poked his body halfway through the window.

With a silently mouthed *help*, Robert frantically waved his arms. Behind him, the starfish on the Mocha El Grande sign waved just as frantically.

The cars moved into position. Drexel pulled Robert back inside.

Trying not to look directly at the beige-stockinged shadow beside him, Robert slowly exhaled into the intercom, 'Welcome to Mocha El Grande. Your order is our command. How can I ... *help* ... you today.

'Ye ...' An electronic voice whined. '... ree ... caps ... ee ... rie ... eese ... nish.'

Robert punched in the order. The total flashed up on the screen. 'That'll be nineteen dollars and thirty-five cents. Please drive through.'

'You understood that? All that beep, bop, eep, eese stuff?" Drexel ripped open a cello-wrapped package of biscotti and started crunching. 'It sounded like you were talking to R2D2 or something.'

'Electronic Linguistics. Standard training.'

Drexel choked down the rest of the biscotti. 'Well, tell dude there you'll throw in one of these stale biscuity things for an even twenty. Cash only. We got to make some quick cash.'

'Biscotti. They're called biscotti,' Robert muttered while leaning into the intercom. He switched to his best announcer voice. 'Beg your pardon, sir, we're having a special promotion today. Add our one cappuccino raisin flake ... *biscotti* ... for an even twenty-five dollars.'

'All right. Mr Employee of the Month.'

'Associate of the Month. We're not employees. We're partners.'

'Partners eh? Are you partners in the profits? I'm thinking no.'

Robert ignored Drexel and pointed to a plastic wood-grain plaque above the drive-through window with Robert's picture on it.

'Associate of the Month. Three times in a row.'

Drexel ignored Robert and turned towards Rufus. 'Best help Shorty get that order together. We'll get outta here faster.'

Rufus tucked his gun into his waistband and sidled up alongside Stacey.

'Hey Shorty, best I help get that order together. We'll get outta here faster.'

'Shorty eh?' Stacey rapidly twisted the steam wand with a damp cleaning cloth. She straightened to her full height and looked down at Rufus. 'Well, maybe if you stand ... over there.' Stacey indicated the farthest possible distance from her that was still behind the counter. 'There by the coffee dispenser ... to pour coffee ... when needed.'

'We need four grandioso mochachoco-frappelinos.' Robert blurred past carrying a tray of brie cheese Danishes toward the takeout window.

Drexel drifted out of the shadows. 'Do people actually buy regular coffee at this place?'

'Some do.' Stacey lined up a half-dozen shot glasses by the espresso machine as Robert called out for six doppio caramalachiattas.

'I'm thinking no.' Drexel grabbed a frothed drink from a customer's order. 'So, I'm thinking it might be a good idea to get my partner on that expresso machine with you.'

'Espresso,' Stacey corrected him.

'Yeah, what I said.' Drexel lifted the nylon veil above his lips and gulped. He wiped his mouth of the foam. 'This is seriously good shit.'

Rufus turned towards Drexel. 'The swears, bro.'

'But, this *is* seriously good shit.'

'Look, Mr … what should we call you guys?' Stacey's hands moved rapidly over the chrome control panel of the Z28.2 Robusta Deluxe. 'It'll be easier to get the product out if we can call you a name, preferably a fake one. The less I know about you, the happier I'll be."

'Call me …' Drexel touched the Lady Smoothskin pantyhose on his head. 'Mr Smoothskin.'

'Well, Mr Smoothskin, welcome aboard.' Stacey nodded over to Rufus. 'And you?'

Rufus scratched his face through the fishnet stocking for a few minutes. 'Gimme a second.'

'Wait, wait, almost got it.…' Rufus tugged at the black seam of the fishnet stocking, which was now running down the middle of his nose.

Rufus brightened.

'Call me … Mr …' Rufus touched his fishnet mask again and casually leaned against the Thermo-Nuke Coffee Roaster behind him. Black smoky tendrils of roasting flesh scent quickly permeated the blue-grey haze of roasting beans.

'F-f-f …' Rufus stuttered.

'Starts with an F. I get it,' Stacey encouraged. 'How many syllables?'

The soft sizzling sound of frying flesh intermingled with the delicate plaint of forced fricatives.

'F-f-f …'

'One syllable? Sounds like?' Stacey cupped her ear.

'F-F-FUUUCK!' Rufus screamed.

Rufus shot forward into the open doors of the Muffinator Convection System. The doors closed with a sizzle, clasping his shoulders against blue-hot steel.

Rufus's mouth flapped open. No sound.

Stacey continued, 'Okay, if Mr Smoothskin and Mr … Fuck could line up the cups according to the order and size, that would be super-helpful.'

Rufus's mouth flapped open. No sound.

Stacey thumped a spent espresso pod into the garbage and carefully refilled the chrome filter cup.

'Sure.' Drexel reached for a straight shot of espresso and gulped it down. 'That would be super-great, and I would super-love that.'

Robert sniffed. 'Does anyone smell something burning? Is the roaster on too high? It'll scorch the flavour right out of those beans. Is anyone listening?'

All eyes turned to the Muffinator ... and Rufus.

Tiny orange flames fanned along the surface of his grey synthetic hoodie. Complex polymer chains burst, melted, flickered into gobs of fire — hissing and snuffling as they dribbled to the floor. Rufus staggered backwards out from the Muffinator's embrace.

'Ffffff.' More foam spittled from Rufus's lips.

'Didn't we already go through this?' Robert offered.

'Fffffff.' Foam spittled from Rufus's lips.

'This is like some mind game right? To exploit our sympathies?' Robert offered again. 'Is this how the Stockholm syndrome works?'

'Fire!' Drexel shouted, and tackled Rufus to the ground. With each slap and pull at the hoodie, the flames splattered further, igniting Drexel's poly-cotton sprint pants.

Rufus slapped and pulled at Drexel's pants.

Drexel slapped — hard.

'Are we quite finished?' Robert grabbed a fire extinguisher and aimed a cold foamy blast over both. Grey-white smoke swirled up into the exhaust fans. 'I have a dozen more orders and —'

An electronic whine staccatoed over the drive-through intercom. With uncanny precision, complete words fell between the intermittent drops in frequency: 'Hey buds, it's Benny Tak ... from Potboiler Productions ... same order as ... yesterday ... twenty-five El Grande Mocha ... cocoa chinos ... seven ... of which ... almond foam ... ten ... reduced-sugar soya ... milk ... another twenty-five iced-butter-bomb green teas — skinny ...'

Robert's eyes glazed. His fingers skittered and poked over the touch screen like dancing crabs. On the overhead monitor, the order flashed in a series of jumbled coded text and numbers.

'Sounds like he'll be dropping a lot of cash.' Drexel stood up and brushed off the last of the embers. He tried to pull the pantyhose back down over his head, but only the waistband remained intact. The rest had fused into his foam-frozen ginger dreds, which now looked vaguely squid-like.

'Yeah, that production company has been in the neighbourhood for a week now. Every day they come by and drop over four hundred ...' Robert stopped talking and stared at Drexel's hair.

Rufus pulled himself up to his feet and leaned against the counter. His blond hair had clumped into a large pointy shark fin, with a foamy white tip. His face was blackened with soot around the eyes like a raccoon. He looked like an animal hybrid experiment gone wrong.

Stacey continued to work the espresso machine and did not look up. 'That guy is a smug hipster jerk. He had the nerve to ask me out, and then not show up.'

Stacey studied the monitor and started setting up the order. 'He's been in here every day this week, waving his money around and acting like he owns the place: "Just a touch more foam with this, just a little less foam with that." Grrrr! I hate him.'

'I would ask you out, and show up,' Drexel mumbled through the pain.

'Aww, that's so thoughtful,' Stacey said sarcastically.

Stacey studied both robbers for a few moments. 'Look, you two want to get your money and run. Rob and I want to finish our shift and go home. Let us do our job. You can do yours by sitting down and staying out of the way. Any questions or anything?'

Drexel noticed that most of his pants had melted into a puddle on the floor.

'You got any spare clothes?' Drexel asked.

Stacey marched into the storage room and marched back out. She dumped two uniforms on the counter. 'They're old uniforms. I don't know if they'll fit but it's all we have. Meanwhile, you can keep your "disguises" on. People might think you're some kind of promotional mascots.'

Drexel and Rufus slunk away to change.

'Hey everyone!' Benny Tak leaned out of his van window as he rolled into view at the takeout window. His purple bangs flopped across his eyes. 'As I remember, yesterday's order was obviously a little overwhelming, so I'll park in front and you can give me a shout when it's all ready. Ciao bella, and go easy on the foam please.'

Benny's metallic-blue van shimmered away.

'Asshole.' Stacey fumed.

'He didn't pay yet, did he? That ain't right.' Drexel poked his head out from the storage room.

'Don't worry, he'll pay as soon as the order is ready, and to his satisfaction.' Stacey scalded the milk. A faint whiff of burnt sugar permeated the air.

'I smell something that begins with delicious.' Rufus squeezed past Drexel and strolled up to the front in his uniform: a bright orange jumpsuit with an embroidered sheriff's star appliquéd with googly eyes.

Drexel followed in the same outfit. 'Seriously? This is wrong on so many different levels.'

'It's amazing what you'll do for a buck,' Stacey said.

'There's gotta be something else for me to wear.' Drexel stalked back to the storage room.

Rufus stood up to the espresso machine.

In rapid succession, he made a single, a double, and a triple-long espresso. Pausing to crack his knuckles, he winced momentarily before frothing a coconut milk cappuccino and a skinny smoka-chino — simultaneously.

'You learn fast when you're on the street.' Rufus winked at Stacey and gave a clumsy thumbs-up, inadvertently knuckling the emergency kill switch.

The Z38.2 cycled down into a slow descending throb, punctuated by the angry hiss of escaping steam. Hot black liquid dribbled and stopped.

Stacey elbowed the fin-headed menace out of the way and switched the machine back on.

'Super-great, that'll take five minutes to warm up again,' Stacey huffed.

Rufus slunk over to the cups and started lining them up according to size and order.

An insistent tapping on glass drew Robert's attention to the front door. Through the partially opened slats, Robert could see Benny Tak waving and pointing to an imaginary watch on his wrist.

'Trouble brewing,' Robert said quietly out of the side of his mouth while pretending to ignore the P.A.

Benny mimed an imaginary drink being poured into an imaginary cup. Benny mimed drinking from the imaginary cup. Benny mimed surprise that the imaginary cup and drink were imaginary.

Robert mimed back with an extended middle finger.

Benny mimed shock and disappointment.

'Plan B!' Drexel shouted as he walked briskly out of the back room to the front door. He was wearing black slacks, an electric-blue collared shirt, and a black clip-on tie. 'Looks like I'm associate manager now!'

Drexel twisted the deadbolt open, hauled the startled P.A. inside, and snarled, 'Now this is what's going down — you're giving me your cash, your van, and you ain't getting no fancy coffee drinks.'

Drexel chugged a triple-long espresso with his free hand and shouted, 'I feel motherfucking great! Time to amp it up, bro.'

Rufus drew his gun. 'Everyone into the back room where we got some nice chairs and duct tape.'

Stacey cleared her throat and looked at Drexel, then at Benny, then back again at Drexel.

'Okay, okay, I get it.' Drexel sighed. 'The girl and Mr Associate of the Month into the back room. Mr Movie Big-Shot into the broom closet. No funny stuff.'

Drexel drew his gun and clicked the safety off.

'So cool.' Benny nodded. 'Just like in the movies. Even the dialogue. Wow. They're gonna love this story when I get back to set.'

'Which won't be for some time.' Drexel pushed Benny in the direction of the broom closet.

'Oh, Benny. You might just miss your free catered lunch — so sad,' Stacey said as she dragged a comfortable-looking leather club chair to the back room.

'You know, they're going to miss me pretty quickly. The whole magical moviemaking process will grind to a halt. The actors can't function without caffeine. They'll lock themselves in their trailers and refuse to come out. I've seen it before. It's ugly.'

'Actors eh?' Rufus rolled the duct tape around Benny's wrists and the chair arms. 'So, who's in the movie? Anyone famous?'

Stacey exploded. 'Who cares! Just tape him up. Tape us up. And get out of here … before you get caught.'

'Hold on, I'm the one calling the shots.' Drexel turned to face the production assistant. 'Is there anyone really famous?'

Benny leaned back in the chair. 'Oh yeah. Denzel Washington. Christopher Walken. Nicki Minaj. Nicki's getting into acting in a really serious way these days. Making the big jump.'

Drexel and Rufus whistled.

Robert rolled his eyes.

'C'mon guys,' Stacey pleaded. 'We're losing our focus. Isn't this all about the money?'

Stacey cut and stretched out lengths of duct tape and hung them in neat rows on the broom closet door. They looked like pretend prison bars.

'How would you guys like an autograph and a selfie with Nicki?' Benny asked. 'I'm not really expecting you to release me … but if you did … I might just be able to arrange something. She's totally down to earth. Nothing like her videos.'

Drexel and Rufus looked at each other.

Benny contemplated the half-filled order on the counter. 'But I can't go back empty-handed.'

Drexel followed his gaze. 'How do I know that you aren't gonna turn us in soon as you get a chance?'

'If I turned you in, I'd have to spend an hour or two answering questions with the police. I wouldn't get paid for that time. I'm a lowly production assistant. In fact, production would replace me on the spot and I'd be out of a job. A year or two down the road when the trial happens, I'd have to go to court and testify, and not get paid for that either. If I'm working on a show at the time I would be let go. Precarious employment sucks.'

Drexel and Rufus nodded.

Stacey and Robert nodded.

'Deal,' Drexel, Rufus, Stacey, and Robert said simultaneously.

Benny squinted at Robert's and Stacey's name tags, then turned towards Drexel and Rufus. 'Give Robby and Stace their store back. We finish the order. You and your partner help me take it back to set. I claim it's a freebie promotion. Everyone's a hero.'

'And the money to cover the cost of this "freebie promotion" comes from …?' Robert grumbled.

'I'll kick in some cash.' Rufus dug into his pockets and threw a wad of fifties on the counter.

Rufus removed the duct tape from Benny's wrists.

Benny looked at Drexel.

Drexel took a stolen wallet from his knapsack and placed it on the counter. He peeled off several twenty-dollar bills and a few hundred-dollar bills. 'Who said crime don't pay?'

'Excellent, let's get down to business. Rob and Stace are in charge of the espresso machine, and … um, what names do you two want to go by?' Benny looked at Drexel and Rufus.

'Call me … D-Rex.' Drexel looked over at Rufus. 'Call him … Roofie.'

'Cool. The Roof-man can oversee line production—lining up the cups according to size and order.' Benny gathered up an armful of napkins, creamers, sugars, and stir sticks and dumped them in a box. 'Mr D-Rex, 'cause you are clearly the man, you will manage the others so that the finished product gets safely and accurately to my van. You can start by grabbing that box of creamers and stuff and coming out with me. Oh, and you're in charge of pastries as well. Nicki loves the big Danish.'

As they walked out to the door, Benny pressed the remote. The side doors of the van trundled open.

Drexel held the box of napkins, creamers, sugars, and stir sticks. 'So, tell me again, why should I trust you?'

Benny gave the remote to Drexel and took the box. He placed the box in the van. 'As I see it, you're not much different from most of the producers I know. They take the money and the credit while everyone else does the hard work. And don't get me started on actors—they commit all sorts of crimes and get away with it. It's called cinematic immunity. Look it up.'

'I'm in the wrong business.'

'You're in the right business, you just have the wrong clientele.'

Drexel watched Rufus inside the store as he clumsily stacked drinks into cardboard takeout trays.

Robert and Stacey were a blur of efficiency.

Drexel turned to Benny.

'Do you think I'd fit in?'

'Of course. It's show business. Where else can larceny, murder, and other bad behaviours be counted as entertainment? And be richly rewarded?'

GHOST NOTE

Strobe

    lights

    trigger.

A memory: a flash mob of pale green skullcaps and white masks huddle over my body, fists pumping to the beat. I float above them, serene. I observe everything.

Where are we today? A bar in Goodwin, Ontario—the gateway to the north. The music is loud. We are into our second set. The stage is crammed with gear. Barely enough room for the three of us.

I rumble thunder on a black Warlock bass. Dougie's drums pulse. The crescendo builds.

Lars, half-brother, halfwit, total asshole, steps towards the microphone. His scuffed Flying V dangles momentarily before he picks it up and starts arpeggiating 'Enter Sandman'.

The crowd goes wild.

Goodwin is a strange place. A tiny fishing hamlet with a reed-choked lake and no decent coffee shop. It has three bars that 'pack 'em in' every weekend.

Tonight: Friday at the Giidhouse Tavern. No umlauts required. All hail the Labour Day Weekend! A sop to the working poor as the wealthy consume the rest of the world.

I notice a few bikers by the bar. Black leather vests, bandanas, beards. Laughing. Chatting up the female bartenders.

Outlaw bikers inhabit the same fractional universe as the elites: one percenters meet the one percent. The first gang screw you up. The second gang screw you over.

I contemplate all this as we hit the chorus.

The crowd undulates: mullets and metalheads, a riptide of testosterone, a swirling sea of white arms and black T-shirts. A sea of trouble.

Tatts and piercings. Ink and metal anchoring rudderless lives.

I thrash my head up and down. Sweaty strands of bottle-black hair whip and cling across grey stubble.

Words I cannot control slip through the turnstile of my mouth: 'Asshat! Sorry! Fuck-wad! Sorry!'

The litany continues.

I have Canadian Tourette's.

My lawyer swears it's true.

Lars gives me the stink eye but continues singing.

The band is so loud no one can really hear me anyway. My brothers won't let me anywhere near a live microphone. They always disconnect mine after the sound check.

The urge surges. I lock down a little tighter on the bass knowing that my fingers will soon thread and weave on their own. Pierce. Puncture. Pull through. Not seamless but exhilarating.

I notice women in the crowd — splashes of pink, purple, blond — flashes of sparkle in an otherwise pitch-black room. I bite my tongue hard. I taste blood: 'Pouvoir de la chatte! ... Je suis desolé!'

Canadian Tourette's in both official languages.

I grimace over at Dougie. He does not look up from his kit. His arms blur between snare, toms, cymbals. A vicious double kick on the bass drum vibrates our logo of a smoky black rose into a shimmering mirage. We are Ashthorn — too old to rock-and-roll, too young to die, too mediocre to care.

We finish the song and quickly launch into the next, an original number called 'Tim Whoretown' — a caffeine-amped ode to donuts and collective consumer guilt. Lars grimaces into the microphone. Singing our own stuff is risky. We usually slip a few into the middle of a set when everyone is totally wasted.

Lars sings in a screechy falsetto worthy of Geddy Lee: 'Palm oil is napalm oil drilling deep into donut fashion. / Cookies crumble, pussies rumble, monkeys die in de-rainforest jumble.'

The guitar seesaws at his side. Lars clutches the stand and strikes a pose, stretching his black T-shirt inches above his hairy white belly.

Imagine a really pissed Lorax.

'The hole in the circle is the whole of my head / Jam it bang it / I'd rather be dead / The blood on my hands is a broil on the brain / Oozing jam jelly, oozing insane.'

I hate this song. Doug hates this song. Lars hates this song, and he wrote it.

'Bavarian Nazi / Creme-filled hate!' Lars screams. The house P.A. system crackles and pops. *'Donut dream puff masturbate!'*

Lars's voice drops a full three octaves, and all coherence, as he launches into the chorus:

'Bubblebubbletoilandtrouble
Washdowntheguiltwithadoubledouble.
Bubblebubblethirstandslake
Nakedandwrithinglikeamoultingsnake.'

Dougie crams through enough frills, fills, and microbeats to make Neil Peart blush; and more importantly, to distract the audience as much as possible from the asinine lyrics.

We are Ashthorn, painfully straddling the razor's edge between self-importance and self-parody.

The gig is over.

The lights, swaddled in chicken wire, are up and humming. Ugly tubes of fluorescence sing harmonies, soft with the ringing in my ears.

I look down at the floor. It's a revelation of shredded suicide wings, crushed plastic beer cups, torn condom wrappers, bile, vomit....

Lars sits at the edge of the stage with his legs dangling towards the murk. A young woman with iridescent purple bangs chats with him. Lars swings his legs like a little boy and nods.

'Yeah, I ...' Lars stops to think a bit.

No one wants to take credit for our original material.

Lars starts again, *'We* wrote that one 'cause I ...'

Lars pauses again. *'We* was really ticked off about how we exploit nature and consume everything without really giving a shit … sorry … a crap about, you know, consequences. Tims is the, you know, Trojan horse metaphor that allows us to put the … er, jelly-like meaning in.'

'Oh yeah, that's super cool.' Purple Bangs nods. Her voice is quite husky. I am transfixed by her large Adam's apple as it bobs with the hard *c* in *cool*.

'It's not that we're slagging Tim Hortons,' Lars continues. 'I love their coffee, and it always seems we got a box of Timbits rattling around somewhere in the van, but … you know, metaphor.'

Purple Bangs nods. I am now transfixed by her large conical breasts. They can't be real.

Lars shrugs and stares at the floor. 'Whadya think of the show? It wasn't our best. Sound system sucked. It was the house P.A. I couldn't hear myself singing most of the time.'

'We'd all be so lucky!' Dougie shouts way too loud. It was meant to be a joke but comes across as a hysterical declamation. Dougie's eardrums are as badly beaten as his kit.

Lars gives him the finger but smiles.

The motel room is small. I am in the bathroom brushing my teeth. Dougie stretches out on top of one of the two single beds. He is dozing off in his clothes.

The duvet is dusty rose with patches of moth white speckled throughout — probably bleach stains.

'Out, damned spot,' I mutter to myself, imagining what the original source of the stain was before the bleach got to it.

I consider getting my sleeping bag out of the van.

Lars and the Purple Girl — Candy or Candice, I think — are in the next room making out. On the road, Lars, Dougie, and I usually share one room, or sleep in the van.

Money is money.

But sex is sex.

Springs squeak. The headboard slaps. I expect their bed to come cresting through the thin drywall like the triumphant figurehead on the prow of Odysseus's ship.

Epic sex.

I am aroused and horrified at the same time.

'Aieee!' Candy's call.

'Uhhhhh!' Lars's response.

The squeaking slows and stops.

It will be quiet now. Lars does not do encores. There will be pillow talk like, 'Can I get you a taxi,' or 'Can you call a taxi,' or 'Does this small town have taxi service?'

In some towns the talk turns to Uber.

Tomorrow we'll clear out by 10:30 a.m. and drive six hours north to Hatcheta Falls for the next gig and do it all over again.

Scuffling and banging.

'Aieeee!' Lars's call.

I turn the faucet on and rinse my toothbrush. Maybe Lars is doing an encore after all.

'AIEEEEEE!' Lars's call again. His voice is loud but muffled, like someone standing beside you and shouting with a sock in his mouth.

'FUUUUCK!' Lars again. He is clearly not using his indoor voice.

The sounds of large heavy objects being overturned and smashed.

Lars screams.

Dougie and I bolt from our room and step outside into the motel parking lot. The light above our door pulses momentarily, brightens, pops.

Loose filament. Old-school incandescent.

Purple Candy steps outside Lars's door. Red lipstick smears down the side of her mouth.

She pushes a black fingernail into my chest and easily shunts me aside. Dougie tries to block her. She grabs his arm and twists.

'Drummer?' Dougie whimpers.

Purple Candy lets go and kicks him in the balls. Dougie drops to his hands and knees on the concrete sidewalk like a dog.

Dougie howls.

I look in the room. Lars is collapsed on the floor. The room is trashed — rock-and-roll style.

Purple Candy turns slowly towards me. She is prettier than I remember. She smiles. Her teeth are blaze white. Her eyes, blaze red.

'Whadya gonna do, Mr Bass Man?' Purple Candy asks. One hand rests on her hips.

'It's *bass* — long *a*. Instrument — not the fish,' I say.

My lips are swollen, and I can barely see out of my right eye as I drive. Lars slumps in the passenger seat. His face is covered in blotchy scratches and bite marks. It is an improvement from his usual pale, undead-looking self.

'Did you see her eyes?' Lars asks.

Dougie moans from the back of the van, something vaguely affirmative.

I nod.

'I think she slipped them on ... the contacts ... in the bathroom ... before getting into bed. They actually glow ... in the dark. That is some high-end shit. She's got a kinky bag of treats, man.'

I nod.

Lars pauses. 'That was pretty near the best pussy I ever had, and it damn near killed me.'

I had my own near-death experience when I was nineteen years old. It had nothing to do with cats. It was a burst appendix during a battle-of-the-bands performance at high school. The crowd went wild as I doubled over on the stage during the chorus of 'Smells Like Teen Spirit', smacking the headstock of my Ibanez bass against the back of Lars's head. It was '91. New Wave had danced itself dead and Grunge was grumbling to life.

The band got honourable mention. I got septic shock.

Rushed to hospital in the back of the principal's station wagon, I almost died. I remember the operating table and floating above my body as the doctors and nurses saved my life. I remember an out-of-body experience with me drifting into the waiting room and watching Dougie eat a bag of chips and drink noisily from a can of Coke. I remember Lars sulking.

I don't remember our parents showing up.

'Your destination is to your right,' the GPS asserts cheerfully.

To our right is a massive shoulder of bruised granite crested with dirt and spindly shrubs. The horizon is curtained with dark green pine.

'It doesn't look like a tavern,' Lars observes.

'*Your destination is to your right,*' the GPS asserts again. The cheerfulness is almost a provocation.

It is 6:30 p.m. We have forty-five minutes to find the Hatcheta Falls Tavern, set up, do a sound check, and grab a few beers. Doable, but the tavern doesn't have a P.A. system or sound man. We are going in cold.

'Whazzup?' Dougie leans forward from his swaddling bed of sound blankets. His crotch is double-packed with bags of ice. He has a stupid grin on his face. He's been into the Tylenol 3s again.

'I think we took a wrong turn at the fork a couple of kilometres back,' I say. 'Multi-path error. The forest can act like a canyon and bounce the signal all over the place. The tavern is probably parallel with us, but on the other side of the forest. Sometimes you can't see the tavern for the trees.' I attempt a witticism.

'GPS sucks.' Dougie yawns. 'Digital sucks.'

'Ha-ha! Yeah! Right! Digital sucks donkey dicks!' Lars fist pumps, and adds, 'They can try to pry that dirty analog Fuzz Box out of my cold dead hands before I go digital.'

'Can they pry that iPhone out of your hands too?' I ask.

'Fuck you,' Lars huffs.

I stare at the forest, the trees, and the rocks as we double back to the fork and follow right instead of left. After twenty minutes bouncing along a corrugated dirt road, we pull into a parking lot jammed with pickup trucks and ATVs. The Hatcheta Falls Tavern is busy, and in need of a good makeover. The board-and-batten siding is the colour of a dead horse's ass and the wraparound porch out front is all bright white pickets and broken teeth.

Sound check.

It is going to be a rough night. A wall of chicken wire stretches across the front of the stage. We are the fluorescent tubes of our last gig. Fragile beams of light. On the other side of the wire — lumberjack men and Daisy Duke women eat, drink, and otherwise ignore us.

Lars gazes out at the crowd and plucks his guitar, morphing a G major into a diminished 7th. 'I'm thinking they might not dig our type of music out here.'

'Yeah, the beards and Thunder Bay dinner jackets don't look ironic.' Dougie tightens the nut on his hi-hat. 'Let's just do covers. No Death Metal. And no Metalcore either.'

'Yeah nothing with "metal" in it,' Lars adds.

'Or "meta",' I quip. Another witticism. Another dull response from my brothers as they stare at me blankly.

Dougie adds, 'Definitely nothing we wrote. I'm thinking Stones and Beatles and maybe some good old Nirvana.'

I nod. 'I'll park the van by the back door for an easy out if things go south.'

The first set goes well.

Some *Sticky Fingers.*

A whole lot of *Rubber Soul.*

Bits of *Nevermind.*

Intermission.

Victoria, one of the waitresses, sets three Coronas down on a small table at the back of the stage. Her long dark hair is clipped with a turquoise cabochon clasped within hammered silver.

'That was awesome, guys. I never heard "Norwegian Wood" with all those drum solos,' she says.

I pop the lime wedge into my beer and watch the fizz bubble up to the lip.

'Yeah, we're trying something a little different,' I say. 'Stuff from when we first started playing.'

'Hmm.' Victoria tilts her head slightly. She is doing the math.

'Look we're old but not that old,' I say. 'When we were growing up in Toronto — well technically Scarborough, but we'll call it Toronto generically — most rock radio stations were ten to twenty years behind on their playlists. Nirvana and Soundgarden were on tour, but The Mighty Q was still playing Journey and Boston.'

Lars puts one hand up. 'Hello, the seventies just called. They want their playlist back!'

'Yeah,' I add. 'It seems all the radio stations out here still wanna play that old-timey rock-and-roll. Not that there's anything wrong with it, but, you know ... 2017.'

Victoria backhands my shoulder. 'Oh, you Trono folk think we're all a bunch of backwoods types out here. We got the Internet, you know.'

Victoria nudges me with her hip. 'Do you guys have any, like, original stuff? I mean your covers are good, but everyone's got at least one good song in 'em.'

'I don't think we even have one good chorus,' Lars laments.

'True that,' I say.

'Oh, c'mon, throw the dogs a bone.' Victoria gestures towards the seething mass of rib-shucking, wing-crunching, hirsute humanity. 'You can't get a leg up without taking a chance.'

We get a leg up. A few legs in fact. Both of mine are up and over a couple of empty guitar cases in the back of our van as it careens out of the parking lot. The good townsfolk of the Hatcheta Falls Tavern funnel out of the bar—hurling sticks and stones, empty beer bottles, and many hurtful words. Doug is silent. Lars jabbers with a bloody fat lip.

'Am I really an ass suck?' Lars's mouth bleeds over the words. 'We didn't even get through the first couple of verses of 'Tim Whoretown' and someone tried to pull me through the chicken wire for Christ's sake ... I'm missing a tooth I think ... all our equipment is still on the stage...' Lars trails off.

'I said covers only.' Dougie spits. He is krumped on Red Bull, suicide wings, and Smirnoff. His face is boil red.

Victoria drives.

'Sorry, guys. I steered you wrong,' Victoria apologizes. 'You can go back tomorrow and pick everything up. Bert, the owner, is really good about keeping the performance area off limits. You'd have been safe there, although they might've wrecked your van a little if they got to it, but not by much. Most everyone knows how important a set of wheels is out here. No other way to get around. They're respectful that way.'

Silence.

'No worries,' Victoria continues. 'You can crash at my grandparents' place. That's where I live, with my sister, Candy. It'll be totally cool.'

'Candy?' Lars straightens up and repeats the name wistfully a few times.

'What's up with him?' Victoria looks at me as the van edges into the on-coming lane.

'Love sick. Bitten hard, I'd say. Met a girl named Candice at our last gig.'

'Well, if it was my sister, he'd have my sympathy. She's a wild one for sure. A free spirit.'

Lars gently touches the scratch marks on his face and smiles.

The van edges back into its lane.

For an hour, we bounce. No talking. The thin-tread tires of the van loop a percussive beat beneath our breathing. I imagine it as a bed track for my new song: 'Beat Lars with a Tire Iron and Leave Him in a Ditch'.

It will be a ballad.

Or a rap.

Or a rap-ballad.

The possibilities are endless.

'See that mailbox up ahead with a reflective wolf silhouette on the side? That's the place. The driveway is a bit bumpy so hold on.' Victoria takes her foot off the gas and slowly applies the brakes.

The driveway is really a walking trail. It downward-dogs past lashing branches and aggressive underbrush. The tires lock into deep ruts as the van's axle grinds on the crest between. At the bottom of the hill, I see a front porch lit up with cold white LEDs. The house is long and narrow, and made of rough-hewn logs. The roof peaks high and extends like a spine, disappearing into the dark forest.

We park behind a silver pickup truck with dual rear tires.

Victoria's grandparents get up from their chairs and introduce themselves as we walk in. We nod our hellos and shake hands. Like most old people, they seem hungry for company, but they are a little different, not everyone's idea of grand-parents.

Isabel Néebear is wearing a flowing white dress that scoops generously below the neck. A purple crystal suspended by a long, thin silver chain swings like a pendulum between her breasts. She has high cheekbones, full lips, green eyes, and white hair cut in an asymmetrical bob. Her skin is tight across the face, loosening below the neck, tightening again at the depth of the pendulum — like she had trouble getting into her skin this morning.

Moses Néebear has a white goatee and long black, braided hair. His broad barrel chest extends into a broad barrel waist. He wears board shorts, a red Tribe Called Red concert T-shirt, and moccasins.

I am not sure if Moses is Indigenous, or a hipster, or a Indigenous hipster. I scan the room looking for a fedora.

Isabel sits back down, sips her tea, and discreetly places a glossy *Hello Canada* magazine on top of a worn copy of Jane Austen's *Northanger Abbey*.

'So ...' Moses relaxes back into his chair. His eyes crinkle with laugh lines although he is not laughing or smiling. 'Tell me about your gig. What was the ... umm ... set list? I used to play guitar back in the day, you know.' Moses gestures towards a worn-looking black Fender Strat hanging on the wall. 'I'm a little rusty now but, you know, once bitten by the music bug, it's in you forever. I got a drum set packed away somewhere too. Isabel plays. Maybe we can jam tomorrow. That would be awesome.'

Moses momentarily plays the air drums while addressing his wife. 'Honey, where's that drum kit? I haven't seen it around for a while. You didn't put it in storage did you?'

Isabel raises an eyebrow and blows on her tea.

I look around.

Their home confounds expectations as well. Beneath the rustic lodge exterior is a modern, open-concept living space: high cathedral ceiling with three large solar-powered copper fans, monochromatic slim-line furniture, muted-colour accents, spare white walls hung with several large canvases. The canvases pop. Four are in the First Nations Woodland style — bright colours swimming within dark outlines, geometric shapes morphing between living things. Two other paintings are vaguely Picasso-like. The last one could be a Basquiat.

Moses's guitar is the only object in the house that looks old and worn.

Isabel sips her tea.

'Oh yeah, the set list,' I begin. 'You know, the usual — Stones, Beatles, anything you might hear on the radio out here.'

Moses says, 'You know I haven't listened to the radio in years. Even for the local weather, I check my iPhone.'

'Yeah, I told them that,' Victoria interrupts.

Lars turns to Victoria. 'Where's your sister? You said you have a sister, right?' Lars is always on the prowl.

Moses looks at Victoria then at Lars. 'Oh, Candice comes and goes as she pleases. We don't expect her home tonight though. Sleepover with some friends.'

'Candice,' Lars murmurs wistfully while touching the scratches on his face.

'What's with him?' Moses asks.

'Long story, but the Candice we met made quite an impression on him.'

'Sounds like my granddaughter.'

Lars puts his hand up. 'Do you have a bathroom?'

'Yep.' Moses points past the kitchen. 'Out the back door. Twenty yards. Motion-sensitive light. It'll light up when you get close.'

'The bathroom is outside?' Lars asks.

'Yeah, I know our place looks like it might have all the amenities of a modern home, but we're totally off the grid. Solar everything. Rechargeable everything. A diesel generator just in case. Unfortunately, our ultra-modern, eco-friendly composting toilet is on the fritz, so we have the outhouse for backup. No pun intended.'

'None taken,' I say.

'It's pretty dark out there.' Lars doesn't move.

'Take the flashlight with you. It's on the shelf by the back door. Oh, and take the airhorn that's beside it. It'll scare anything … bears, wolves, fishers, zombies. It makes me jump every time I use it. Unfortunately, it has no effect on mosquitoes or blackflies—those buggers are the ones that'll eat you alive.'

'What's a fisher?' Lars stands up.

'Weasel family. Total badass. I've seen lumberjacks run from them. They sneak down a tree trunk headfirst and rip into your face.'

Moses turns to Victoria. 'Ours might be on the prowl for a new mate soon. Sleep with anything. Watch out! Ha!'

'Gramps!' Victoria scolds. 'She won't appreciate that.'

'Oh okay.' Moses Néebear bows his head a little. 'Don't tell her I said that.'

I think the weasel talk is code for something else. Neither of my brothers seems to care.

Lars moves a step towards the back door and stops.

Lars looks at me then Dougie.

Imploring.

It is a look I remember from our childhood: asking for backup when things weren't going well in the schoolyard.

This time Dougie and I do not move. Lars can deal by himself.

'Okay then.' Lars skulks past Victoria.

I hear his sneaks squeak through the kitchen. The screen door bangs shut.

'Zombies?' I ask Moses.

Moses laughs. 'Yeah, your brother didn't bat an eye on that one. I'm joking of course. I say crazy shit every so often to see if people are listening. Most of the time they're only half-listening.'

Isabel sips her tea. She makes a slow sucking sound. My eyes drift to her neck and chest again. She reaches out to Dougie and holds his hand for a moment. It is a weird gesture. I'm not sure if it's a 'grandma' thing. Dougie always seemed the most vulnerable amongst the three of us, and in need of guidance, or a slap upside the head.

Isabel looks deep into Dougie's eyes. Dougie blanches.

'Ha! Zombies.' Moses laughs nervously. 'Like real life isn't scary enough. Bears, wolves, rutting moose — actually any wild animal that's rutting — that's scary.' Moses leans forward. 'Wendigo — that's scary.'

'Wendy who?' I ask.

'Wendigo. Worse than zombies. Fear not the zombie that eats the flesh but cannot eat the soul. Fear the wendigo that consumes both.'

'Oh Gramps,' Victoria scolds.

'Oh Gramps yourself.' Moses settles back into his chair and crosses his arms. He looks at Dougie and me.

We lean forward.

Moses begins, 'The wendigo is a forest spirit that roams the deep woods, usually in the winter when food is scarce. Although, with global warming ... who knows? Mother Earth might be drumming a different beat these days.... Where was I?'

'Wendigo. Forest spirit,' I say.

'Oh yeah.' Moses shifts forward in his chair now for dramatic effect. 'Wendigo — a nasty creature: tall, gaunt, head of a stag, bulging eyeballs, sharp teeth. It eats people. If it possesses you, *you* eat people — mostly friends and family, mostly raw. Think Hannibal Lecter without the spice rack.'

'Seriously?' Dougie perks up. His face is flushed. The perma-bags under his eyes are now white, ghost-like.

'Seriously. Of course, no one believes in an actual Wendigo anymore. Settlers decided that it's only a wickedly good folk tale we came up with to warn against the dangers of cannibalism.'

'So, are you saying it's true?' I ask.

'I am not not saying it's not true.' Moses relies.

Victoria interrupts. 'Anyone feel like some rice crisp squares? I made them today from a totally authentic and awesome recipe.'

'Authentic as in Kraft?' Dougie asks.

Moses answers, 'Authentic as in edible wild plants and natural ingredients. The common mallow makes a tasty meringue. With a bit of honey, wild rice, and dried cranberries it is delicious. Funny enough, it's soothing on the stomach too. Not like that abomination of sugar, water, and dead-horse glue you call a marshmallow.'

'I thought marshmallows were basically an edible chemistry experiment — like hot dogs,' I say.

'It wasn't like that in the olden days. Ancient Egyptians used *their* indigenous marsh-mallow plant for food, and that tradition continued for thousands of years until some genius in France decided to mimic the *idea* of marshmallow and ignore the substance.' Moses stops a moment. 'Hey, I think I said something very clever there — but I'm not exactly sure what. Vicki, you're good with that stuff. Help me out here.'

'Sorry, Grandpa, I stopped listening at "olden days".'

Moses shakes a finger at her in mock consternation, then continues, 'Some people have a problem with common mallow though. Treat it like a weed.

Poison it. Rip it out by the roots. Like dandelions—which I might add are edible and medicinal. But hey, that's what you people do, right? Kill off anything that's indigenous.'

'Ooh burn,' Victoria says.

Moses stares into my eyes and smiles.

I counter hesitantly, 'Dandelions came over with the *Mayflower* as part of their medicinal supplies. They're invasive.'

'Well maybe that proves my point as well. They just take over, like the settlers did.'

'Hey!' Dougie thumbs through his iPhone. 'Wikipedia says the common mallow is also invasive—came from Europe at some point.'

'And that is why we should all learn to get along, and not argue so much,' Moses says.

We all awkwardly study one another's shoes for a moment.

Eventually, I ask, 'So, the wendigo thing. Do you believe it?'

'It is what it is,' Moses says. 'It doesn't matter what I believe.'

Dougie stands up. 'Lars is taking a long time.'

The forest is dark. We stand a moment and let our eyes adjust.

'Lars!' I yell.

'Lars/L/ar/L/a/L/ars/ars!' The voices of Moses, Victoria, Dougie, and myself overlap. It sounds like we are calling out *le arse*.

Isabel gives two sharp whistles like she is calling a dog.

No Lars.

The exterior light on the outhouse blinks on as we get closer. Moses pushes the door open. No Lars. Memory of Lars, perhaps.

'Should we phone the cops?' I ask.

'Let me think about that.' Moses pretends to pick up a telephone. 'Hello, Officer, this is Moses Néebear ... yes, that Moses Néebear, anyway I would like to report that a friend just wandered off to the outhouse and hasn't come back yet.... Yessir, you don't give a shit either.... Ha-ha, I get it.... Call if I find a body? ... Yessir!' Moses hangs up the imaginary telephone.

Moses walks back towards the house. 'We'll get a few flashlights and make our way down to the stream. I doubt he would try and get past it. He'd know enough to head back up the hill. Right?'

'I don't know. It is Lars,' I say.

Dougie nudges my shoulder and points at the house.

Lars is standing on the back porch, eating a rice crisp square.

'Wassup?' Lars says, spraying out bits of black rice and white meringue towards us as we make our way back to the house.

'Where were you?' I ask. 'We were actually worried and went looking.'

'Long story.' Lars shrugs.

We file inside.

I watch Lars devour a plate of cold sausages smothered in yellow mustard.

'Smoked venison.' Moses nods. 'Hunted the deer and smoked the meat myself. Good, eh?'

Lars nods. His hands are almost shaking as he stuffs the greasy meat into his mouth.

Isabel pours water into the kettle and plugs it in.

'I can taste …' Lars gazes past Moses's shoulder like the answer is hanging behind him.

'Pork. I add pork shoulder. Game meat is usually pretty dry, so you need the fatty domestic stuff. And fennel seeds. Fennel is a sausage's best friend. Salt and pepper are good friends too.'

'I thought I tasted liquorice,' Lars says.

'That's the fennel—similar but different.' Moses nods to the rest of us. 'Just like how the world goes 'round.'

'Okay.' Victoria sighs. 'I'm hungry now. Anyone want a sausage? Hot on a bun. I'll heat them up in the microwave.'

Dougie and I put up our hands. Moses shakes his head. Isabel steeps another cup of tea.

Lars puts his sausage down, chews carefully, swallows.

'Néebear is an interesting last name. What does it mean?' Lars asks. 'I mean, I get the "bear" bit.'

Dougie and I shoot him a look.

'Oh c'mon, man. I love hearing about last names. For instance, our last name — Cooper — refers to someone in the family who built barrels. Probably in Ye Olde Merrie England times. Probably beer kegs. How awesome is that?'

'Yes, beer kegs are awesome,' Moses agrees. 'And yes, the "bear" is … umm, sort of self-explanatory. I'm all for hibernating during the winter. Ha!' Moses stops. He places both hands on the table, interlocking the fingers. 'The "Née" part is different.'

Lars, Dougie, and I nod. We don't know how it may be different, but we are being polite.

'First off let me start by saying that naming is more fluid in our culture. You can have a lot of different names depending on who you are with, and where you are at. There is your family name, ancestor name, spirit name, and nickname. Bear is my spirit name. It was given to me in a naming ceremony, decades ago.'

'Cool.' Doug, Lars, and I nod.

Bear is a cool name in any culture.

Moses continues. 'I grew up in a residential school and my real name was something the sisters and brothers at the school could not pronounce. I was so young I cannot remember it either. They gave me something more pleasing to their ears — something more civilized and Christian in their minds — Moses Jones. Of course, Moses, and for that matter, Jesus Christ, are really anglicized Jewish names, but hey, who am I to argue with two thousand years of cultural appropriation? I digress.'

Victoria rattles around the fridge looking for hot sauce. She has probably heard the story too many times.

Moses continues, 'Appropriation. Misappropriation. You say potayto. I say potahto. Anyway, not knowing my birth name, and because Bear Jones sounded goofy, I improvised — dropping Jones, keeping Bear, adding Née — spelled N-E-E with an acute accent.'

'I find accents adorable,' Lars interjects.

Moses arches an eyebrow.

I sigh.

'No, an acute accent is a mark above the first *e* that indicates that the sound is modified and extended,' I correct my brother.

Moses adds, 'Funny enough, it also indicates that the word has been — not to belabour the point — appropriated from another language. Although, having said that — I realize that an appropriation can be useful and add something to the ... conversation. Don't stop me now; I'm on a roll.'

'Rock-and-roll!' Lars fist-pumps.

Moses arches an eyebrow.

I sigh.

Lars sputters, 'No guys, seriously. I just realized that rock music is kind of the ultimate appropriation. One that works. Thanks to a bunch of white guys that ripped off a bunch of black guys, the world is a better place. It's a language we all use. I should write that into a song. I can have it ready for our next gig. It'll write itself.'

Dougie and I look at each other in horror. We will die at that next gig.

Dougie steers the conversation back to its original lane. '*Née*? Oh, I thought it was *Nay*, spelled N-A-Y — as in "no", like "not a bear".'

I nod.

Moses smiles politely.

'Why N-E-E?' Lars asks.

'I was being clever, but obviously way too clever for you English-speaking folks who borrow freely from other cultures then forget about it.' Moses takes a deep breath and continues. '*Née* is Latin by way of France. It means "born". You see it in those obituary columns that refer to a woman's maiden name before she got married. Of course, that naming ceremony has plenty of issues too. Maybe we should all be like the Purple One and adopt a sign that can't be spoken.'

'Wouldn't work. Everyone still called him Prince.' Lars shakes his head.

Moses takes a glass of water and gulps it down. He gazes longingly at a bottle of Scotch on the shelf.

'Talking is thirsty work. Feel free to join in the conversation.' Moses looks around the room. Victoria is marshalling the condiments on the kitchen counter. Isabel has a glazed look in her eyes. My brothers and I are rapt.

'That reminds me of a story Dad used to tell where — ' Lars begins.

'But I digress,' Moses interrupts. 'Of course, the English language being what it is — and the English-speaking peoples being who they are — when anyone meets us for the first time and calls out our last name from reading it on paper, they say "nee" and not "nay".'

'Right on! That's how I saw it,' Lars says. 'Without even reading it on paper. It was in my mind like ... right there.'

Lars points to different areas of his head, trying to decide which is the most accurate.

Moses stares at Lars for a moment.

'You're killing me,' Moses laments.

'Your name sounds like "neighbour" — as in next-door neighbour. Which is kind of nice,' I say.

Moses claps his hands. 'Yeah, I'm the neighbour you keep borrowing stuff from and never returning it. As in the land! Ha!'

I visualize the words *Naybear, Neighbour*, and *Néebear*. I also visualize Moses doing a stand-up routine.

In an empty club.

The microwave chimes.

I salivate.

I visualize food.

It is Sunday morning. Dougie, Lars, and myself are on the floor of the house, in sleeping bags, lying on a slim air mattress that we pulled out of the van. Dougie snores. Lars thrashes in his sleep. I stare at the ceiling. The sun is rising. A skylight glows at the far end of the main floor, casting a slash of light across a painting of a boggle-eyed thunderbird screaming up towards a bright yellow orb. The wing feathers look like tightly packed people with mouths open, heads tilted back. They have sharp teeth. Maybe they are screaming. Maybe they are waiting to be fed. It is not a restful image.

The rooms on the upper split level remain quiet. Victoria and her grandparents had gone to bed soon after we ate, and they said, 'good night, love you' to each other before retiring. I was impressed. I don't think my dad or stepmom ever said that to anyone, ever, at any time, when I was growing up.

'You know.' Lars rolls over towards me. 'I didn't get lost last night.'

Lars's voice is clear and not blurred with sleep.

'Jesus!' I jump a little. 'I thought you were asleep.'

'I was. You know me. Everything is like an on or off switch.'

'Yeah, I forgot—you and Bela Lugosi.'

'Anyway, I didn't get lost on my way to the outhouse. I saw something that freaked me out.'

'Really?' I yawn. 'Everything freaks you out.'

'Yeah, I got to the outhouse and somebody was already inside.'

'Was it an animal? We're pretty well out in the middle of nowhere.'

'I know. At first I thought it might be an animal too. There was plenty of animal noises coming out of the outhouse, for sure. So I just start peeing against a tree, then I hear the toilet paper roll spin and a hand sanitizer pump being pressed—it makes that squelchy sound. Animals don't use toilet paper or hand sanitizer. Anyway, just as I'm at my peak freak, the door slowly opens and—'

'Good morning,' Dougie interrupts. His voice is rough. His breath reeks of acetone.

I gag.

Dougie breathes into his cupped hands and sniffs. He reaches over and waves his smelly hand over Lars's face.

'Gaaaa!' Lars ducks under the sleeping bag.

'Did you sleep with a mouth full of nail polish and raw meat?' I ask. 'That's worse than Dad when he had diabetes.'

'And he died.' Lars's voice is muffled under the protective barrier of the sleeping bag.

'I heard you get up in the middle of the night. Were you in the kitchen eating?' I ask Dougie, ignoring Lars.

'I don't think so. I had a really good sleep—best ever. Although I dreamed I was in a kitchen—a dream kitchen—all chrome appliances and white marble countertops. It even had a Wolf gas range with twin convection ovens.'

'Those red control knobs add such a delightful pop of colour.' Dougie's eyes mist over.

I have never ever heard my brother rhapsodize about anything coming out of a kitchen except maybe a plate of nachos.

Dougie chokes up but continues, 'There was food everywhere. I ate everything. My jaw still hurts. It was like I was eating the plates too. I might've been grinding my teeth.'

'Great, you had a freaky dream that involved food. Big surprise.' Lars pulls himself out of the sleeping bag. 'Let me finish my story. It is freaky, and it was not a dream.'

Lars sits up. 'So I'm in the forest, by the outhouse, and I hear weird noises. The door of the outhouse opens ... and it's that crazy chick from the Goodwin gig!'

'I get it. It's not a dream. It's a fantasy,' I say.

'Shut up, Mr Fancy Words. Anyway, I hide behind a tree and she walks out, looks around, sniffs the air, heads back to the house. I don't think she saw me. She might have smelled me though. I pretty well shit my pants.'

'She walks back to the house?' I ask. 'The one we are in right now?'

"Walks back to the house. The one we are in right now.'

'Why didn't you say anything?'

'Maybe she had a curfew. I don't know. I'm not gonna rat her out. Anyways, I was totally psyched—their Candice was my Candy.'

Dougie and I nod. We are psyched, but in a different way.

Lars whispers, 'Besides, she didn't go into the house directly. She climbed up—really fast like a spider—to one of the second-floor windows and slipped in. As I remember, she was quite the gymnast in bed if you know what I mean, so I wasn't surprised. Anyway, I tried waiting up for her just in case she came down the stairs at some point and I could surprise her, but I fell asleep. I was a little disappointed—I thought we had something.'

Dougie and I had something.

Fear.

Our van stealthily grinds up the hill towards the main road. Lars seems more lovesick than anything. It is eight in the morning. Saplings and branches lash at the side panels, ripping and scratching the white paint. We don't care.

In the daylight, the reflective silhouette of the howling wolf on the mailbox is a pale silver shadow, barely noticeable. The red flag is up, and a Sunday newspaper hangs half out of the box.

'I dunno, shouldn't we have woken up the Néebears, or at least Vicki?' Dougie asks. 'Doesn't she have a shift today or something?'

'You heard me call out thanks as we left.' Lars sighs. 'We did our bit.'

'The front door barely hit you in the ass before the words were out, bro. And it was more of a whisper. You are as chicken as chickenshit,' Dougie says. "I am embarrassed to be a member of our family.'

'Yeah, well, I noticed you were in the van with the seat belt on before I turned the ignition over ... bro,' Lars retorts.

I interrupt. 'If that was really Candy that you saw climbing the outside of the house we'd all be pretty well-beaten, or well-fucked. Neither is true.'

'Yeah, except for that weird kitchen dream, I slept pretty soundly.' Dougie smiles. It is a weird sour smile.

Dougie, still smiling, turns to Lars. 'Did you really see anyone climbing that window or was that an acid flashback?'

'No, seriously, that's what I saw. There is something weird going on at that house. I knew it from the get-go. Did you notice that Victoria's grandma drank a ton of tea and didn't have to pee once? That's unnatural. She drank so much, *I* had to pee. And what kind of old lady wears a low-cut top. I could see her boobs. I don't want to see old-lady boobs. I might've seen a nipple.'

'You must've been looking hard. I couldn't get past that purple pendulum banging back and forth between the two sisters. I'll never un-see that,' I say.

Dougie clenches his jaws.

'I think she's in really good shape regardless of her age. Nothing wrong with being proud of all that hard work.' Dougie's voice seems to have tightened up a bit. A bit churlish, or girlish. Snippy.

Yes, snippy.

Lars is relentless. 'Notice how her skin was tight in some places and loose and wrinkled in other places. Weird! Like it wasn't really hers ... What's going on with that?'

'Yeah, I noticed that,' I say.

'Getting old isn't easy. The skin has a mind of its own, you know. Not everyone can afford to run out and get plastic surgery.' Doug is on a tear. He can be quite defensive about women's issues. He is our de facto feminist as he is the only one amongst us who has had a girlfriend for longer than three months.

Lars will not relent. 'And she wouldn't let on where the drum kit was. I bet she got rid of it and didn't tell Moses. That's just mean.'

Dougie purses his lips and arches his eyebrows. 'Well, I bet Moses ain't no saint either.'

Dougie is sounding like our stepmom.

'Okay, okay,' I say. 'Let's calm down a bit, collect our gear, collect our thoughts, eat breakfast, and figure out what's next. Our gig isn't till Saturday up near Dryden, so we got an extra day or two to stick around here if we want. Maybe we'll drop back in on the way out and drop off some Timbits.'

'Or not,' says Dougie.

'Or not,' I agree.

Officer Nate Wilson pulls over on the side of the road. It is late Sunday evening. The sky is a deepening blue. The ground is awash in shadow. Through the tops of the pines, he can see pink spreading from the sinking sun.

Officer Wilson talks into his radio: 'Checking on the Néebears at 2525 Concession Road as requested, over.'

The radio fizzles. 'Copy.'

'I'll say a big hello to Moses for ya. I know you all love him so much.' Nate Wilson steps out of the car. He looks in the mailbox. The Sunday paper is still there. It is 8:00 p.m.

Not good.

Nate has been patrolling up and down the highway for most of his shift. His legs need a stretch. He looks down the driveway towards the house. Too many ruts and ridges for the patrol car anyway.

It'll be nice to see Vicki, Nate thinks as he picks his way down. *It's been a while.*

Moses's truck sits in the driveway. Nate notices another set of tire tracks within the dual ruts. There is fresh loose dirt kicked up all around.

The front porch light is off. The lights are off inside the house. Nate knocks on the door and peers through the large window to the left. No answer.

'No one home.' Nate talks into his radio. 'They're not on some vacation, are they? Moses's truck is still in the driveway. But Vicki's car isn't here.'

'Vicki's car is still at … work.' Dispatch is scratchy. '… didn't show up … this morning … Bert's worried … she left with … losers from out of town.'

'I'll go around back,' Nate says.

Nate walks past an overturned white wheelbarrow. The rubber tires are deep black and there is no rust on the rims. Except for the daubs of reddish-brown paint flecked along one side, the high-gloss enamel barrow glistens like it was new. Nate remembers a poem from high school about a red wheelbarrow and white chickens.

One sentence, one wheelbarrow, many meanings.

One meaning is sinister as hell now. Red on white.

The daubs of paint look like dried blood.

Nate notices a lot of flies in the air, but they're not the usual blackflies or deerflies.

Rounding by the back porch, Nate stops.

The flies thicken near the open back door. Most are flying in. None are coming out.

Nate unholsters his gun.

'I can't believe Dougie drove through the dead-end sign and right into the river.' Lars sulks.

After we'd spent Sunday night and Monday night camping in a provincial park, Dougie decided we needed to find someplace even cheaper.

He found it.

A river in the middle of nowhere.

Our van is grille first and axle deep in that river.

The sun is beginning to set. It is warm. The mosquitos are out. The mosquitos are hungry.

'Hey Dougie!' Lars shouts. 'I don't mind roughing it, but this is ridiculous.'

Dougie gives him the finger.

Dougie paces along the grassy bank, staring mournfully at our van as the river pushes against the chassis. A dented hubcap works loose and floats away. Dougie panics.

'That Big Bend campground was a little spooky,' I say to Lars. 'Notice how most of the campsites around us were deserted by Monday morning.'

'Yeah, Labour Day weekend is a big party blowout generally. It was real quiet early on Sunday night too. Weird, that.'

Dougie wades into the river towards the van, rips out the GPS, and, with a surprising combination of brutishness and finesse, beats it with a tire iron.

'Quid pro quo,' I mutter.

Lars picks up a Styrofoam container of cold BBQ ribs and starts chomping. 'I guess we don't need the GPS anymore, seeing as how the van is stuck and we're probably gonna starve to death by the time someone finds us. By the by—you have a signal on your phone? My batts are dead.'

'Nope.'

'Oh well, remember when Dad used to say, "When one door closes another door opens?"'

'I don't see any doors out here.'

Lars gnaws thoughtfully on the gristle. 'Yeah, Dad was an idiot.'

Dougie scoops up a handful of water.

We watch him drink it with middling success.

I turn to Lars. 'You remember when you found out that Dougie and I were your half-brothers?'

High-pitched whining hovers around my left ear. I slap the side of my head. The whining switches to my right ear.

'Yeah. Good times.' Lars lifts his head up from licking the Styrofoam container. Sticky, sweet sauce rims his mouth. 'I was seven. Dad shows up with you two on Christmas Eve, says "Merry Fucking X-mas", then disappears for a month.'

Lars picks up a gnawed rib with one hand and waves it back and forth at the mosquitos like a sword. He slaps his face with the other hand, leaving a sauce-red palm print.

'Best Christmas ever.' I slap my face.

'Yeah, Mom was really pissed though—especially after finding out you were the same age as me, and worse still, Dougie was a year younger.' Lars stands up and dances around, slapping his body in multiple places. He is in full Bavarian/alpine/*Schuhplattler* mode.

Lars shouts, 'Mom would have gutted Dad if he stuck around that day. Good thing he was always on the road!'

'Dad was smart that way!'

The whining is back. I slap both cheeks in rapid succession. I feel welts rising.

'Good ... ol' ... dad!' Lars nods and slaps between each staccato burst. 'Disappears ... for ... months ... at ... a ... time ... returns like a hero ... carrying ... a bunch ... of ... lame ... gifts, filling us with big stories ... when ... all ... he ... was ... doing ... was ... dicking around!'

'A modern-day Odysseus!'

Lars stops slapping. The mosquitos cluster around his face like a beard. 'Does everything have to have a freakin' literary reference? Don't forget you *dropped out* of college.'

I stop slapping. The mosquitos cluster around my face like a beard. 'I withdrew without academic penalty, and you couldn't *drop in* if it bit you in the ass.'

'Fuck you.'

'Fuck you.'

'Maybe you two could stop being so "learned" for a moment and give me a hand.' Dougie is hauling our equipment out of the van and spreading it onto a large granite outcropping. Lars and I stop arguing and watch. The mosquitos buzz around Dougie's head like a black halo. He ignores them. They are reluctant to bite.

Dougie smokes a lot of dope.

Dougie lines up the guitar cases on top of the rock, then lays them flat in four groups of two, lids open, instruments exposed.

Crushed-velvet eyelids. Glinting steel-stringed irises.

The drum kit is exploded over the rest of the surface, each piece like a pitted carbuncle. Amps and speakers rim the bottom of the rock like broken teeth. Black cables and power cords tentacle out to the side.

Lars points at the equipment on the rock. 'Hey Dougie, kinda reminds me of Pink Floyd's *Ummagumma*. You know the back of the album with the band's equipment laid out on the road like a rocket, except in this case it's more squid-ish.'

'Scylla and Charybd-ish,' I say.

'Jesus! Again with the lit shit.' Lars shakes his head. 'Sting called. He wants his lame-ass lyrics back.'

'Yeah, well, if you would let *me* write the lyrics you might have something worth singing about.'

'Fuck you.'

'Fuck you.'

Dougie sighs and wades back into the river towards the van.

He opens the glovebox and pulls out a bag of weed. As an afterthought, he grabs a bag of Doritos from the dash.

In the distance, I see the shimmer of a vehicle coming towards us. It is kicking up some dust, but not much. The driver slows down every time he crests a hill, allowing the wind to carry the dust forward for a moment, before he accelerates again — punching through puffs of dirt.

'Must have the same model of GPS,' Lars ventures.

The dust gets closer.

The silver lining in our cloud: a metallic-grey, sun-dappled pickup with a bone-white camper cap anchored to the bed.

The truck rolls to a stop in front of the crushed 'dead end' sign. The man inside is chunky faced and breathing heavily. He wears a tattered baseball cap that perches on his head like a beak.

Staring at the sign, he cannot see our van which is on the other side of a steep drop. He cannot see Lars and me. We are hidden behind a dense cluster of dogwood.

He will be seeing Dougie very soon.

Dougie ambles through the brush on the other side of the road, puffing on a joint and eating Sweet Chili Heat Doritos. He has tied his hair up in a man bun. His shirt is off. His pants are off. His skin is translucent road-rocker white — like milk-infused jellyfish.

Dougie sees the pickup and jogs towards it, waving his bag of nacho chips.

Dougie's large, hairless testicles squid-jig up and down.

The man slams his vehicle in reverse and fishtails backwards into a shallow trench on the south side of the road. Lars and I jump out from the bush and wave our hands. The man struggles to get out of the vehicle, but the weight of the door and the angle of the truck keep closing the door against his shoulder. The man's face flashes between ghost white and bluster red. His mouth opens and closes. A fish out of water. He might be having a heart attack.

'Wait! Wait!' I screech.

The Tourette's is about to kick in, so I jam a balled-up fist in my mouth. The torrent of bilingual swears and inappropriate sex comments translates into a series of *hmmms*, *mmphs*, and *aaghs*, like I'm getting off on sucking my hand.

Chunky-faced truck man frantically locks the doors.

'We're in a band! We lost our van! Can you lend a hand!' Lars shouts.

His best lyrics to date.

I look at my reflection in the driver's-side window. My long, bottle-black hair is matted and scraggled to the side of my head. I am wearing a tattered Iron Maiden T-shirt with my right nipple poking out from the eye socket of the leering Eddie mascot.

Mosquito bites and self-induced welts pockmark my cheeks.

Did I mention that I am sucking my fist?

I look at Lars. The welts and bites on his face are smeared with dull red BBQ sauce. The same dull red BBQ sauce is smeared across his dingy white T-shirt, looking like bloody palm prints.

We could be demented cannibals, or a lost tribe of Juggalos.

Dougie jumps up on the passenger-side running board and rocks back and forth. His testicles slap against the window, leaving greasy streak marks.

The driver hunches down and drops the transmission into reverse. The wheels kick up stones, dirt, twigs.

It is a smoke show of blistering pain.

Moses Néebear lopes through the forest on three legs. Phantom pain spasms below the stump of his bloodied back paw. A full yellow moon floats between the silhouetted pine boughs above. Moses lifts his snout and sniffs. A bear can smell a rotting carcass twenty miles away. Moses smells the death behind him, the death he barely escaped, the death that took his loved ones, the death that …

Moses smells blueberries.

Moses pivots, angling in the direction of the berries. His bloody back stump bangs against a tree trunk. The phantom pain spasms and morphs into real pain.

'Jesus, motherfucking, cock-sucking, fucking-fuck-fuck-fuck!' Moses says in a series of indistinguishable growls, barks, and yelps.

He sits back on his fat, furry ass and weeps.

He remembers.

Insatiable. Rancorous. The Hungry One was unstoppable.

At first, She toyed with Moses, throwing him up and down like a baby in a blanket. Tiring of the game, She bit off his foot, moccasin and all, and spat it out. Then She threw him out the second-storey bedroom window. Moses landed on his ass, on the jagged teeth of a rake.

Moses experienced fear, humiliation, and deep physical pain—a lot of deep physical pain.

Now Moses experiences hunger.

Moses sniffs. He senses the soft roundness of tiny raspberries clustered under serrated green leaves. Raspberries are rare at this time of year.

Hunger.

Moses remembers.

The noise woke him up.

It was two a.m. Sunday.

A loud subsonic rumble.

Isabel remained asleep beside him.

Isabel could sleep through a car crash, and once did. Moses was a light sleeper. His own snoring woke him up.

He was on his back when he woke up. He might have been snoring. He was loosely draped in the comforter, still wearing his moccasins. Isabel was tightly wound in the bedsheet. Not swaddled. Shrouded. He should have known.

The rumble started again and continued for several seconds. It was a droning boom, like a deep-voiced deity uttering OM.

Eventually the sound dampened and disappeared.

Moses was worried. Victoria might be awake. Unlike her half-sister and himself, she was not a shape-shifter. As a result she was not immune from the Appetite. It was always a danger with her proximity to Isabel.

Thank god for herbal teas.

The musicians were another matter. There was something deeply unsavoury about them—apart from their questionable hygiene and poor lifestyle choices. They could be a source of infection of the settler/colonialist strain. Potentially virulent and unstoppable—like smallpox.

But Victoria had brought them home and generally she was a good judge of character. But then again, she had all those posters of Chad Kroeger on her bedroom wall. Freddy Krueger might've been a more wholesome choice.

If they had come home with Candice, he would have thrown them out as soon as they crossed the threshold.

Moses slipped out of bed, walked to the bedroom door, and put his hand on the metal doorknob. It was cold—so cold his palm stuck.

The deadbolt above the doorknob slid open.

He had not touched it.

Thrown back onto the bed by an unseen force, Moses rolled over to Isabel's side, but she was already cold.

The spirit had moved on. Drummer to drummer. He should have known. Drummers are easily seduced by the rhythm.

Oooommmm. The sound reverberated through Moses's body.

The door remained shut.

Why was no one waking up?

Pinned to the bed, Moses's vision glazed over. He saw the gauzy outline of a hulking beast bend over him. He felt its cold breath against his face—acetone and rotten fruit.

The toying began: lifted, thrown, caught in mid-air, gently dropped, caught again, thrown again. The bite. The spit. The toss. The rake.

Ass impaled on metal teeth, Moses's blindness fell away like scales from his eyes. Pain could do that—teach a person to see more clearly. It was biblical wisdom, something he had learned from the kind Brothers and Sisters at the residential school.

At that point, satisfied with his insight, Moses shape-shifted into a bear and then passed out.

Blueberries. Raspberries.

He is back in the moment.

Moses's shin pulsates. Beneath the thick fur, tarsal bones push downward and extend the outline of the stump into a bear claw.

It is time to shape-shift again.

Moses rises on his hind legs and winces. He spreads his arms. Long sharp bear claws soften, shrink into black wing tips. Coarse black fur thickens, extends into barbed black feathers. He curls inward. Each limb, each appendage, each bear part slowly morphs into the body of a crow.

A large crow.

An embarrassingly large crow.

Moses caws. His wings flap, barely lifting him skyward.

He knows where the wendigo is going. He will meet Her there.

Moses dips below the tree line and smacks into a bough.

The last ten pounds are the hardest to lose.

Nate Wilson is sitting at his desk at the OPP detachment outside Hatcheta Falls. It is Tuesday evening. A couple of days after the Néebear incident. He is staring at the notes in his officer's notebook. It was designated a crime scene at first, but after a half-assed investigation on a holiday Monday, the assessment changed to a wild animal attack.

A neighbour of the Néebears had reported an enormous black bear, fat and out of shape, galumphing — that was the neighbour's exact word — galumphing — through her backyard early Sunday evening, just before Nate arrived at the Néebears's to check up on Victoria.

The animal left splatters of blood on some of her plants and ate a few of her squash.

Nate knew that a wounded, hungry, and angry bear could be capable of great mischief, but disembowelling and eating a family was a stretch.

Nate thought the musicians were more suspect. They were from Toronto after all. They left with Victoria late Saturday night halfway through the gig. They had poor hygiene. They played metal.

But...

According to Bert, they were back at the tavern the next morning picking up their equipment, eating a leisurely breakfast, and arguing with Bert about the money owed them for the previous night's aborted gig.

Not the typical behaviour of murderers.

Bert did note they were agitated and a bit wild-eyed towards the end of their breakfast.

Bert also noted that they drank a carafe of coffee each.

Coffee-sucking, Toronto-bred, Scarborough-born degenerates.

The musicians were expected in Dryden for a show on Saturday. All police detachments along the way had been alerted.

Nothing yet.

No white Econoline van. No musical persons of interest. It was as if they had dropped off the edge of the earth, or at least off a steep incline.

Nate sips his tepid coffee and taps the space bar on his laptop. The screen lights up ... again. He has lost count of how many times the computer has defaulted to sleep mode. He has already submitted a copy of his notebook and a summary incident report. Now he must write the full narrative.

Writing full narratives is hard.

Nate consults the point-form in his notebook once again:

- Sunday, September 3, 2017/ 18:25.
- 2525 Concession Road. Néebear residence.
- Responding to a courtesy request by Bert Smith, owner of Hatcheta Falls Tavern, to check on Victoria Néebear who has not shown up for work.
- Park cruiser on road and walk down to house.
- Moses's pickup is still in driveway.
- Deep fresh tire tracks beside pickup.
- Dirt spray kicked up against front of house.
- Front door closed and locked. Back door unlocked and open.
- Main floor clear.
- Bloodstains and human remains on upper floor, bedrooms, hallway.
- Miscellaneous dents and holes in the walls in upper bedrooms.
- Severed foot in master bedroom.
- Bedroom window smashed, and screen pushed out onto backyard below.

• Blood and fur on rake in backyard.

Nate's stomach churns. Days later and he can't get the images, or the smells, of that house out of his mind. The severed foot was not the worst thing he saw but it disturbed him to the point of obsession. He had spotted it in the master bedroom. It was sitting atop Moses and Isabel's bird's-eye-maple dresser like a treasured memento. At first, Nate thought it was a hand-carved miniature canoe with a little man piloting it, something out of *Paddle to the Sea*.

Paddle to the Sea was a 1966 NFB short film and a complicated memory for Nate. His dad, a retired teacher, loved the movie and put it on whenever Nate was sick and home from school. Watching the movie involved an elaborate ritual of setting up the 16mm-film projector, tacking a white tablecloth across the living room wall, closing the blinds, turning off the lights — stuff you never had to do with television.

Soon after Dad died, Mom threw out the projector and the movie. She never remarried.

So...

Nate was startled to see a childhood icon sitting daintily on a dresser in a room full of blood and guts.

The toy canoe and paddler looked very detailed: a narrow, light brown birchbark canoe with an elaborately carved ivory paddler, festooned with a shock of dark red hair.

Nate bent over to get a closer look.

The smell hit him first.

And then he saw it.

It was a stump of flesh-clotted tibia, attached to a severed foot, in a blood-soaked moccasin.

Not an iconic childhood memory.

Nate threw up.

* * *

'What did you say your name was again?' I ask.

The chunky-faced man from the camper truck straightens. 'Joel. Just call me Joel. My surname is hard to pronounce. Polish. No one ever gets it right, so Joel is fine.'

'Sorry for freakin' you out, Joel.' Dougie leans towards the bonfire with a big stick and pushes a log farther into the flames.

Dougie has put his clothes back on.

I have brushed my hair.

Lars has changed his shirt and wiped the B B Q sauce from his face.

'Yeah, yeah, no worries, man.' Joel pulls out a hot dog from a cooler and impales it on a stick. 'I'm sorry for putting the truck in the ditch. It's got a tow line and a winch, but I think it'll be better if we try it in the morning when the sun is up. You don't want to fuck around or that steel line will cut you in half. Doing anything in the dark is dangerous. I tried shaving my beard off without the lights on and I damn well near slit my throat. Ha-ha-ha-ha-ha-ha!'

Joel continues to laugh for a long time. It is awkward.

'Yeah, yeah, sure,' Lars, Dougie, and I mutter. We are dead tired and stuffed. Earlier, after we sorted out all the miscommunications, Joel pulled out a beer cooler and hot dogs and we gorged on fire-roasted wienies and ice-cold brewskis.

Joel had a monster appetite.

He was still eating.

'So, you guys are in a band, I gather. What do you call yourselves?' Joel asks between mouthfuls of hot dog.

'Ashthorn mostly. Although we do change our name from time to time to keep it fresh and to trick people into seeing us more than once,' I say.

Lars adds, 'At one point, we called ourselves Canada Postal Service, but only old people showed up at the gigs to complain about missing packages.'

'Canada Post?' Joel's left eye twitches uncontrollably for a few moments.

'Then we got a cease-and-desist order, so we changed to the Delivery Agents, but apparently CP had dibs on that too.'

I hear a weird grating sound in the darkness — like someone grinding their teeth. I can't see anything except Joel's dyspeptic smile.

Lars continues, 'Name a small town anywhere in Canada or the northern states and we've played there.'

Joel spits, 'Magog, Quebec? My family is from there. The Gogs of Magog.'

'Except there. We don't do well in Quebec for some reason.'

Dougie nods. 'Except the time we ordered a bunch of tour posters from Montreal and they printed our name as "Asshat". Those were sold-out shows—all the way from Gatineau to Rimouski.'

'They thought we were a parody metal band and went crazy. We played all of our originals. It was a blast,' I add.

'It was humiliating.' Lars shakes his head.

I stare at Joel's feet. He's wearing red Yeezy boots. They don't match his ratty, drab cargo shorts, or his Old Navy tank top—in price point or style. One of those boots would buy groceries for a week.

'Yeah. What can you do? You make your choices and get on with it,' Joel agrees softly, and then chirps, 'When's your next gig, fellas?'

'Saturday in Dryden,' I say.

'A couple of days driving to be sure. And it's only Wednesday. You got a bit of time to get there. Any expected layovers? Visits to friends or family along the way? Long time between here and there, eh?'

'We show up when we show up. We're booked as Ashthorn, but we might re-book as a straight-ahead cover band—something more obvious like Bone Jovi. We do a pretty good job on a bunch of their tunes,' I say.

'Yeah, I'm a little tired of experiencing life through a chicken-wire filter,' Lars says.

Joel scarfs a flaming hot dog down his throat. Tiny puffs of dragon smoke escape between gritted teeth. Joel's eyes are bulgy and red.

Dougie looks wistfully up at the sky.

A large grapefruit moon floats above us.

'Full one tonight, fellas?' Joel continues to cough out smoke.

'Harvest moon,' Lars says.

'Corn moon, barley moon, or bean moon depending on your Indigenous affiliation,' I explain. 'This year, because the autumnal equinox is so early in September, they don't call it the harvest moon. We go straight to the hunter moon on October fifth. It's complicated unless you're in the know.'

'Fuck you, Mr In-the-Know-It-All,' Lars says.

'Fuck you, Mr In-the-Know-Nothing,' I counter.

'Fuck both of you,' Dougie corrects.

We sulk as Joel goes to the back of his truck and disappears into the camper.

'I'm sorry, bro,' Lars says.

'I'm sorry, bro,' I counter.

'I'm sorry for both of you,' Dougie corrects.

It is time to break out the acoustic guitars for some campfire magic and a little brotherly harmony.

Joel reappears with a bottle of screech and a pitcher of mixed punch.

'My own secret concoction—call it the cat-o'-nine-tails. You'll need nine lives to drink this one.'

Lars and I grab our guitars and tune up. This may not go as expected. The wood is still damp, and the heat of the fire may warp the necks.

We start playing 'Harvest Moon' by Neil Young. It's as if Neil plucked that song out of the ether and breathed it to life. Simple and perfect. After playing it, one always asks, 'Why couldn't I write that?'

The long answer: simplicity is harder than it looks—it requires an ability to filter out unnecessary complications and focus on the essence of the expression.

The short answer: you are a talentless hack.

After mixing our drinks with great drama, Joel dances around the fire, drinking straight from the bottle of screech. Occasionally, he disappears into the darkness outside our circle of light.

Joel begins chanting.

'Kneel! Kneel! Kneel! The Great One has arrived.'

He must be totally hammered.

Everyone knows that 'the Great One' is Wayne Gretzky's nickname and has nothing to do with Neil Young.

Lars continues to strum. I arpeggiate. We reach the third chorus.

I am feeling woozy.

Dougie slurs, 'Hey Larsh, yer A7 ain't shounding right.'

'Am in tune—fer sure.' Lars's head lolls to the side.

'I hear ghosht notes.'

'Feck you.' Lars rests the guitar against a charred log at the edge of the fire pit and tries to stand up. He falls backwards onto the grass.

I watch the headstock of his Martin guitar light up. It is magical.

Joel is all up in my face suddenly. 'Ghost note! What's a ghost note? Is that like a deadwalk? It sounds like the metaphorical equivalent of a deadwalk!'

Joel gibbers unintelligibly for a few moments longer then screams, 'I hate deadwalks!'

I fall backwards off the stump.

My brain is mush.

'A ghosht note!' Dougie begins, and then stops.

Dougie tries again. 'A ghosht note is ...'

Dougie stares off into space. It seems like he is listening to something.

Joel stalks over to Dougie and prods him with the bottle of screech. 'What are they? Omens? Portents? Harbingers? Needlessly repetitive actions? Must I strut and fret this hour upon the stage delivering what I have already delivered — fear and a handful of dust? A clutch of admail? Bills, bills, and more bills? I have a degree in English literature for fuck's sake. Lay it on me. It is not beyond my ken.'

Joel sounds surprisingly sober; and yet surprisingly insane.

'A musical event that contains ... zounds ...' Dougie struggles.

Dougie smiles vacantly.

'Zounds?' Joel hisses.

'Zounds ...' Dougie trails off again.

'Zounds? Zounds? Zounds?' Joel yammers.

I want to make a witty comment about how 'zounds' is an archaic oath meaning 'God's wounds' and Shakespeare used it to great effect in various character speeches in his plays.

I gurgle instead.

Just as well. I suspect that our friend Joel already knows about zounds.

'Oh Jesus! I'll look it up myself.' Joel takes out his iPhone and thumb-hammers away.

'No signal,' I croak helpfully.

'Got a cell booster in my truck,' Joel replies.

After a few minutes of walking around in circles with his phone held aloft like a torch: 'There, I found it on Wikipedia. "A ghost note is a musical note with a rhythmic value, but no discernible pitch when played!" Also called a dead note. Dead note!' Joel shrieks dramatically.

I suspect he is milking the moment. We are not his first audience.

Joel puts away his iPhone. 'Thanks for nothing!'

Dougie lies down on the cold dirt beside the fire. He takes a deep breath. 'You might not notice the ghost note on the first listen; but if you pay attention, the second or third time you will hear it clear as mud, propelling the musical narrative onward. You cannot unhear it — ever.'

Dougie's voice is clear, although his words are a bit vague and confusing — typical Dougie. He must be sobering up.

I try to add to the conversation with an insightful observation about the cosmic interplay of chance and structure and the musicality of life's vibrations.

'Music of the spheres,' I say.

'Britney Spears,' everyone hears.

I pass out.

I wake up. It is light. I can barely move. My eyes burn. I squint and look around. Lars is duct-taped to a tree. His mouth is taped. A nest of brambles is on his head.

Dougie is duct-taped to a tree. His mouth is taped. A nest of brambles is on his head.

I try to move.

I can't.

I am duct-taped to a tree. My mouth is taped. Something scratchy rests on my head.

At least we have our clothes on.

The sound of whirring and machinery.

Joel is hooking up his camper truck to a large tree on the opposite side of the road. The winch pulls the truck slowly up the side of the ditch.

My head pounds.

Eventually, Joel walks over.

'Morning, gents. Sorry about the makeshift crown of thorns. I've decided to change up my MO this time around. "Keeping it fresh till death" as they say. You like?'

Joel looks at us expectantly as he pulls on powder-blue latex gloves.

'Oh yeah. Kind of hard to talk, isn't it?' Joel removes the tape from across Dougie's mouth. 'Don't bother yelling. It just makes it more exciting for me.'

Dougie does not make a sound. He licks his lips instead.

Joel pulls out a sharp-looking filleting knife and holds it with great delicacy between thumb and forefinger. 'Well, fellas, we are at the end of the road. *Auf Wiedersehen.* Until we meet — no wait, wait, wait — until we "meat" again — spelled m-e-a-t. God, this stuff almost writes itself. I have to tell you guys: it's not the killing I enjoy so much as the great speeches and the terrific audiences I have come to expect.'

Joel begins to swagger around. 'And yet, I would give all my fame for a pot of ale and safety.'

Joel is multi-tasking: murdering Shakespeare and me.

My Tourette's kicks in — all swears, no apologies, one official language.

Unfortunately, the tape blankets my eloquence, smothers my ambition. I cast darts with my eyes instead.

'You don't have to do this.' Dougie flexes against the binding.

'But I do.'

'At least tape over our eyes so we don't have to see each other getting killed.'

'Good. I like that.' Joel jumps on a stump and waves his arms around. '"Justice is blind," the detectives will say. "And so is injustice," I will rejoin. The quality of mercy is boiled, strained, ladled over with much red sauce.'

Joel is clearly mad, and a butcher of words.

Joel steps down. The animated glee is gone. He leisurely stretches out the tape, covering my eyes, pressing firmly against the ridge of my eyebrows and lower sockets.

I hear the stretch of tape a few feet over to my right. Lars.

The tape dispenser moves to my left.

Dougie murmurs something. I don't recognize any of the words.

Joel stretches out the duct tape.

The stretching goes on, and on.

It seems for … ever.

Silence.

Then some snapping and popping, like random twigs breaking, followed by a bit of crunching.

Silence.

Steps coming in my direction.

Warmth floods my body. Everything, and I mean everything, rushes for the final exit.

'Bro!' Dougie rips the tape off my eyes. The strip hangs limply for a moment, then flutters to the ground. Both eyebrows and a great many lashes are on that strip.

Dougie rips off the tape on my mouth.

I scream.

Joel is gone.

According to Dougie, Joel jumped into the river, swam to the other side, and disappeared into the forest after Dougie broke from his bonds, all Samson-like, and started kicking his ass.

A fishy tale.

I've never seen Dougie make a fist. He is the peacemaker in our family.

Dougie walks back from the silver pickup. 'We got a full tank of gas and our gear loads in the back with room to spare. We are ready to go.'

Because Lars and I are missing our eyebrows, we continue to look at Dougie with perpetual surprise.

It throws Dougie off.

'We still got that gig Saturday, right?' Dougie ventures. 'The show must go on, right?'

Lars and I continue staring.

Dougie tries a different tack. 'Maybe if we freshen up a bit. Maybe try on a new outfit. I know that always gets me in a better mood.'

Lars and I exchange glances. Dougie doesn't freshen up or get into better moods. His outfit has always been blue jeans and a T-shirt—as grungy as his attitude.

Dougie gestures to the back to the truck. 'There's a bunch of clothes that

Mr Nut-Job left behind. It's all piled beside the truck. Had to get rid of it to make space for our gear. Some nice stuff there.'

Lars and I search through the mound of clothes. It is disturbing.

Lars picks up a yellow sundress and grimaces. I pick up a black camo hoodie with YOLO in blaze red across the front. I grimace.

I go to the river to salvage some clothes from our van. I get a pair of ripped jean shorts, a vintage Zappa concert tee, and a leather jacket. They are fresh … enough.

Lars stays onshore. He says he is just fine.

I see a pair of red Yeezys bumping along the bank of the river, caught in an eddy. They are like little lost boats.

It is Thursday morning. Nate is supposed to be off-shift. Instead, he sits in an unmarked suv with three other police officers on their way to hunt down the 'Beast of Hatcheta Falls' as it is now nicknamed at the station. Benny Tak—a rookie transfer from the Ottawa detachment—sits beside Nate in the second row. Staff Sergeant Lydia Finch is driving. Her common-law spouse, Sergeant Jay Compton, stares down the road while eating an apple. Everyone is wearing orange camo jumpsuits: criminals on their way to wilderness prison. Two hounds lounge in crates in the back.

'What kind of gun you bringing?' Jay asks Nate.

'I got a … uh … Winchester bolt-action .30-06. Been in the family for years.'

Jay nods. 'Classic. Your mom was a Winchester kind of gal.'

Jay turns to Lydia. 'I remember the church potlucks growing up—before you and your dad moved here. Mrs Wilson always brought in the best venison stews I ever tasted. Man, she bagged those critters herself and cooked 'em up to perfection. Nate's dad was a lucky man.'

Lydia looks in the rear-view mirror at Nate and raises one eyebrow ever so subtly.

'"Lucky" isn't the word,' Lydia says.

Jay continues, 'So this bear is big, maybe pushing close to three hundred pounds. I'm surprised no one has shot it yet. The head must be enormous. That would be a good-looking trophy.'

'Yes, the head must be enormous. And no, that trophy will not be coming into our house.'

'Not even in the garage? What about a nice bear-skin rug in the bedroom?' Jay makes a clicking noise with his tongue and winks back at Nate and Benny.

'No. Normal people don't keep trophies of dead things. Serial killers do.' Lydia's tone is calm, matter-of-fact.

'Oh, okay.' Jay sulks momentarily.

Jay is a lean bullet: over six feet tall, bald, with an action-hero jaw. It is funny to see him pout.

Eventually Jay shrugs. 'Happy wife, happy life. Am I right, fellas?'

Jay and Lydia have been together for seven years. They have no children. A good thing.

Nate says, 'Yeah, Mom used up every part of the animal, not just for food. She made leather jackets from the deerskin. No trophies though.'

Nate does not enjoy hunting, but he understands it. When he was growing up, it put extra food on the table. Mom thought hunting was useful. Dad did not. Dad went along on the hunting trips to be supportive and usually brought one of Mom's extra guns—just in case things got hairy. He used it once, to shoot a squirrel that was foaming at the mouth, or maybe eating a marshmallow. No one was ever sure. There wasn't enough left of the squirrel to do a post-mortem.

'So, what is the strategy for hunting down this bear?' Nate asks.

'Shoot first. Ask questions later.' Jay laughs.

Lydia laughs too. She is bubbly and blond, but no one ever tells her that to her face. She competed for many years in track and field and made it to the Commonwealth Games—twice.

Lydia has a wicked javelin throw.

Lydia's tone becomes serious. 'We're going out to the Big Bend campground where it was last seen—yesterday evening. Funny enough, a bunch of campers disappeared a couple of days before that. It might be related but we're keeping it hush-hush right now as it's close to the end of camping season anyway. All the missing campers were from Toronto except two from Ottawa.'

'Probably forgot their solar-powered espresso machines at home and had to leave. Wah-wah.' Jay pretends to wipe away tears with his meaty fists. With his big, bald, baby head, the cry-baby face looks more macabre than mocking.

Lydia glances at her partner for a moment. She seems to be reconsidering her life choice.

She continues, 'Now, where was I? Oh yeah, at the Big Bend, we'll pick up its scent with the dogs. All reports indicate that the bear has been travelling in a straight line since Sunday which, I might add, is unusual for a bear. Not the travelling-on-Sunday bit, but you know … they usually establish their territory and keep to it, avoiding humans whenever possible. This bear is on a mission. It has been running across people's backyards, across roads and parking lots. No fear. At one point, it knocked someone's lunch right out of their hands and ate it on the spot. Witnesses say one of the back paws is missing. That would make one angry bear and link it to the blood and fur found near the original crime scene. Maybe it's got some degenerative brain thing going on to boot.'

They all grunt in agreement.

After a few minutes of quiet, Jay starts to fiddle with the radio. It's all April Wine and Bachman-Turner Overdrive. Jay plugs in his iPhone and scrolls through his playlist. Drake's 'Passionfruit' starts playing. Everyone bops along.

'I love this song,' Jay says. 'Drake sings it so cool and casual but bang on. He sings without overselling. Sometimes it's almost like he's singing without singing, but he is singing — make no bones about it.'

Everyone nods.

'The William Shatner of hip hop, maybe.' Lydia is the absolute queen of left-handed compliments.

Lydia's cell phone rings. She takes it out of her pocket and hands it to Jay as he leans forward to turn off the radio.

'Sergeant Lydia Finch! … Yeah funny … yeah, it's me, Jay … what's up? … Really … no kidding! … Wow! … Maybe … Yeah … I guess not … no … no way … no way … no … way.'

Jay puts the phone down.

'That was Mike at the station. We got a prelim from forensics. Our body count was off by one. Four victims, not three. To be honest, there was so little left to collect, it's no wonder we underestimated. Anyhow, two of the victims are women, and related. Probably Victoria and Isabel … as expected. The other two victims are male ... one is Moses — expected — or at least his foot — I'd recognize that moccasin anywhere. The fourth victim is a bit of a mystery. It is a male, or part of a male ... the pelvis really. Couldn't find anything else that matched. That's all we have. Weird eh?'

'Weird that you got all that info in a thirty-second phone call.'

'Mike's a fast talker. It's like a one-sided conversation with an auctioneer.'

Lydia pulls in to the Big Bend Gas, Smokes, and Guns Variety Store parking lot. The Big Bend Conservation Area is across the road.

'And it gets weirdlier — as they say,' Jay continues. 'Forensics couldn't identify the bite marks on the victims. The bite marks are large, widely spaced, and have a serious pound-per-square-inch crush force. It's not a bear, not a cougar, not a wolf, not anything we see around here. A few bone fragments had human teeth marks on the exposed marrow ... can't figure that one out. Could be the impact of someone's mouth on someone else's leg when the animal was ripping them up.'

'That is one badass animal. Did Mike really have time to say all that — seriously?'

'Okay, I'm filling in the blanks a bit, but not by much.'

Benny leans over towards the gap between the two front seats and pushes into Nate's personal space. Nate feels agitated.

'Does this mean we revisit that cold case we've been talking about?' Benny asks.

Lydia nods. 'Yeah, it does. The horses have left the building, my friend — time to close the doors.'

'Copy that.' Nate leans into the gap between the two front seats trying to reinsert himself into the dialogue, but Benny does not budge. Instead, Benny smiles. It is the first time Nate wants to punch a fellow officer.

Nate offers, 'What if the bear ... the one sighted over the past couple of days ... is ... running from whatever *that* other animal is? Wolverine maybe? Mustelids are fearless. They'll take on anything including bears — and win. I'd be running in a straight line to get away too.'

Neither Lydia nor Jay answers. Lydia gives Jay the side-eye.

After a few moments, Lydia says, 'Nate, you may be right on that, and if that's the case, we'll need bigger guns, and a different strategy. We better head back and regroup.'

The drive to the station is quiet. No music. No chatter. Nate feels like the odd person out. Lydia, Jay, and Benny are in the loop. Nate is not. Benny is the newbie. It's not how the police services are supposed to work.

That cold case we've been talking about.

A surprising statement coming from a rookie and addressed to a superior, a statement inappropriately infused with casual familiarity. Even Jay, who fancies himself the alpha male of the Hatcheta detachment, defers to his wife when they are on the job.

The horses have left the building. Time to close the doors.

Nate has no idea what that might mean. It is the opposite of common sense. He mulls over the possible interpretations as they pull into the police station parking lot.

Jay and Lydia hustle into the building and disappear into Lydia's office. Nate loiters at the front door. A few other officers are milling around their desks, early for their shift, making small talk. Benny walks over to the Bunn coffeemaker and pours the last of the coffee into a Styrofoam cup. He looks at the empty carafe for a moment and puts it back down on the hotplate. A few spilled drips sizzle. Benny adds a squirt of agave nectar and a splash of soya milk from his personal condiment rack in the mini-fridge.

Nate is about to ask Benny if he's spent any time in Toronto.

Lydia and Jay step out from the office.

Lydia says, 'So it looks like this is a much bigger problem than originally anticipated. We're calling in some expert wildlife authorities to assist, and maybe get a chopper in the air. Benny, you can go out and finish your shift in a patrol car. Nate, I need you to go over a few things with me about your report on the Néebear residence. And then everyone tomorrow morning, zero five hundred, at the station.'

Jay ambles over to the Bunn coffeemaker.

Nate follows Lydia into her office.

As the door closes, Nate can hear Jay cursing out the empty coffeepot.

Lydia's office is spartan. On the desk is a laptop, a stapler, a plain white coffee mug, and a stack of paperwork in a black tray. On the wall is a black-and-white photograph of a young Queen Elizabeth II, a framed Ontario coat of arms, and a Canadian flag. There is only one chair and it is behind the desk.

'So, Nate, we have a very complicated situation now and I need you to wrap your head around what I am going to tell you. You do not breathe a word to anyone else. Do I have your word?' Lydia paces.

'Yes.' Nate remains standing in front of the desk.

'I knew Moses Néebear ... let me clarify ... I *know* Moses Néebear.'

'Yes.'

Jay enters the office and slurps noisily from a hot cup of tea. He seems disappointed in his beverage choice. He goes to sit down on the only chair. Lydia shoots him a look. He remains standing.

Lydia continues, 'Moses is still alive. I know it. Apart from his foot, nothing else of his body was found at the crime scene. And yeah, I'm calling it a crime scene now. Moses is not necessarily the perp, but he is definitely a person of interest.'

'We're looking for Moses then?' Nate asks.

'Moses might not be Moses.'

'Not following.'

Lydia takes a deep breath and sits down.

'That thing back at the house that did all the killing and eating.... I'm thinking it's something we're not accustomed to looking for as regular police officers. As I said before, I know Moses. My dad and him had an understanding about some of the stuff that can go wrong out here in the wilderness. And I think that is what this is. Something that went wrong. Someone that fell in with the old habits. The Anishinaabe call it wendigo. In Europe, the locals might have called it a vampire, or a werewolf. In Africa, they call it an adze. Most cultures like to project their own particular brand of demon out into the world. It's a psychological mechanism to save us from looking in the mirror. A scapegoat of sorts.'

'And Moses?'

'Moses is a shape-shifter. The real deal. But he's always been friendly and, in fact, he introduced my dad into this crypto-crazy world a while back.'

'Shape-shifter? What?' Nate looks from Lydia to Jay and back. Jay is nonplussed although he is warming up to his tea. Lydia is earnest.

'I'm surprised your parents didn't tell you. They knew about Moses too.'

'My parents? What?' Nate's ears feel hot and tingly. His stomach bottoms out. Mom and Dad rarely spoke of Moses in any detail when he was growing up. Everyone in the town knew of Moses. His name was a placeholder for various unarticulated racist sentiments about 'Indians' and the 'Indian problem'. Nate's mom had a soft spot for Moses's family. In high school, she made sure Nate understood that the 'Indian problem' was a problem created by white people. That view made Nate unpopular with his peers, but it did help him score points with Victoria. He had crushed on Victoria all through high school.

Nate's parents also knew Lydia's dad. Nate had met Mr Dale Finch a few times. Dale was a police officer in the Hatcheta detachment, and formerly served with the Thunder Bay OPP, homicide division. Dale transferred to Hatcheta when his daughter had finished high school in the T-Bay. She was going to a university in Toronto and Hatcheta was a compromise. It was closer than Thunder Bay but still far enough from Toronto. While Toronto fancied itself the centre of Canadian culture, everyone outside Toronto suspected it just fancied itself.

Dale settled in comfortably with the Hatcheta community. He was easygoing for a police officer. Even Moses liked him. They would go hunting together occasionally. Everyone would go hunting occasionally with Dale. He was that kind of guy.

It is the Thursday that never ends.

Nate wads a Kleenex and jams it up his nose. His brain hurts. His nose bleeds. Nate, Lydia, and Jay are still in their fluorescent hunting gear and are now standing outside the Néebear home.

Benny is not with them. Lucky Benny. He would be finishing his shift soon and going home.

Nate was surprised that they hadn't included Benny in the new plan; but when they drove over to Lydia and Jay's house to load up with some very unusual gear, it made sense. Benny would think they were nuts.

Crossbows, silver-tipped bolts, aerosol cans, bags of dried sage.

One of these things is not like the other.

Okay, none of these things really belong.

Nate wishes he wasn't included but he grew up in Hatcheta Falls so by default this odd toolkit must make sense to him.

It did not.

It does not.

At the Néebear residence the yellow police tape is already down.

'We should set up close to the Hollow and wait for sundown.' Lydia pulls out her iPhone and begins texting, turning away from Jay and Nate.

Nate is curious about who she is texting. They are supposed to be in a closed loop.

'Hey Lyd.' Jay smiles. 'Who would have known all those *Twilight* movies were prep for this.' He taps his crossbow: a silver-tipped bolt pulled back, taut, ready to fly. 'Booyaah! I'm stoked.'

Jay's professional deference to his boss/wife has disappeared.

'Yeah, about that, the wendigo uses your own thoughts against you, so be careful. It gets under the victim's skin,' Lydia says.

'Before ripping off that skin to wipe its slavering jaw, like a moist towelette.' Jay nudges Nate.

'Actually, Jay, that warning is mostly directed at you. It turns loved ones against each other.'

'My love is too strong.'

'Exactly my point.'

Nate remembers the hunting accident that gravely injured his dad and broke his mother's heart. It was February 14, 1999. It was cold. Lots of snow on the ground. A large pack of wolves had entered the area and were being a nuisance to a few of the local farms. Sheep, cows, and even an old horse had been attacked and eaten within the first week of that month.

Nate was ten and didn't quite understand the panic of the adults.

His parents joined a posse of sorts to hunt down the wolf pack. Everyone rode snowmobiles and carried walkie-talkies. Nate's parents had cornered a large wolf down by the Hollow—a series of small caves with an underground river rumoured to lie beneath. They had radioed for backup and were waiting for

Moses to join when Dad's gun discharged, shooting off the dimple in his chin, as well as most of his lips and nose. Dale Finch arrived soon after. Moses arrived a little later.

Dad eventually died from sepsis.

Mom stopped hunting.

Almost two decades later they were back.

The Hollow is several miles behind the Néebear house.

Nate and crew trudge past the outhouse, across a wide and shallow stream, and into a brindly forest of conifers. The land slopes gently upward. Five miles in, Nate notices a large grey boulder squatting among the trees and shadows. The boulder is the size of a small house. It would have been left behind by the retreating glaciers tens of thousands of years ago. The boulder is smooth except for a fracture on one side that has cleaved away, leaving a small heap of rubble.

Eventually the forest dwindles to a palisade of dead bone-bleached trees surrounding a large meadow. The resinous smell of pine gives way to intense waves of mulch and grass. The Hollow is ahead. It is at the bottom of a large outcrop of black granite with a wide, deep gash on one side. The gash drops five feet, then opens into a series of small caves. Nate knows. Every teenager in Hatcheta Falls knows.

Cigarette butts and a few empty mickeys are strewn about in the tall grass.

Lydia gently drops her backpack on the grass and pulls out a crossbow. She checks the safety on her shotgun and slides it over her shoulder. 'Well, I know that both of you boys being Hatcheta bred have a familiarity with this place, but not being from here, I didn't find out about it until well into a month on the job. I had to come out here to investigate a missing persons report. Quite the party place.'

'Yeah, it has a reputation.' Jay looks over at Nate. 'Mostly drinking, making out, and some wicked ghost stories though. Am I right?'

'Yeah, I remember those days.'

Nate remembers something else. Smoking weed and drinking beer with some buddies at the Hollow when he was fourteen. He was sitting on top of the granite outcrop and trash-talking a teacher when he blacked out. His buddies said it happened in mid-toke. His eyes rolled up and his jaw dropped down to his chest like a Christmas nutcracker. It freaked them out. After a few minutes, he snapped out of it like nothing had happened. He had the munchies for a week.

'You see how the lichen grows on all sides of the rocks out here?' Jay asks Nate.

'Yeah, that's a bit weird. It usually clings to the north side. I remember learning that as a kid — you know, in case you got lost in the woods and needed to figure out compass directions without a compass.'

Jay bends down and flakes a bit of the blue-green lichen with his fingernails. 'Well, here's the thing. Lichen is not really a single plant. It is algae and fungus that have worked out some sort of co-survival strategy. The fungus draws up the moisture and raw nutrients while the algae gets the sun to photosynthesize it into usable food. It grows on the north side because up here the sun shines from the south and would dry out the moisture. The north side gets just enough light without drying up the food source. A win-win situation.'

'I kinda remember that from biology class ... and why are you sounding like a biology teacher all of a sudden?'

Lydia lights up a bundle of dried sage and waves it slowly in the air. 'Jay and I have been trying to figure out this wendigo thing for a while. The missing persons case I mentioned earlier was never solved. We found some bones. Foot bones! Poor girl. Never found the rest of her body. The case went cold. Moses helped but I knew he wasn't telling me everything. My dad insisted I back off. I really wanted to run Moses in. Make him sweat just a little bit. But I didn't. Still regret that decision.'

Lydia carries the burning sage towards the cave entrance. 'Getting back to the lichen bit — the wendigo is sort of similar. It creates a symbiotic relationship with the host. You won't detect it until it is too late. Even the host may not be aware of it at first. Nature certainly likes to get its freak on.'

The first cave is the size of a two-car garage. Nate remembers some pretty epic parties in this chamber as a teenager. He looks around. The vibe has changed. The technology has evolved. Bright, stackable poly-resin Muskokas and mildew-resistant antibacterial fabrics purchased from Amazon have replaced the trappings of yesteryear: battered aluminum-frame lawn chairs, moldy wool blankets, and cast-off pillows liberated from someone's basement.

Gone is the derelict but completely functional battery-operated boom box. Nowadays everyone has their own smartphone and personal playlist courtesy of Apple or Spotify. No one has to listen to the same music although you're in the same space.

'Sweet Jesus, they have a recycling bin!' Jay exclaims, pointing his flashlight at a large blue box in one corner. 'These kids are uptight even when they're letting loose.'

'They probably compost their own party vomit.' Lydia pushes the smoking sage in front of her. 'We gotta move down a bit farther to the last chamber.'

Twenty feet down, through a narrow passage, the rock opens into a second chamber much smaller than the first. Only four people might be able to stand together because of the cramped footing. Above the knees, the space gradually extends into a large bulbous mushroom shape that then rapidly narrows again into an arching crevice. Water weeps down the sides.

Because of the bulky backpacks they are carrying, Jay, Lydia, and Nate remain in single file as they pass through.

The third chamber is considerably deeper, colder, and creepier. No one parties in the third chamber. Nate remembers being spooked when he entered it on a dare from his buddies — that same day he gapped out in mid-toke. The third chamber is very large. In one corner, a four-inch crack extends from floor to ceiling like a scar. Lydia brings the smoking sage close to the scar. The sage brightens, bursts into flame, and quickly burns out.

'Just as I thought.' Lydia shakes the smudge stick in seven directions. The ashes fall into darkness on the floor.

'Not methane, I hope?' Nate shines his flashlight down into the scar. The light dissipates into dark grey after several metres. 'I'm told there's a river that runs somewhere deep down. I can sort of hear it. Fresh air must be getting in that way too.'

Nate, Jay, and Lydia stand quietly. Nate focuses on the soft, deep rumble of water. It seems louder than when they first walked in.

Lydia turns to Nate. 'I know that's what everyone thinks but I've looked it up. They've done numerous geological surveys and there is no underground river here. It's pretty well bone-dry bedrock.'

'That sound though.'

Jay holds the flashlight steady under his chin. 'The roar of a thousand hungry souls.'

'Knock it off, Jay,' Lydia says.

'The roar of a thousand hungry souls,' Jay repeats, strobing the flashlight under his chin. His mouth opens and closes in rapid succession: each time getting larger, the teeth sharper.

'Jay?' Lydia turns to her husband. 'Look at me, Jay.'

Out of the side of her mouth: 'Nate? Gun.'

Nate reluctantly unholsters his gun. At such close range, a bullet would tear through a body and ricochet helter-skelter off the walls—probably killing or wounding all three of them.

'Jay, honey?' Lydia again. Her voice is softer.

The air in the cave is colder.

'A thousand hungry souls.' Jay's voice deepens as he lunges at Lydia, knocking the crossbow out of her hands. Lydia sidesteps to the left and redirects Jay's momentum straight into the slab wall. His face bounces off the rock with a wincing crack. Jay falls onto his back. Both arms flatten out, one to each side in a cross shape. Jay's body quivers. His eyes remain open, staring up into the darkness.

'Hand me the crossbow quick!' Lydia pants.

Nate scrambles over to the weapon. The whipcord has broken. The bolt is lodged in the nut.

Jay's arms snap backwards at the elbows into right angles. Palms rotate slowly like landing gear. Wrists extend, pushing the torso upwards and causing the body to bend first at the waist, then at the knees. The angle is so extreme that his kneecaps pop.

Nate's stomach churns. The adrenalin surges. It's fight-or-flight mode, with a little side trip on the good ship nausea.

Jay's disjointed ascension continues: ankles grind, foot bones snap, crackle, and pop.

The side trip is now the main destination.

Jay vaults over Lydia and lands on Nate, knocking him to the ground. Jay grabs the crossbow and crushes it with hands grown large and gnarled. The dislodged bolt skitters across the rock floor. The silver tip breaks. The remaining iron stump sparks on contact with the rock floor.

Jay is momentarily distracted by the sparks.

Lydia pulls another bolt from her backpack and jams it into her husband's neck. Jay lurches forward, his face morphed by rage and a good deal of hunger.

Nate can see the silver tip protruding past Jay's Adam's apple. 'That went right through!'

'I hardly pushed. It felt like it was slicing air.' Lydia pulls another bolt and stabs it into her life-partner's spine below the shoulder blades. 'This one's a little harder. Hitting a lot of bone.'

Jay twists and knocks Lydia off her feet. Several bolts scatter from her backpack onto the cave floor. Some tips break. Some remain intact.

'Do you think you could be a darlin' and give a hand? I got five more chakras to nail before this beast slows down.'

Nate grabs two bolts while kicking the remaining ones towards Lydia. Jay swings back towards Nate and smashes him in the head with a fist that is now the size of a large boulder. Nate instinctively turns away but catches some of the impact. A few of Nate's teeth loosen and rattle around in the hollow of his mouth. Jay's other fist roundhouses Nate to the side of the temple. Nate falls back onto the cold stone, clutching the bolts like a punch-drunk cherub. The cave spins. Nate swallows — teeth, spit, pride.

Nate passes out.

'Snap out of it.' Lydia slaps Nate across the face.

Nate looks up. He is lying on his back in the grass outside the cave. Lydia is kneeling over him. It is dark.

'Are you hungry?' Lydia asks. She shines a flashlight in Nate's eyes.

'Peckish?' Nate says hesitantly, unsure if that is the best answer under the present circumstances.

'That'll do. I'm glad you didn't say "voracious" or else you might've ended up like Jay. I'm surprised how quickly he got infected. That wasn't part of the plan.'

'Plan?'

'Yeah. We thought you might be the one. Wouldn't be the first time, right?'

'What? How do you know?'

'Small town.' Lydia walks back to the cave entrance with her backpack. She takes out two aerosol cans and sprays intertwining lines in slow descending curves across the rock and open space. They look like ephemeral DNA strands.

'Is that holy water? What symbol is that? Shouldn't you be making a cross or something?'

'Pffft, please. It's a fungicide and an antibacterial spray. I'm disinfecting the opening. What, are we in the Middle Ages?'

'What about the crossbows and silver-tipped arrows?'

'Silver has natural antibacterial properties. Plus, it's bioactive, which means microbes cannot develop immunity to it. And the crossbow is an excellent delivery system, better than a gun. Silver bullets aren't practical, or affordable.'

Lydia lights a flare and places it on the ground in front of the cave entrance. The sparks are intense. Nate turns his eyes away and focuses on the treeline to the south. The stars are bright pixelated dots. Orion's Belt hangs in the darkness. The moon is pale orange.

'Full moon,' Nate observes.

Without looking up, Lydia answers, 'I think the full moon was yesterday. Still pretty awesome, eh?'

'Harvest moon, right?'

'Corn moon. The harvest moon is October fifth.'

'I thought October was the hunter moon.'

'They threw the hunter moon under the bus this year.' Lydia has her back to Nate as she guards the cave entrance. 'You can google it when you get home.'

'Are you waiting for Jay?'

Lydia shakes her head. No words.

Nate watches the moon float in a sea of stars. Grey wispy clouds scud past.

Another moon cleaves from the first and swoops down, skimming above the tree line towards them.

'I think the hunter moon is driving the bus,' Nate observes.

* * *

It is late evening, Thursday. Dougie pulls into the parking lot of the Waffle Waffle House. There is a sandwich board on the gravel shoulder with two badly painted fried eggs sagging beneath the words 'All Day Breakfast'. There is a wide, shallow drainage ditch surrounding the paved lot on three sides. A moat to keep the riff-raff out, or in.

I count five cars and three pickup trucks parked in front of the restaurant entrance. The rest of the lot is empty. Dougie parks in the far corner closest to the road and the sandwich board.

Dougie's stomach grumbles.

'I smell bacon,' Dougie says.

I smell the bacon too.

I also smell smoky maple syrup, and the dense scent of griddle-cooked pancake batter.

'Bacon,' I agree.

Lars shouts something from inside the camper cab in the back. The word is muffled but the excitement is unmistakable. It is 'bacon'.

For men it is easier to talk about bacon than about mysteriously disappearing families, strange creatures in outhouses, or near-death encounters with serial killers.

Dougie does not disappoint.

'Remember how Dad used to love bacon so much, he would eat strips of it, raw out of the package, while Mom cooked ours?' Dougie says.

'Yeah, and he would wash it down with a cup of hot black joe, burning his mouth — always,' I say.

In the background, Lars is pounding his fist against the camper walls and shouting, 'Bacon.'

'Mom didn't like bacon. Did you ever figure out why — apart from the occasional grease fire?' Dougie asks.

'I have my theories. Have you ever noticed that women in general don't like bacon as much as men? Oh sure, they may say they "like" bacon, but they don't love bacon. Men love bacon. And have you ever wondered why some religions won't let you eat bacon? They hate bacon — as if that's possible.'

'Your point?'

'Let me illuminate. Prepare to be amazed. Bacon is a metaphor for ...'

'Sex?'

'No ... I'm thinking that the prohibition against bacon is really a prohibition against human sacrifice and cannibalism.'

'I'm sticking with sex.'

'No, seriously, hear me out on this one. I have read from a very reputable source—on the Internet—that pork is similar in taste and texture to human flesh; therefore, it makes sense that these ancient cultures were being proactive by banning pigs. If you start eating pigs, what's to stop you from eating babies? Women and most religions do not want you to eat babies.'

'Not buying it.'

'There is a very thin line between civilization and post-apocalyptic baby eating,' I argue.

Lars taps on the driver's side window, startling us. He is eating from what looks like a jar of brown, wrinkly, dried-out raisins. They are not raisins. As Lars jostles the jar to loosen up the contents, a yellow sticky note dislodges from the side and flutters up against the window. NIPPLSE is written in uneven block letters on the yellow sticky-note. The note flutters to the ground.

Lars chews like a maniac and swallows. 'These raisins suck. And by the by, that Joel guy has quite the collection of toupées. I didn't realize he wore a piece.'

'Those probably aren't toupées.' Dougie then points at the jar. 'And those most definitely aren't raisins.'

* * *

The interior of the Waffle Waffle House is rustic pine with a nod to rustic hygiene. Flypaper spirals hang randomly throughout the open kitchen.

Lars picks up a paper napkin and scrubs his tongue.

'Have you ever eaten a raisin?' I ask.

Lars glares at me. 'I thought they were fancy—like those salted caramels —you know, they add salt to almost anything these days and call it gourmet.'

Dougie pats Lars on the shoulder. 'Listen, bro, we had to tell you. You were hell-bent on scarfing down as many as you could. At some point, you would've figured it out. I mean, that Joel guy was pretty twisted.'

The waitress slides three menus down the table towards us and quickly steps back. 'Would you like to start with a drink?' She breathes in sharply and holds her breath. I look around. Everyone else in the restaurant appears to be holding their breath as well.

'Yes, please. We'll start with a carafe of your finest — coffee that is.' Dougie pulls out the knife and fork from the rolled paper napkin.

'We sell it by the cup.'

'Three cups of your finest then.' Dougie tucks the pristine paper napkin into his dirty shirt collar and clutches the knife and fork in separate hands, sharp ends up. He has a serene grin on his face.

I know how bad we look.

I sense how bad we smell.

We are Cortés and the conquistadors, smelling up the halls of Montezuma — oblivious to our stink. When the conquistadors first arrived, the Aztecs accompanied them everywhere with burning incense. The conquistadors thought it was a sign of honour. It was not.

The cook swivels an industrial-sized floor fan towards where we are sitting. The greasy, warm air of the kitchen flows into the restaurant. Everyone leans towards the greasy, warm kitchen air and breathes deeply.

'I'll have the wild blueberry pancakes — they are *wild* blueberries, right?' Dougie asks.

'You're in wild blueberry country,' the waitress assures him. She steps back a little farther.

Lars nods. 'Yeah, don't you remember all those blueberry stands at the side of the road? We must've passed at least ten in the last couple of hours.'

I know those stands. Every year they proliferate up and down Ontario highways from early August to well past Hallowe'en. Variations on a theme: tables neatly arranged with stacks of small white Chinese takeout boxes brimming with tiny berries; a vintage Shasta trailer in seafoam green parked nearby with flat tires and a broken axle; clusters of quaint 'hand-painted' signs offering 'Wild Bluebarrys' or 'Wild Blubberries'; white, middle-aged man and woman sitting behind the table, reading books — always something by Stephen King or Dean Koontz. So much cuteness. So much set dressing. So much bullshit.

A front for something far more sinister.

The Mexican blueberry cartel. Muscling in on our home turf.

'And you?' The waitress looks at me.

'Wild blueberry pancakes, please.'

'I should've ordered tea,' Dougie frets after the waitress walks away.

'Tea? Since when did you start drinking tea?' Lars asks.

'Since right now. It's good for you.'

Lars and I exchange glances.

'Good for you? Since when did that enter your vocabulary?' I ask.

'I dunno. I feel all of a sudden that I should be thinking more about my health. I'm going to wash my hands.' Dougie gets up. 'Because hygiene is good for you too.'

Lars and I watch Dougie, in his filthy, torn jeans and T-shirt, stride towards the bathroom. A sign in front of a long dark corridor reads 'Restroom Is for Customers Only'. A gender-ambiguous symbol of a half man, half woman block figure dangles beneath. A silver arrow points into the darkness.

The waitress brings our three orders of pancakes and coffee at the same time. She produces the bill before I manage my first bite.

Dougie is still in the bathroom.

'Pay whenever you're ready.' The waitress remains standing three feet from our table. I hunch forward over the pancakes and eat — clusters of hot purple berry burst sweet juice in my mouth. Lars digs in too. I think I hear the waitress's foot tapping, or maybe it's the clock ticking. It is distracting.

Dougie is still in the bathroom.

The waitress looms in my peripheral vision. She is in her thirties. Blond hair sloppily pinned up into a bun. Full lips. Wide hips. A hard life. Shiv you just as soon as fuck you. My kind of gal.

'Hey honey, is it possible to get a refill? I know it looks half-full still, but …' I point to my cup.

Silence.

'Half-full? I meant half-empty.' I point to my now miraculously transformed 'half-empty' cup of coffee. The power of perspective.

Silence.

My kind of gal.

Dougie is still in the bathroom. I have noticed a few other customers leave their table and go down the same corridor towards the bathroom. None have returned. Maybe there's another exit. Maybe it's a rash of dine-and-dash.

'I would love a slice of coconut cream pie,' I say dreamily, lost in the dark, limpid, and hostile gaze of our waitress.

'The kitchen is closed.'

I glance behind her and notice that the cook is gone. I catch a glimpse of someone's hand desperately reaching out from a hidden corner, grasping the chrome edge of the chafing station, knocking over a pack of smokes, slowly disappearing back behind the corner.

'Okay, we'll pay and leave as soon as my brother gets back from the john.'

Lars and I stare at Dougie's full plate of pancakes. The syrup has disappeared, fully absorbed into the stacks of doughy deliciousness — like it was never there.

I am full. Lars is full.

'Can we have a to-go container?' I suggest. 'If it's not too much trouble?'

It is too much trouble. The waitress stands with her arms folded.

I schlep self-consciously across the tiled floor to see what's up with Dougie. There are now only five people sitting in the restaurant: each at a separate table, waiting for their friends to return to finish the meal. Their expressions flicker between disdain and unease.

The bathroom hallway is long, dark, and narrow. It is panelled with cheap beadboard: black burls printed on shit-brown veneer. Claustrophobic. Like an abattoir chute. The smell is terrible. I cover my nose and mouth with one hand and twist the bathroom doorknob with the other. The door opens a crack. Slivers of bright light cut along three of the edges — like a celestial moat ... to keep the riff-raff out, or in.

I push, but the door only budges slightly. It feels like there's a sandbag or dead weight on the other side.

'Doug, bro! Are you okay?' I yell through cupped hands.

The occasional sound of water dripping.

'Dougie?' I ask softly.

The occasional sound of water dripping.

BANG!

Behind me, bedlam: dishes screaming, voices breaking. I recognize Lars's voice—rapid-fire curses with no audible breath between. It begins hoarse and bellicose, then shrills up an octave beyond his best Rob Halford impersonation.

Impressive and alarming.

My adrenalin kicks in, triggering the Tourette's. I run back into the restaurant, yelling profanities, offering apologies, sucking my fist—sometimes all three at the same time—always in both official languages.

I lurch to a stop.

Dougie—a nine-foot grotesquerie of Dougie—is standing in the middle of the restaurant surrounded by carnage: body parts, blood, unfinished blueberries, spilled coffee. Nine-foot Dougie hoists the waitress's severed head up like a trophy, bringing the blood-ooze neck and the vestige of spinal cord up to his mouth. Nine-foot Dougie inhales. The sound is maddening: part Dyson vacuum cleaner, part high-pitched rape whistle. The poor woman's eyes vibrate momentarily before imploding within black sockets. Her nose flattens and inverts. Lips pucker and are gone.

Lars jigs from foot to foot while vomiting.

Staggering backwards, I grasp the edge of a table and slowly slip to the floor. I notice a lot of mismatched shoes scattered around. I notice they all have feet in them.

Demon Dougie belches hard. The curtains flutter. His breath smells of stale ice from the depths of a very old freezer, or maybe the ninth circle of hell.

Slowly Dougie trudges towards the exit. Broad demon shoulders contract and soften. Giant demon claws unclench and relax. Fingers flex, shrink into calloused drummer hands swinging in gawky rhythm. A fucked up metronome.

'Sorry you had to see that, guys.' Dougie's mouth trembles in emotion.

Emotion?

Not emotion. Dougie's oversized demon lips and teeth soften into man mandibles—the crushing organs.

'Get in the truck and I'll explain everything as best I can.'

Lars and I hesitate.

'Don't worry. Couldn't eat another thing.' Dougie rubs his belly. 'I'm good for at least a couple of hours.'

'Actually we're more worried about your lack of pants.' Lars says.

Dougie grumbles and bends over to pick up a pair of blood-soaked jeans. He thinks a bit. He stalks over to the kitchen and grabs the Bunn hot water dispenser and a box of green tea bags.

'One for the road,' Dougie says, and kicks out the restaurant door.

Outside, the angel chorus sings.

Crickets rosin up their wings.

I put the truck into gear and gently accelerate out of the parking lot. Dougie sits in the middle and struggles to put on his pants. Lars is pressed up tight against the passenger door with one hand clutching the door handle. The Bunn hot water dispenser on his lap weeps steaming hot water. Lars weeps as well.

'I have looked myself in the mirror and I can tell you, I am not happy with what I see.' Dougie has angled the rear-view mirror towards his face and he grimaces as he talks. 'I have worked so hard ...' Dougie gestures at his image in the mirror and sighs. 'I've become a monster.'

'Yeah, I've been meaning to ask you about that.'

Part of me wants to console him and pat him on the shoulder. The other part of me fears he will bite off my hand as soon as it gets close to his mouth.

I continue, 'You ate everyone at the diner and you looked like you were getting beat with the ugly stick while you were doing it.'

Lars interjects, 'You have a hollow leg or something? I was full after five pancakes.'

'I'm not sure. A compulsion? Filling an existential void? As a certain step-bro would say.' Dougie shakes his head. 'I *can* tell you that it is something dark and pre-human — with a wicked-fast metabolism.'

Dougie lets that statement sink in for dramatic effect.

The drama doesn't have far to go. I read a lot of H. P. Lovecraft in school.

Dougie continues, 'That night at the Néebears's, when Isabel touched my hand, I felt a part of me ... diminish ... and part of Isabel become stronger and enter me ... but Isabel isn't Isabel either. She has been ... enhanced.'

Dougie's tongue rolls out like a fat snake and languidly plays at the radio controls.

'Am mot thure ith ay can geth thru thith,' Dougie lisps, mangles, and clutters the English language in syncopation with the rapid cycle of partial phrases and song snippets on the radio.

'I'm not sure if I'll get through this either.' I lean forward and switch off the radio.

'We're family,' I add without much conviction.

Dougie draws his shredded and blood-stained T-shirt up to his face and wipes away the tears. The tears go. The blood remains. Thankfully, he does not blow his nose.

'Yes, blood is thicker than water.' Dougie nods while resting his hand on my thigh. He squeezes a little too hard — like he's gauging the fat-to-lean ratio. I do not appreciate it.

My leg spasms.

The truck accelerates, decelerates, accelerates — puncturing through puffs of dust kicked up by our wheels. We have been down this road.

'Are you still Dougie?' I ask.

'Not sure.' Dougie smiles. His teeth look sharp. 'Are you still Angus?'

'Pretty sure, yeah. Why?'

'After you died on the operating table. You remember? You were different.'

'Didn't die. It's called a *near*-death experience, not a death experience. I floated away a bit but didn't go anywhere exciting.'

'No, you died. I can tell now. That's why you were passed over for this.' Dougie points to himself. 'I can't even eat you. You're like tainted beef.'

'Burn.' Lars sobs as much from the physical pain of scalding-hot water dribbling on his legs as the metaphorical implication of the word.

'And Lars, well … Lars has a different fate awaiting him, courtesy of my granddaughter Candice.'

'Since when did you have kids, let alone grandkids?' Lars looks bewildered and turns to me. 'I bang this Candy girl once and now her name pops up everywhere. That's like coincidence, right?'

'Cognitive bias,' I say.

'Lars, Lars, Lars.' Dougie shakes his head. 'It is neither coincidence nor cognitive bias. The Candy you "banged" — not a term I approve of — is the half-sister of Victoria and therefore, the granddaughter of Isabel — me.'

'Jeez, get with the program, Lars,' I add sarcastically while turning my head away from Dougie and looking desperately at Lars.

I mouth, *What the fuck?*

Moses perches on a Jack pine. The stars are bright. The moon is bright. A sliver of shadow cuts along the side of the moon's face. The corn moon was yesterday. It will be another twenty-nine days before the next full one. Below Moses, the Ouimet Canyon drops one hundred metres into deep darkness and a rubble-rock floor strewn with small pockets of rare flowers and plants. It is a remote geographical marvel in a sparsely populated region. A handful of walking trails, boardwalks, and viewing platforms proliferate along the lip of the gorge: a beautiful and breathtaking sight. Visitors are not allowed down on the canyon floor itself because of the ecologically fragile flora and fauna unique to that environment.

Visitors are not told that the ecologically fragile flora and fauna might try to kill and eat them.

The canyon extends almost two kilometres north–south and is one hundred and fifty metres wide in parts. Split open by advancing glaciers millennia ago, then washed out as the glaciers retreated, the gorge is located almost sixty kilometres northeast of Thunder Bay. From Hatcheta Falls, it is over twelve hours of driving, and slightly less than three hours as the crow flies; but Moses is no ordinary crow. With people to see and things to eat, it took a little longer.

Unfortunately, a lot of his fellow shape-shifters were busy fighting other injustices, or just being generally distracted. Snapchat, Facebook, Instagram, and Twitter are major spirit vampires it seems.

At least Candice offered to help.

Moses preens his feathers and relaxes into a near dream state. The musicians will probably arrive sometime tomorrow morning. Isabel will lead them here. It is inevitable. It is where She was born. It is where She will be reborn. Moses shudders. It might get ugly. If only he had paid attention to Candice's warning that evening. Victoria would be alive, and those damn musicians would be dead.

Isabel will fix that.

Nate rests in the back of the helicopter glaring at the back of Benny Tak's head. Benny Tak is piloting. 'Show-off,' Nate mutters and switches his attention to Lydia. She reads a topographical map while periodically checking the GPS. Every square inch of the helicopter's control panel is jammed with toggles, dials, and lights.

Lights.

It was the large searchlight under the nose of the helicopter that Nate mistook for a second moon. Nate was already seeing stars after being punched in the head by Jay's boulder-sized fist. Why not see an extra moon?

'Where are we going?' Nate yells over the noise in the cabin. No one hears him. Benny and Lydia are wearing flight helmets and talk to each other through their mouthpieces. Nate stares past them, out through the front windshield. He recognizes the Cygnus constellation.

The helicopter is travelling north.

Nate grew up watching the night sky and knowing all the constellations. His dad believed in the beauty of the cosmos. His mom believed in the practicality of knowing how to find your way out of the woods at night.

To his dad, constellations were a secret language: random points of light in the universe, arbitrarily connected by the human need to impose meaning and order. An ancient Greek myth told the story behind the Cygnus constellation: it was made of the bones of the musician Orpheus, gathered up after his murder and cast into the night sky, transformed by the gods into the shape of a swan. His star-shaped lyre close by.

Famous dead musicians were immortal — even in ancient Greece.

To his mom, Cygnus hung in the north sky and pointed with one wing to Polaris — the true North Star. All the constellations rotated around Polaris. Find it, she would say, and you can find south, east, west, and home.

To Nate, Cygnus was all that, and more.

It was — it is — an awesome Rush song.

Nate whistles the atmospheric bell sounds of Rush's 'Cygnus X-1: Book 1'.

Suck, pucker, blow.

Nate vocalizes the chunky bass line: 'Duh, duh, duhduh. Duh, duh, duhduh, dada.'

Nate spastically thrashes at an imaginary drum set.

The roar of the helicopter engine, the whirring of the blades, the persistent bleeps and blips of the console instrumentation meld nicely with the music in his head.

'Hey sunshine!' Lydia has turned around and is yelling at Nate. 'Sorry to interrupt your ... whatever the hell it is you're doing back there, but we'll be landing in less than an hour and I want you to put that helmet on so we can talk without me losing my voice. Capisce?'

Nate grabs the helmet and gingerly fits it over his head. With a possible concussion, he is not sure the added pressure is such a good thing. He looks up at the front cabin. Lydia and Benny don't seem to care.

He can now hear their chatter: a lot of crazy talk about wendigo, cannibalism, and lichen. Lydia throws the word 'symbiotic' around like a Frisbee. Benny throws 'weaponize' back like a lawn dart.

Nate wants to ask Lydia if Benny is old enough to fly.

Instead, Nate asks ... again, 'So, Lydia ... where are we going?'

Benny replies, 'Ouimet Canyon.'

Lydia only nods.

Nate senses a power shift. 'Hey Benny, why are — '

Benny Tak interrupts. 'Ben. Call me Ben.'

A real power shift.

'Ben ...' Nate sucks in all his contempt for the new guy and continues, 'Why Ouimet?'

'Why not ... Ouimet?'

If it is a joke, Nate doesn't get it.

'No seriously,' Nate persists. 'Why Ouimet?'

'What happened to Jay at the Hollow is related to something in the canyon. We've been tracking some odd murders and disappearances out here in the boonies and believe they're related to a plant-based hallucinogen — maybe a specific type of lichen—located in a few areas on the canyon floor. We've had our suspicions about the Hollow as well, going back several years. Right, Lyd?'

Lydia nods.

Nate watches Lydia's face. Her jaw tightens then relaxes. Nate returns his attention to Benny.

'Jay's reaction in the cave confirmed it.'

'So how did my face hallucinate the boulder-sized fist that crushed it? Or Jay's body bending at all the wrong angles?'

'You experienced the stimulus differently. Lydia tells me that Jay fell into a sudden rage and became super-strong, super-agile, super-murderous. On the other hand, you got super-spaced-out and super-uncoordinated. She didn't mention anything about an actual physical transformation on Jay's part.'

Nate looks over at Lydia. Lydia's jaw clenches again.

'Anyway, we need to track down and isolate a live specimen.'

'Track down? Why don't you just dig up the plant?'

'It's more complicated, and a little bit classified. Suffice it to say, the plant's toxins remain inert and unidentifiable until they bind with a human host—which appears to be randomly selected as per your experience in the cave vs. Jay's vs. Lydia's. My people need to get verifiable and reproducible stats.'

'Your people?'

'That's really classified.'

Nate notices four M4 carbines latched against the rear bulwark. The M4 carbine is a heavy-duty assault rifle used by the U.S. military. They're as rare as palm trees in Canada.

Benny's people are not Nate's people.

Nate decides not to ask any more questions.

Nate watches the stars.

It is early Friday morning as we roll into a gas station outside Marathon. We have been driving for most of the night. Dougie stays in the vehicle while I get out and gas up. Lars walks over to the chip truck. It is closed, but the blueberry stand is open. A middle-aged couple sit behind a table stacked with white Chinese takeout containers brimming with tiny blueberries, and rows of white-boxed blueberry pies. I hear Lars haggling over the price of a blueberry pie.

Two OPP cruisers zip by, heading southbound.

I pump seventy bucks of gas into the tank and act casual as I walk into the convenience store to pay. Our credit cards are missing, and we are down to a fistful of green deuces and red kings — mostly liberated by Dougie from the abandoned wallets and purses at the Waffle Waffle House. The next gig is tomorrow, and I don't think we can pull it off. Lars is a jittery mess, I can't focus, and Dougie will eat everyone in the audience.

I line up behind a young woman and her daughter waiting to pay. Behind the counter is a small flat-screen TV running the regional 24-hour news channel: multiple feeds, tickertape lines, cartoon weather icons.

The sound is off.

'Do you have a lavatory?' the young woman asks the clerk. The young woman's pronunciation is clear, crisp, British. She is wearing a light-blue hijab, jeans, and a tight black sweater. Her daughter clings to her side and stares at me with a mixture of awe and horror.

The clerk, a middle-aged white male with a Colonel Sanders complex, squints and puffs his lips forward. 'What?'

'Water closet, toilet, bathroom.'

'Paying customers only.' The clerk points to a sign behind him with the message 'No Gas, No Ass'.

'My husband will pay when he finishes.' The woman points past the sign and out the window at the pumps where a tall black man in dark grey dress slacks and a mauve dress shirt pumps gas into a red minivan.

Lars is on the other side of the pump, shoveling pie into his piehole. I watch Dougie step out of the truck and saunter towards the blueberry stand.

Colonel Clerk stares at the woman.

'I will buy a bag of crisps then?' The woman is vexed.

'Crisps?'

'Po-tay-to chips,' the woman enunciates. 'Ketchup flavour.'

'That's more like it.' The clerk nods. 'All righty then, the bathroom is in the back of the store. Go past the jerk station, past the fireworks display, past the Pepto-Bismol stand … then look for the signs.'

It will be a good five-minute walk with a few getting-lost detours for that woman and her child before they find the bathroom. These stores dot the rural wilderness of Ontario and are always a minotaur's labyrinth of aisles, shelves, dead ends, dust, detritus, desire. Everything you need and don't need. Hardware and software. Food and fallow.

'Crisps, eh? Foreigners and their foreign foods,' the clerk mutters as the woman and child disappear down an aisle. Behind him, the 24-hour news channel streams grainy surveillance footage of Dougie, Lars, and myself walking from our stolen truck, across the parking lot, and into the Waffle Waffle House. Captions running underneath declare, 'Persons of Interest', 'Do Not Approach', and 'Considered Dangerous'. I guess they didn't want to show the footage of us running out of the restaurant covered in blood and throwing up, or of Dougie morphing from monster to man. That would've been a shit show for sure.

'Yeah, foreigners,' I pretend to agree. 'We all came here from the old country to get away from them, and then they just follow us here.'

Colonel Clerk looks at me and nods. Irony is not part of his vocabulary.

The TV news feed has switched to the seven-day weather forecast. It's looking good. Temperatures will be in the low double digits well into next week. Big smiley suns sporting big black sunglasses all in a row.

Nothing like a pleasant weather forecast to put a little pep in your step.

The red minivan has a lot of pep as we roar down the highway. Dougie is driving. I am sitting behind him with a take-out tray filled with four cups of steeped green tea. The man with the mauve shirt and dark grey dress slacks is in the passenger seat. His name is Awamiri. It means 'life'. He is terrified. Lars is near catatonic in the back seat. He has smeared blueberry pie filling across his cheeks and forehead in symmetrical lines in a misplaced gesture of tribal tokenism, or perhaps an homage to *Apocalypse Now*.

Same diff.

'What will my wife and daughter think when they come out and see that I am gone?' Awamiri asks. His accent is rootless and pleasantly un-American—a Torontonian for sure.

Dougie answers, 'Well, at first they will be mystified, then they will be angry. When they stumble upon the blueberry stand, I think they might experience something akin to horror. And by the way, I must say blueberry makes an excellent compote that goes well with many savoury cuts of meat.'

Lars tries to wipe the blueberry filling off his face. It smears into his skin instead. He looks like a Smurf.

I pass a cup of green tea to Dougie who sips it with one hand while driving with the other.

'Thanks, bro. That'll take the edge off.'

'Where are you taking me?' Awamiri asks. He is trying to be calm, but the question has a tremulous uptick on the last three syllables. His cologne — a citrusy, cedar mix — diffuses with the tang of sweat.

Dougie puts down his tea and pats Awamiri on the leg, occasionally squeezing the fleshier parts with a little too much enthusiasm. 'We ... no ... I ... I am takin' you on a journey into a world that predates the quaint platitudes of the Abrahamic faiths. A world that is red in tooth and claw. A world that is full of—'

'Juggalos?' Awamiri interrupts. Sweat stains spread beneath his armpits. 'You are Juggalos, right? This is part of the whole 'dark carnival' thing? I've read about it. It's all role-playing. Nothing to worry about, right?'

'Right, absolutely, nothing to worry about,' Dougie soothes. 'Whoop, whoop, as they say in the hood.'

I notice that Dougie's diction and accent have come unmoored from his Scarborough roots. At times his sentences sound genteel and feminine — like someone who has read Jane Austen ... for pleasure. That must be the Isabel spirit rising to the surface. Other times, it's reverting to the grunts, clipped syllables, and dropped consonants of our local Brimley neighbourhood. Sometimes it's a bit of both.

Dougie smooths over Awamiri's anxiety with a bit of social engagement. 'So, what is it that you do for a living? And what brings you and your lovely family up to Marathon?'

'Holidays. Heading to Thunder Bay to see relatives. I'm an orthopaedic surgeon at Sick Kids Hospital in Toronto. My wife works there as well. She is a specialist in autoimmune disorders. Also, a doctor. We're doctors. We help people.'

'A doctor, eh? Well, maybe you can help find a cure for what ails me.'

As human Dougie finishes the last syllable, demon Dougie's tongue snakes out, wraps around Awamiri's neck and snaps it. The tongue pulls at Awamiri's body. Awamiri's body twitches and roils but remains strapped in by the seat belt.

Demon Dougie smiles. His teeth are like sparkling stars, backdropped by an expanding universe of darkness.

Demon Dougie looks at me, then Lars. 'Chan youth guyths gif a handth?'

Dougie's fat tongue undulates with each syllable.

'No!' Lars crosses his arms. 'That guy was all right. He worked at the children's hospital for Christ's sake. And all you want to do is eat him? You're a racist. Fuck you.'

'Anguth?'

'Sorry, Dougie, Lars is right. You're out of control. You ate less than twenty minutes ago.'

Dougie's tongue unravels from Awamiri's neck and slithers back into the cavernous maw. Awamiri's body slumps forward.

'Hypocrites.' Dougie seethes. 'You and your ilk...'

I have never heard Dougie use an archaism. I am speechless.

Dougie resumes, 'You and your ilk strut the earth: day players consuming everything the mother gives, and then shitting it in her face. No respect. God did not give you dominion over the world and everything in it. You put those words in her mouth. You are nothing — nothing more than pathetic, ungrateful ...squatters.'

Wow. Dougie/Isabel is on fire: a little bit of Shakespeare, a little bit of biblical exegesis, a whole lot of existential venom.

'Well then, brother, what do you propose we do?' I ask. 'We are captives to your capricious and capacious appetite. And remember: you murder and eat people. We do not. For all your rhetorical flourishes, you cannot ignore that your acts are real, not metaphorical.'

'Yeah, what he said,' Lars adds.

'Great, lost my appetite.' Dougie sulks. He reaches over, unbuckles Awamiri, opens the door, and pushes him out. Awamiri doesn't quite clear. The red van's back wheel bounces over Awamiri with a gut-churning crunch.

Lars begins to sob.

I lapse into silence and watch the road signs—and potential signs of Dougie's awakening appetite. We're heading to Dorion and not Thunder Bay. That'll take us hours out of our way.

'It's faster to get to Dryden, and our next gig, if we go through Thunder Bay,' I suggest.

'More places to eat too,' Lars adds before turning pale.

'As opposed to people,' I snark.

Dougie lets off the gas and coasts to the shoulder. We roll to a stop.

'Are we a band anymore, or merely a moving buffet?' he asks.

'Well, considering all our equipment is still in the camper van back in Marathon, I'd say the latter.' My fingers feel for something sharp or vaguely weapon-like in the seat beside me. Instead I grasp Lars's leg. Lars screams.

'Oh, for god's sake lighten up.' Dougie laughs. 'We're going to Ouimet Canyon. A tourist attraction that doesn't attract many tourists. We will be safe there. Everyone will be safe. We will find a cure for me or you'll die trying.'

The rest of the drive is uneventful. Lars and I move from the middle bench seat to the back bench seat and set up a makeshift barrier of suitcases and pillows.

Dougie talks to himself.

As we get closer to Ouimet Canyon, Dougie starts copping my Shakespeare angle full on.

It has been relentless: a lot of 'out, damned spots', 'tales told by idiots', and 'Great Birnam Wood to high Dunsinane Hills' interspersed with witty observations on life, love, and death—but mostly death.

Dougie has gone full soliloquy.

He is stepping on my toes, but at least he is not ripping them off my body.

Finally, Lars asks the question I've been meaning to ask.

'Why don't you eat feet?' Lars asks. 'I mean, at the Waffle Waffle House, you left them all over the place—still inside the shoes. What's up with that? You seem to have no problem eating everything else. I mean, I didn't see any penises left around, so obviously you eat those without any problem.'

'Ouch!' I say.

'Ouch, indeed,' Dougie adds. 'And perhaps … touché as well.'

I miss the mute drummer boy Dougie.

'Why don't you eat the feet?' Lars persists.

Dougie mulls over the question for a while before answering. 'One quarter of the bones in the human body can be found in the foot — twenty-six of them. Think about it. Too much effort for such little payoff.'

Dougie glances into the rear-view mirror and smiles. 'Not worth the pound of flesh — right, bro?'

Cain meet Abel. Abel meet Cain. I move up to the middle bench seat, ready to punch my brother in the mouth, or at least reassert my dominance in all things learned.

'Stop! Stop! Stop!' Lars shouts.

Lars bounces from the back seat to the middle seat to the passenger seat. 'It's that Candy chick. She's hitchhiking! You're gonna pass her. Pull over! Pull over!' Lars is frantic, hitting Dougie in the shoulder.

At first, I don't notice anyone at the side of the road. We are in the middle of nowhere: forests and trees, rocks and boulders, far between points of human habitation.

But now I see.

Candy is standing on the soft sanded shoulder. She is wearing a black leather motorcycle jacket and carrying a black motorcycle helmet under her arm. Her hair is as purple as ever.

I don't see a motorcycle.

Dougie slowly pulls over, fifty or so metres past Candy.

Lars gets right in Dougie's face. 'I swear if you so much as lick your lips, I will rip your balls off and stuff them down your throat.'

'Love is all-consuming,' Dougie observes cryptically. 'But don't worry. She is untouchable.'

Candy jogs up to the sliding passenger door and yanks it open.

'Hey boys, long time no see.' Candy hops in.

Lars giggles like a schoolboy.

The sun has not yet risen, but the sky is shimmering purple, with small streaks of light orange along the horizon. Moses is tired. He has been resting on this perch for many hours but unable to sleep — always some part of the brain awake to danger.

The life of an animal.

He is hungry as well.

The stomach that never sleeps.

The life of a human: always consuming, never satisfied.

A breakfast of flying insects and worms awaits. Moses considers changing back to a bear. He could do with a nice bit of fish, or a bird like himself. It is better to eat like a bear than a bird. Someone wise said that, at some point, sometime long ago.

A helicopter swoops up from the southeast and descends to the mouth of the gorge. The navigation lights blink red, green, and white as it disappears into the dark. Beyond the gorge, beyond the valley, Lake Superior's black surface fractures from the sky as daylight quickens. Moses ruffles his feathers and preens. He was expecting Isabel, or at least her latest incarnation, by car. She doesn't like flying. Moses flaps his wings and lifts off. He will greet Her nonetheless and try to remedy the situation as best he can.

The air is cool, the view, serene. Moses flies over a large rock column resembling the profile of a man. It is Omett, a giant turned to stone by Nanabijou, the Spirit of the Deep-Sea Water. Punishment for causing the death of Nanabijou's daughter and then having the audacity to cover it up.

A guilt that Moses understands.

Ben lands the helicopter at the southernmost part of the gorge where it opens to a rolling expanse of boreal forest and a fat serpentine river. The engine shuts off, but the blades continue to rotate as Ben and Lydia jump out.

'C'mon, Nate, let's go,' Lydia says.

'Where?' Nate looks out.

It is a valley full of shadow.

'It'll lighten up soon enough, but here you go.' Lydia hands him a flashlight.

Nate steps out and gently removes his helmet. The air is cold and stale. It smells of freezer burn. To his left, a stand of Jack pines cluster at the edge of a small pond. Here and there, a few roots dip into the water.

Those roots are blanched. White rot creeps up along the trunks and towards the branches.

Nate knows that Jack pines are survivors. The cones remain dormant in the soil for years until a fire routs the elder trees. The heat from the fire opens the cones and the forest rises again from the ashes — like a phoenix.

Ironic.

Fear death by water.

Nate remembers the poem from high school. *The Wasteland* by T.S. Eliot. The narrative was long, hard to follow, and ridiculously obscure.

But it had some kick-ass lines.

Rock-and-roll lines.

Nate recites two in his head: *April is the cruelest month* and *I will show you fear in a handful of dust.*

He knows differently now: September is fucking sadistic, and water is way scarier than dust.

Nate walks closer to the pond.

A carpet of iridescent blue-green lichen sweeps past the exposed roots of the pines and into the pond. Below the surface, the lichen luminesces.

Algae lives underwater. Fungus doesn't. Nate knows his lichen. And that is not lichen.

'Hey dreamboat, let's get a move on. Our perps will be here soon, and we have to set up our welcoming committee.' Lydia unloads two of the M4 carbines. She hands one to Nate. 'Not standard issue on our side of the fence, but I'm sure you'll get it. Keep it on semi. Might heat up and jam otherwise.'

Benny pulls out a flame-thrower and straps on the backpack.

Nate hefts the assault rifle. He has used a C8 in training at the firing range. The M4 seems similar but different, like Canadians and Americans in general.

Nate asks, 'Two questions. What perps? And why a flame-thrower? There hasn't been a lot of rain this summer and I'm sure Parks Canada has a sign up somewhere telling campers to avoid open fires. This place is probably a tinderbox. Parks Canada will fine us for sure.'

Benny points north towards where the gorge is strewn with crumbled rock and scatterings of alpine greenery. 'We're going that way. Into Ouimet Canyon proper. Not much will catch fire there. The forested area behind us is of no concern really.'

'Okay then, the M4 carbine seems lethal enough. Flame-thrower? Really?'

'Bullets stop the unholy host, but a frozen spirit needs a roast.' Benny punctuates his odd little rhyme by unleashing a scorching flame of liquid fire on the dead Jack pines. The pond bubbles. The Jack pines smoulder.

The underwater lichen recoils and dives deeper.

Nate asks, 'So, perps then. What perps are we looking for? Jay is dead, and that wendigo thing didn't leave the Hollow as far as I can tell.'

'Jay will live forever in my heart — and then some.' Lydia pops a full magazine into her gun and checks the scope. 'You weren't listening to the scanner in the whirlybird obviously. The three musician scumbags that murdered Moses's family are headed here. One or all of them are infected. They are also tied to a massacre at the Waffle Waffle House outside Espanola. Same MO: ritualistic cannibalism and footwear fetishism. The camper truck they later abandoned at a gas station outside Marathon also has forensic links to several disappearances in the Central Ontario region. We have three missing persons reports related to the gas station as well: a couple of blueberry vendors and one doctor from Toronto. It's a whole can of apocalyptic whoop-ass and we're aiming to shut it down quick.'

'Why would they come here?' Nate asks.

'Moses told my dad a long time ago that this Ouimet Canyon area is sacred but also deeply troubled. The spirit of the canyon is restless as a result of everything from Nanabijou's missing and murdered daughter to the invasion of Nanabijou's narrative by white people.'

'Oh, I've heard about the Omett rock formation legend. I thought the Omett character *accidentally* killed Nanabijou's daughter while he was trying to impress her with moving a bunch of mountains around.'

'That's what they'd like you to think. The fact that Omett hastily buried her in a shallow grave makes us think otherwise. Crime of passsion.'

'Okay, so the invasion of Nanabijou's narrative. What's that about?'

'Being of European stock, I feel some guilt over this,' Lydia begins. 'As you know, Nanabijou is the Spirit of the Deep-Sea Water and was a central character in many Ojibwe legends before European explorers arrived on the Great Lakes.

After the cultures intersected around the eighteenth century, the Ojibwe began telling the legend of the Sleeping Giant.'

'Oh yeah, I've heard that one, too. Explains that odd rock formation at the mouth of the bay. It looks like the profile of a giant dead man resting on his back with his arms folded. Funny how the only two stories I know about Nanabijou involve death and rocks.'

'Death rocks.' Benny Tak does an odd little fist bump.

Nate and Lydia look at each other. It is not the first time Nate has felt like punching his fellow officer. Lydia's expression reveals the same.

'Anyway, as I was saying.' Lydia leans against a large boulder. 'The short version is that Nanabijou showed a large silver deposit to a loyal Ojibwe tribe and made them promise to never tell the white man where it was hidden. Unfortunately, through trickery, the whites found out and Nanabijou abandoned his people. He lay down in the bay and turned to stone. In the versions I've always heard, the Ojibwe were never really at fault, but they got burned anyway. So, I guess that's kind of like life in general. Makes it more realistic.'

'Bummer.' Benny tries to make the word sound vaguely philosophical.

He fails but continues talking. 'This, my friends, is cultural appropriation par excellence: insinuating yourself into someone else's narrative and taking out their hero with your own tired tropes. No wonder they hate us.' Benny's mood brightens. 'Anyway, on with the business at hand. As Lyd says, the three musicians may all be infected in some way or other with this ... thing. We've been studying it for a while. The Centers for Disease Control believe it is confined to this geographical location in Northern Ontario. People disappear. Families disappear. Small towns disappear. We keep it on the down-low 'cause Toronto isn't affected directly. In the meantime, we are left with a lot of questions: Is it biological? Psychological? Spiritual? Is it something they ate? Is it something that eats them? We hope to preserve at least one of the musicians and bring him to a secure lab for further study. The CDC has a secret facility out in Manitoba, on a lake, near a bunch of kids' summer Bible camps. Popular with hunters and anglers too.'

Nate has seen this movie. It never ends well.

'Why are you studying it? Does it have an essential medicinal, cancer-curing application?'

'Maybe. Didn't think of that. When we submit our annual budget, we'll probably throw in something about using our studies to cure disease, but mostly we hope to weaponize the phenomenon. You know — infect one enemy soldier with an insatiable hunger to consume all his co-combatants, then sit back and relax. No need for direct engagement on our part until after it's all done. Then we march in and neutralize the lone survivor — which we haven't quite figured out how to do yet; but, you know … we're working on it.'

'Jay seems pretty dead. Whatever we did there seemed to work,' Nate says.

Benny looks at Lydia.

Lydia shakes her head. 'Not dead, just hurtin' real bad. I imagine all that silver will be keeping his infection busy for a while. Soon after we left, an evacuation team arrived to stabilize him.'

That made sense, sort of.

Nate had wondered why Lydia seemed so casual after killing her partner of seven years. He had put it down to relationship fatigue — the seven-year itch, or something like that. Now he knows that Jay is alive and kicking whomever was sent to rescue him.

Nate panics: one person infected with the wendigo spirit was serious shit. Jay Compton threw Nate and Lydia around the cave without breaking a sweat. It would take more than the three of them to capture three wendigos.

Nate relaxes: the three wendigos were musicians. They would be out of shape, stoned, and lazy as a bag of hammers.

Nate panics: musicians could be malnourished and slaves to their appetites at the same time.

Nate looks behind him, past the helicopter, past the dark green river, past the dark green forest. The sun is rising, casting a pall of mist-infused light across the river. He could follow the river to freedom. He would have to escape these clowns first.

Nate turns back to Lydia and Benny. 'Great, so are we setting up a perimeter of some sort, improvising booby traps, shooting anything that moves? Just tell me. I'll secure the treeline behind us. I'll camo myself real good. I bet you won't even see me.'

Nate starts walking.

'Not ... exactly what I ... have in mind,' Benny starts slowly.

Benny points towards a large boulder amidst a heap of rubble deep in the gorge. Scraggly conifers line the crushed-rock slopes, gripping the edges of the sheer rock walls, seemingly determined to avoid the canyon floor.

'Sit down over there and look casual,' Benny says. 'Maybe pretend to study something on the ground — a weed or something. We need the suspect cannibals to think you are alone and unaware. And do not touch anything under any circumstances. As you reminded me earlier, it's a very fragile ecosystem. Parks Canada will be on our asses.'

Nate looks at the smouldering stand of Jack pines behind him and at the desolate boulder alley of Ouimet Canyon in front of him.

'That's it? I sit there and wait? Why would they even bother if I'm wearing a police uniform and holding a gun?'

'We have to make you irresistible.'

'The uniform isn't enough?'

'No.'

Nate does not feel irresistible. He sits on a rock thirty-six and a half metres from the mouth of the gorge. His shirt is off. His pants are on. *Thinker* pose — the sanitized version.

It is cold. Goosepimples on goosepimples.

Nate's hairy chest is matted with smears of raspberry jam from a stale donut found in the back of the helicopter.

Although Nate does not feel irresistible, an increasing cloud of flies have decided otherwise.

Nate watches a large black bird drop from the edge of the cliff. It swoops down and overshoots a boulder closeby, landing in some scrub brush. The bird hops closer and casually pokes between the leaves of a tiny shrub at Nate's feet.

'Man! It's so cold here even the bugs don't want to hang out,' the black bird caws. 'Except for those flies, but I don't do flies. Too greasy.'

'What?' Nate looks around for the source of the voice, but only sees the bird. It is a crow. A big crow, almost as wide as it is tall.

The bird continues to caw. 'Tell your friends that I will lead the three musicians here, but also tell them to chill with the big guns and flame-throwers. I got everything under control. Do a little talk. Do a little smoke. Get down tonight. Ha! First Nations style.'

'Moses?'

'Yep. The one and only. I am here to lead everyone to the promised land. Ha!' The bird tilts his head sideways and fixes Nate with one eye. 'I'm really hungry though. Hey, is that raspberry jam?'

Dougie leads the way to the lip of the canyon.

The view is spectacular. A giant knife gash through volcanic rock. Clusters of shrubs and trees on occasional rocky outcroppings on the sheer sides.

'There's a secret path. Follow me.' Dougie steps off the edge.

Lars and I scream. Candy looks bored.

Lars and I run up to the edge of the canyon and look down. Dougie is standing on a small ledge below us. The top of his head is a foot below my foot. I have an impulse to kick that head.

'This is the deal,' Dougie says without looking up. 'As I drop from ledge to ledge, you guys follow, one at a time.'

Dougie begins a rapid descent. We scramble after.

Halfway down, Lars shouts out, 'Hey guys, there's a bunch of people down there already.'

I look to where he is pointing.

Three small figures dodge and weave between boulders followed by a tiny, aggressive, feathered speck. Occasionally, a flame-thrower goes off, followed by gibberish and screams.

'Don't worry! It's all good!' Dougie calls out. 'Friendlies.'

By the time we reach the canyon floor the three figures are now four. The bird has disappeared. Dougie scrambles over to the fourth person. It is Moses. Moses looks pissed off, but smiles when he recognizes Dougie.

Dougie and Moses hug, for a very long time.

Everyone starts to feel a little uncomfortable.

Lars and I stare at our feet. Candy studies a rock.

'And now it is time to talk.' Moses breaks a foot-long veggie submarine sandwich into eight equal pieces and distributes it among the group. 'I would like to thank Benny for allowing us all to partake of his lunch, which he had the foresight to pack. Normally, I would break out the tobacco and pipe to share but, you know, the crow has no pockets, as they say. And it appears that everyone here is a non-smoker. So, I will say this: What we share is important to some. The fact that we share is important to all.'

Turning to Candy: 'And I'd like to thank my granddaughter Candice, who finally made it here ... in her own sweet time.'

Candy makes a sour face. 'And I'd like to thank Nimishoomis, who is so very understanding ... in his own sweet way.'

Moses pauses a moment to scratch behind his ear. A black feather falls, fluttering to the ground. 'I would also like to thank Staff Sergeant Lydia Finch for lending me a spare camo jumpsuit as otherwise I would be sitting here naked and very cold, because, as you can imagine, the crow does not carry spare clothes either.'

Dougie inhales his chunk of sandwich while everyone else is nodding politely at Moses.

Dougie licks sub sauce off his fingers with loud slurping sounds. Moses shoots him a look, then walks over to a tuft of green plants and mosses, pulling a few out by the roots, scraping others off a rock. He offers them to Dougie.

'Caribou moss to neutralize those nasty prions and some good old *Mayflower* dandelion to quell your hunger.'

Moses is silent for a moment. 'Dandelion is one hell of an adaptable weed. It's best we don't tell the Parks people about this one. They'll freak. Anyhow, I digress. *Mayflower* or not, we're all here now and maybe some useful benefit shall be achieved.' Moses touches Dougie's shoulder very gently.

Dougie tears up.

Moses is silent for a moment. 'Although, now that I think about it, how did that dandelion get all the way out here, deep in this canyon? This is a protected zone. That's depressing. We are truly doomed as a people.'

'It's all good, Mosey.' Dougie née Isabel conjures a bit of Jane Austen by way of some Upanishad wisdom. 'It isn't what we say or what we think that defines us. It's what we do. We can only act. We cannot be attached to the outcome of those actions.'

'The actions being to eat one post-colonial interloper at a time?' I ask.

'Bite me,' Real Dougie responds before returning to Isabel/Dougie. 'Yes, Angus. There is, I believe, in every disposition, a tendency to some particular evil, a natural defect, which not even the best education can overcome. Our only hope is to work together.'

'Eating post-colonial … whatsits as a team?' Lars attempts wit.

'No.' Dougie's eyes light up with a strange glow, not the usual post-party chemical shine that I have witnessed on numerous occasions. It is a light from within. Dougie's face softens into something more feminine. The Adam's apple sinks. The scruffy facial hair remains but the chin and jawline round out slightly. The overall face tightens into a smaller space — becomes more delicate. Dougie's voice demurs. 'Love is the answer.'

I look around our little circle. Moses is tearing up. Lydia is tearing up. Lars and Candy are making googly eyes at each other. Nate glares at Benny. Benny looks bored.

'If love is the answer, I have a question. Why are my brother Dougie and your wife, Isabel, now in one package, and which one of them is responsible for eating all those other people?' I ask.

Moses chews thoughtfully on his sandwich. 'I will answer with a meandering tale that may or may not satisfy. It was late afternoon, August, twenty years ago. Victoria had just moved in with us — for reasons I cannot go into right now. Anyway, Isabel and I were house-sitting a friend's place in Thunder Bay. The three of us decided on a little day trip out here to forage for some wild edibles and mushrooms. It was sunny and hot except for this little slice of sub-arctic paradise. Vicki and I were rooting around the rocks in the gorge, naming all the plants we could find and being very careful not to damage anything. Isabel chose to stay in the green area near the river and collect the food. After a few hours, Vicki and I returned to the river, but Isabel wasn't there. We stumbled up and down the riverbank, looked in the woods. Nothing. Eventually, we found Isabel. She was facedown in a pond in a small clearing. The pond was rimmed with lichen and choked with algae.'

Moses sighs. 'It is the small details that break your heart. Isabel's hair was longer back then, and prematurely grey. It fanned out like a halo around her head. Both hands were within the water, pressed deep into the algae as if she had been trying to wrestle something out. I did what I could. No breath. No pulse. She was cold. Brackish fluid poured out of her mouth as soon as I put her on her side. With the chest compressions her eyes fluttered open, but whenever I tried mouth-to-mouth, the air got sucked out of my lungs as soon as our lips touched. So I kept on with the chest compressions. It took a while. She started breathing on her own, but her eyes were different. No pupils. Just green irises. Only when Vicki knelt and clutched Isabel's hand did I see Isabel's pupils. They exploded like the Big Bang, pushing out the white space, leaving a sparkle of green at the edges. That lasted a few minutes. I was scared.'

Benny starts clapping slowly. 'Bravo, a wonderful story. How am I supposed to weaponize that? C'mon, man. I need a few more details. What is wendigo? Is it extractable? Can I make it into a serum, or better still, a sports drink?'

'Does every story have to answer the question so directly?' Moses huffed. 'Okay. Fine. In a nutshell. The spirit of consumption is in all of us. We can choose to feed it or not. There, are you satisfied? The wendigo ate my homework. It ate most of my family. It ate Vicki. It cast off Isabel like a moulting snake and consumed her. It ate part of Dougie before integrating into his soul like a parasite. No offence.'

'None taken,' Dougie answers.

Moses continues, 'The flesh shall die but the spirit abides. Dougie and Isabel are now one. What the Creator has put together, let no man put asunder. Amen.'

'What do we do then?' Lydia asks.

'We give thanks for our friends who journey along life's path with us. The joy of friends and family is the only treasure our spirit can carry. And even then, we may forget that too. So live your best life—the life that the Creator sent you down to live. That is all we can hope to do. There. You see. I am done like dinner.'

Moses stares at the ground.

The rest of us look at each other and nod. The wisdom of the spoken word has washed through us—cleansing, lifting our thoughts to a higher plane of spiritual awareness.

Except Lars.

Lars turns to Dougie. 'So, does that make you more like my sister? Because that would be cool. I've always wanted a sister. We can bake together. I do a killer Pillsbury turnover. The secret is to buy a good-quality jam and use that for the filling. It's awesome. You'll like it.'

EPILOGUE

Another bar. Another town. Another year. We keep to the far north now. Small, isolated mining towns. Occasionally we'll pass through obscure roadhouses outside of cottage country. Lots of people on their way to somewhere else and never getting there.

We have a new band name.

Ashthorn is in ashes. Thorn is ascendant.

Our first run of posters used the Old Norse variant of thorn, which resembles a lower-case *p* with the spine extending above the bump. Lars's idea.

The printer was unfamiliar with Old Norse.

The first couple of gigs were a little uncomfortable.

A lot of old men in raincoats.

Our trio is now a five / six piece. A challenging time value in and of itself. We do covers. Lars and Moses share guitar and singing duties. I play bass and write most of the lyrics for our original stuff — none of which has been performed. The Isabel / Dougie entity plays drums, and occasionally eats an audience member in the middle of a set. The crowd goes wild.

They think it's some crazy-good CGI.

Candy is our road manager and lead tambourine player. She cannot sing, but we let her anyway. No one gets hurt that way.

It has been a busy year for Lars and Candy. They are in relationship and have four kits already. Lars was a little freaked out at first by their small furry heads and thin weasel bodies, but he has adjusted. Parenthood is a sobering process.

Benny keeps in touch. He is our biggest surviving fan. Although he works out of a secret CDC facility south of Winnipeg, he visits every second week to take our blood samples.

Lydia and Jay returned to Hatcheta Falls. They took early retirement from the police force and run a bed and breakfast now.

I would not stay there.

Nate became super-infected and is at the same CDC facility as Benny. Benny assures us that the place is quite nice. It is on a lake popular with hunters, anglers and children attending overnight Bible camps. It sounds bucolic.

The lyrics.

I wrestle with them every night like Jacob with the angel. Words are bones and sinew wrapped in a little flesh. One day I might prevail, beat the demon into submission, and receive my blessings.

But.

Today is not that day.

CODA

Lars crushes through a series of drop D power chords interpolated with erratic Phrygian dominant scale screeches.

He sings:

> *'It all depends*
> *upon*
> *a surf-green*
> *telecaster*
> *rubbed raw with*
> *sweat*
>
> *beside the black*
> *amplifier.'*

Lars puts down the guitar. 'I'm thinking that would make a good chorus for a song about writing songs. You know, that meta thing you're always on about — things that talk about themselves while pretending to talk about other things.'

Candy nods. She rests her hands on Lars's shoulders. Her face is radiant.

I wonder if she is pregnant again.

'I dunno, it sounds vaguely familiar,' I say. 'Who'd ya rip it off from?'

Candy's eyes flicker with flashes of blaze red.

'But,' I continue, 'music is one big rip-a-palooza, so you might as well giv'r.'

Candy smiles: pearl-white perfection.

Rock-n-roll is as much the answer as the question.

S T .   E L I O T

On the sidewalk in front of the St. Eliot Motel, the snow had been scraped back to reveal a patchwork of grey concrete and black ice. Streetlights angled down and cast their glow in with the evening murk, allowing commuters to shuffle home along pathways sown with salt and strewn with debris. Hats, scarves, and coats were uniformly pulled tight against the cold.

A scattering of the homeless also drifted past. Bent towards the soup kitchens and shelters south of the Allan Gardens, their eyes scavenged the ground for cigarette butts. Great oversized coats flapped in the wind like wings.

Saul Keown, the night manager at the St. Eliot, watched them all as he stood on the porch and prodded a stuttering neon 'No Vacancy' sign that hung below the eavestrough. With each hollow *thok* of broomstick handle on plywood frame, the 'No' jittered into longer periods of darkness. The final blow broke the tubing. Glass scattered across the stairs.

'Jesus!' Saul swore. Breaking the 'No' wasn't part of the plan, but it revealed a truth: there was always room at the inn—on an hourly basis.

'Hey Saulie!' Charlotte waved from where she stood on the sidewalk. Platinum strands of hair whipped across her face as she spoke. 'Don't forget. I got room 16 for the next couple of hours. I want fresh sheets.'

'Getting right on that!' Saul swept the broken glass into the snow.

Between the street and the sidewalk, the snow was piled high into thick ridges with no cutaway access to the street. Charlotte was not impressed. Wearing a white leather miniskirt hiked up to her ass and white patent-leather go-go boots that stopped inches below that ass, she hovered beside the snowbank like an apparition. A hungry apparition.

'Anything for my number one customer!' Saul shouted.

Charlotte ignored him and glided towards a salt-grimed car as it slowed down. She slyly opened her white faux-fur bomber to show the goods. The car stopped. Charlotte kicked at the top of the snow ridge and awkwardly straddled it to get closer.

Saul stopped his sweeping. He might have to intervene. Sometimes she got stuck.

Cigarette smoke wafted out in grey swirls as the passenger window rolled down. The driver leaned over. He was balding. Probably married and 'misunderstood'. Quick blow-jobs or quick sex — in the comfort of the driver's seat.

Those were the good dates.

The bad dates might try to kill you.

Saul heard the stories. The girls liked to dish.

Charlotte stuck her head in the open window. She was aggressive today. Her ass waved in the air as she pushed her tits into the car.

Saul resumed sweeping. He was glad he was past the whole sex thing. Growing up repressed and gay in a Jehovah's Witness family had filled him with self-loathing. There wasn't much room in his heart for lust.

There was plenty of room for the Holy Spirit — straight out of the bottle.

As he stumped back to the porch of the hotel, Saul's breath plumed upward, enshrouding his face and fogging his glasses. He stopped before the oak door with its peeling green paint and scuffed his feet on the festive doormat, paying special attention to the threadbare smile of jolly old St. Nick.

The St. Eliot had always been a 'down-at-the-heels' kind of place. Built in 1910 as a small hotel, it had mostly functioned as a rooming house: daily, weekly, and monthly rates available for those down on their luck. When a city referendum approved the construction of the Bloor Viaduct in 1913, the hotel's owner — Bartholomew Enderby — slapped fresh paint on the porch and upgraded the wooden hotel sign to a neon one.

The new sign was a big deal. Showcased as a cutting-edge invention at the Paris Motor Show three years earlier, neon technology was extremely rare in North America and almost non-existent in Canada. Bartholomew thought it a better investment than upgrading the plumbing. It would drive business to his hotel.

It did, but not in the way he had hoped.

Anyone with money still stayed at the King Eddy.

But they did drive by at some point to marvel at the glowing red tubes.

Within a year of the bridge's completion, the sign sputtered into longer periods of darkness until 'Vacancy' was the only part of it that worked with any consistency. The hotel became a rooming house again, frequented by the Irish spilling over from nearby Cabbagetown.

The Irish.

Saul was Irish. He was also Jewish, Metis, Spanish, Scottish, and most embarrassingly — English. A lot of English. Apparently, the Irish would sleep with anyone. Nonetheless, Irish was the default ethnic background for anyone remotely Irish. Saul's great-grandfather grew up on a farm in County Fermanagh, Northern Ireland; therefore, Saul was Irish.

It did not matter that every subsequent generation of the family was born in Canada; Saul was Irish.

Saul walked into the lobby of the St. Eliot trailing a constellation of tiny snowflakes.

'Cold enough for ya?' Peter, the assistant night manager, looked up from his laptop. Thick fingers thumped across the keypad, then stopped. 'Did you salt the front?'

'Forgot.'

'I'll do it then.' Peter yawned. With the awkward confidence of a circus bear, he walked over to the coat rack and pulled down his jacket. 'I could use the fresh air.'

'Suit yourself.' Saul didn't understand Peter. Nothing seemed to bother him. Peter went with the flow. Saul constantly struggled against it.

Nonetheless, they both found themselves downstream in life.

'What are you working on?' Saul nodded at the laptop.

'School project. A menu based on the regional foods available in my hometown. Part of the Farm-to-Table class I'm taking.'

'You're from Churchill, Manitoba. You got polar bears and beluga whales — not much farm.'

'We got muskeg. I will call it the "Bog-to-Bog" movement and I'll throw in some of my mom's mad Spanish culinary skills. It will dazzle.'

'Seriously?'

'Seriously. It'll be a hoot, bro. The instructors think I'm Indigenous just because I got long black hair and I'm from Churchill. They'll be paralyzed with fear—especially when I roll out my appetizer: baby beluga ceviche in the deep blue seaweed. Fuck. I'll sing that Raffi song too. It'll be epic.'

'Wow, I thought I was cynical.'

'I learn from the best and, as you know, with only a diploma in hospitality services, I'll end up working in some crappy kitchen in Toronto for low pay, with a Gordon Ramsay wannabe all up in my ass.'

'I thought you were Mr Go with the Flow?'

'I am.'

'Oh.'

Saul studied Peter momentarily. Peter's 'flow' had gotten a bit choppy of late.

'Well, if you don't mind, I have a date with some Del Monte peaches.' Saul stamped the remaining snow off his boots, sat down and rummaged through his lunch bag. 'Peaches remind me of summer, of rolling up my trousers and gamboling on a beach. The opposite of now. Do you know what else peaches remind me of?'

Before Saul could answer his own question, Peter slipped out into the cold with a pail of rock salt. Saul could hear the *tromp* of Peter's Kodiaks on the porch and the occasional *ping* of salt pellets on metal railings. Peter's form ghosted across the ice-crusted glass of the bay window before merging into the darkness beyond.

On a lark, and to pump up his own intellect, Saul grabbed an expired Air Miles card from the till and scraped a message into the frosted window. Bits of ice sloughed off as Saul diligently gouged out translucent backward letters. It was hard. It was magic. It was growing up with too many Bible stories.

Mene, mene, tekel, upharsin.

Saul tapped the window and peered outside to see if Peter had noticed. Peter noticed and shrugged.

'Numbered, numbered, weighed, divided!' Saul yelled, his words echoing back into the room, his breath frosting up some of the letters.

Peter cupped his hand to his ear and grimaced.

'The fall of Babylon!'

Peter turned his back and continued salting.

'Fucking Anglican,' Saul muttered. Having writ, his fingers moved on to scratching himself.

'Hey honey, when you're done playing with yourself, I need a room.' Luci, a regular, leaned across the desk and lifted key number 18 from its hook.

Behind her, a man in his fifties pretended to study the mottled greens and browns in the carpet. He wore charcoal-grey slacks and a dark green puffy jacket zipped up to the neck. A royal-blue toque hung out of his left pocket. Brown leather gloves dangled limply in his right hand.

'Howdy!' Saul boomed. 'And what brings you to our fine establishment?'

The man looked up and smiled nervously.

Luci's 'date' could have been the middle-class version of Saul — if Saul had managed to get at least one foot out of the gutter. It was such a low measure of success that Saul immediately became depressed. Like Saul, the man had sky-blue eyes, thinning, combed-over blond hair, and beaver-worthy incisors. Unlike Saul, the man looked well rested and vaguely content.

Saul walked over as the man slid three twenties across the desk.

Saul pushed his tongue against the loose partial plate in his mouth. It made a clicking sound.

'You know,' Saul drawled as he pushed the guest register forward, 'I'm supposed to ask for ID. It's the law. We've gotta protect ourselves from potential terrorists.'

The man scribbled something barely legible on the sheet and slid an extra twenty across the desk. Saul noticed a circular white shadow on the ring finger of his left hand.

'So, Mr ...' Saul looked at the register. 'Mr J. Smith! Well ... John ... if I can be so presumptive as to go by your anticipated first name.'

'Don't be such an asshole,' Luci scolded, and pulled her date towards the fire door by the main-floor hallway.

'For those about to rock!' Saul made a quick fist salute before Luci and her date disappeared.

Saul sat down behind the desk and swivelled his chair towards the window. Outside, Sherbourne Street slithered by on slush and ice. Saul closed his eyes. He heard the murmur of voices, the *thrum* of motors. He felt the sensation of creeping cold. He remembered the walkway he had forgotten to salt and his many other sins of omission. He imagined the lowly crystals of salt clumping together into a tall pillar, full of litigious anger.

'Salty?' the pillar asked.

'Salty,' the pillar cajoled.

'Salty,' the pillar accused.

Silence.

'Saulie Benjamin Keown!' the pillar screeched.

Saulie Benjamin Keown pitched forward in his chair, spitting out his partial dentures in the process.

They bounced across the mottled green-and-brown carpet and slid under the wrought-iron radiator near the window.

Charlotte craned over the front desk and twitched. 'I got no clean sheets. Where are the fuckin' sheets?'

Saul's temple throbbed. His heart palpitated. He hoisted himself from the chair and wobbled over to the radiator. He got down on his knees and reluctantly poked his hand under the radiator. He was Saul on the road to Damascus casting about for a scapegoat, but happy enough if he could find his partial plate without touching anything unclean.

'Peter's got the master key. *He* was supposed to drop the sheets off,' Saul said. Part truth. Part lie.

Saul's hand scuttled over something fuzzy and gelatinous.

Charlotte tapped her fingers on the guest register. 'Don't know. Don't care. Just gimme another room that's ready already.'

Saul pulled himself up and walked over to the desk, gingerly holding his dentures between thumb and index finger. He dropped them into a glass of flat cola.

'How about room 13? I know that one is always empty and clean.' Saul swished the dentures around in the cola for a bit before putting them back in his mouth. He sucked absently on the residue of cola sugar.

'Thank God for superstitious people,' Saul added.

'Whatever.' Charlotte flipped a cigarette into her mouth.

Saul pointed to a 'No Smoking' sign.

'Go ahead, call the police.'

'No need to get hostile. We're all professionals here.'

'Fuck you.'

'You know what I mean.'

'Oh, I do all right. You think I like this job. You'd screw me over the first chance — like anyone else. Money talks. Bullshit walks.'

'I would not screw you over, period, full stop, end of story.'

Charlotte and Saul looked at each other warily. They each had a sense that they were using the same words but with different meanings.

'That's a nice top you're wearing,' Saul said, nodding his head at Charlotte's black lace bustier.

'You like it? I got it at Winners. It's sexy without being too slutty. Okay. It's totally slutty, but it's classy slutty.' Charlotte swivelled her tits back and forth. 'I only got medium-sized boobs and it seems every guy is a tit-man, so this gets their attention pretty quick.'

'Yeah, it's an attention-getter.' Saul was glad to see they were on the same page again.

Charlotte scratched between her breasts. A large blue vein glowed dimly beneath pale skin like slow-leaking neon. Charlotte was a junkie. She shot up along her arms and legs. The tits were mostly off limits. Bad for business otherwise.

'You ever think about … moving on to something different?' Saul asked.

'All the freakin' time, but you know … life,' Charlotte answered.

Saul fumbled the key for room 13 off the board. He turned it over in his hand before giving it to Charlotte. The number 13 looked like a stylized capital B. The one and the three were too close together.

'Hello.' Charlotte snapped her fingers.

'You know,' Saul started slowly. He felt woozy. Everything in the room looked different. The lights burned brighter. The carpet bristled with microbial life. The pockmarked, paint-flaked walls looked beautiful, authentic.

Saul pinched himself. 'As I was saying, you know Peter wants to open a fishing lodge up in Churchill. He's got pretty supreme culinary skills. It could be a fresh start. Lots of fresh fish. People pay big money for those big-fish dreams.'

'My dream is to wake up tomorrow.'

'Yeah, actually that's kind of mine too.'

Saul and Charlotte stared at each other.

'Hey, can you …' Charlotte stopped. 'Can you come around later? I'm not totally sure about my date.'

'The one I seen you with outside in the car? The ethnic? He was salt of the earth if anything. I can tell.'

'Oh, that guy. He was salty for sure. Super-fast too. Barely got his dick out of his pants.' Charlotte shook her head. 'No, this is someone else.'

'Oh.' Saul realized they were reading from a different script again.

Charlotte continued, 'Probably nothing to worry about. I mean the guy's been here before. He was Tatianna's regular for a long time. I've had him a few times too … you know — he gets into these weird headspaces.'

'Sure.' Saul nodded. Tatianna had a lot of crazies for regulars.

'Thirty minutes tops and then come in and change the light bulb or something.' Charlotte walked towards the hallway and disappeared.

Saul waited a few beats, then reached under the counter for his smokes. He pulled out a hand-rolled cigarette and a self-striking match. On the third strike, the match sparked. The heat flared. Sulphur. Smoke. Bliss.

Saul exhaled and watched the smoke drift up towards the ceiling.

'Bro, you trying to get us busted?' Peter lumbered in through the front door, carrying two large coffees and a carton of Timbits. The shot of cold bent the smoke away from the alarm. 'They're like totally enforcing the no-smoking bylaw these days. It's a big fine.'

Saul inhaled deeply while stubbing out the cigarette.

'Busted.'

'You see the guy Charlotte came in with?' Peter asked.

'Apparently not. Why?'

'Tatianna's old date. Smarmy-looking guy. Always wanted to punch him in the face.'

'I want to punch a lot of people in the face. Can we be more specific?'

'Mr Purple Bangs. The ugly-haircut guy.'

'Oh yeah. I remember the haircut—a porcupine's ass slapped upside a cockatoo's quiff. Crappy dye job too. Who does purple anymore except angry grandmas? Pffft.'

'Wow, I think you need some sensitivity training.'

'Sorry, having a bad day. I take that back.'

Peter stared at the propped-open fire door leading to the first-floor rooms.

'You know that's against code too, right?'

'Call me Mr Transgressive.' Saul stared longingly at his stubbed-out cigarette. 'Char asked me to check up on her in thirty minutes. Maybe you could do it. You got the master key. I should stay at the desk as I am the night manager.'

'Sure.' Peter started toward the stairs and then stopped. 'Although, as the night manager, you should have the master key.'

'As night manager I'm delegating.'

'Are you sure about that?'

'Yep. Pretty sure I'm delegating. Besides, I have a lovely fruit cup calling out to me. Peaches in light syrup. Yum. You know that the canning process actually improves some of the nutritional impact of peaches?'

'Yeah, but it would never fly in a restaurant. Unless you did your own canning, then it would be considered artisanal and you'd pay a lot more for it.'

'The cult of authenticity. Wasn't there a rock song by that name?'

'No. You're thinking "Cult of Personality" by Living Color.'

'Someone needs to write that song then.' Saul stared at the window. His hastily scrawled message was quickly greying up with condensed moisture. Soon the window would return to an opaque sheet of milk-coloured ice.

A blank canvas.

'You know, Tabula Rasa would be a good name for a band,' Saul offered. 'Grindcore, maybe.'

'Everyone wants to be in a cool band,' Peter agreed. 'But with a name like that, you would probably find yourself in the world music category, with a heavy bhangra vibe.'

'I could be the lyricist. I'm good with words.'

'Really, what *was* that gibberish you were fingerpainting on the window earlier? "Mene, mene"? Is that a taunt? Like you were trying to say "mean" but spelling it wrong?'

'Read the Bible much?'

'No. My parents were Anglican.'

'"Mene, mene, tekel, upharsin" is from the Book of Daniel.'

'The den of lions guy.'

'Yeah, that guy. Anyway, the words translate as "numbered, numbered, weighed, divided".'

'Oh, that's what you were yelling through the window. I thought you were having a stroke.'

'And you didn't come in to save me?'

'I thought a double-double and some Timbits would be better appreciated.'

'True that,' Saul agreed. He rolled his chair over to the far end of the front desk, pulled a large metal toolbox from the floor, and hefted it onto his lap. It was heavy and mostly empty. Snapping open the lid, Saul took out the entire contents: one pair of needle-nose pliers, one hammer, one multi-bit screwdriver.

'Here, take these with you. You can knock on the door and pretend you need to fix something or other. Or use them as weapons. Go all MacGyver on his ass. I don't care.'

Peter stood still for a few seconds. The pliers, hammer, and screwdriver easily fitting in the palm of one hand. Peter stared at Saul.

'This is all cheap dollar-store stuff. It'd probably break as soon as it breaks the skin. Just sayin'.'

'Okay, okay,' Saul responded. 'I'll run up if there's a problem. I swear. Just walkie me.'

* * *

Charlotte smoothed the bedsheets, but did not bother to tuck them in. Saul was right about room 13. No one stayed there. The folded sheets were so old, the creases looked permanent. Also, Charlotte was surprised to find a private bathroom with a large claw-foot bathtub attached to the room. All the other rooms shared a common bathroom on each floor.

Her date was in the bathroom taking advantage of the luxury.

'You almost ready, hon? We only got the room for an hour.' Charlotte wanted her date out in half that time. She needed to crank it up with a little salty fuck talk.

'I'm so hot. I wanna feel your big hard ...' Charlotte husked, barely getting out the big hard consonant of the next word before her date interrupted.

'Hold on to that thought, babe.' The man's voice echoed off the tiled walls. 'I fucking love this tub. It's a fucking phenom.'

Charlotte imagined her date, shoulder-deep in the tepid water—furiously masturbating. The St. Eliot's water system was old and barely functional, but the vintage cast-iron tub was totally pimping: large silver feet cast as eagle claws dominated the checkered tiles like grotesque chess pieces; the faucet—an elaborate goose neck of pitted chrome—looked menacing and beautiful at the same time.

Charlotte was hoping to take a bath on her own at some point as soon as she could hustle out this date, but now he was in there, sucking up all the oxygen.

Tatianna was right. Some clients were real vampires.

This guy was the worst.

His haircut was annoying. His fashion sense was annoying. Charlotte wanted to run in and punch him in the face—just once—really hard.

'*Branches on water / Black veins frozen in white skin / Touching earth to sky,*' The man mumbled as sloshing-water sounds slipped through the space between door and floor.

Charlotte wasn't sure if the guy was trying to make small talk, or if this was part of the fantasy. He did fancy himself a poet. Charlotte drew heavily on her cigarette. She did not do small talk. She did not do the girlfriend experience. She definitely did not do poetry.

Charlotte's words flowed through mouthfuls of smoke. 'So, sweetie, let me get this straight. When I hear all the water drain out, I come in, pretend you're dead, and fuck your brains out?'

The man mumbled something again. It sounded like 'glub' or 'gahlub', something with a lot of gurgling 'ub' sounds.

'Okay.' Charlotte sat on the bed and rubbed her feet. 'Do you want me to wear the high heels? It might be a little tricky in that bathtub. I might stab you or something.'

No answer.

Charlotte fidgeted out of her clothes and waited. She put her high heels on.

Footsteps trudged outside in the carpeted hallway, getting closer to Charlotte's door. They were heavy footsteps. Peter's footsteps. She recognized his walk. He was a big boy.

Something sharp scraped against the wooden door: metal clinked, slipped, and clattered. Charlotte grabbed her faux-fur coat, pulled it over her shoulders, and quietly walked over to the peephole. The hallway fish-eyed in three hundred and sixty degrees of emptiness. The rattling continued outside the door, beyond her view, down by her feet.

'Everything okay?' Peter's face bobbed up into view of the peephole. His eyes and ears disappeared behind a distended mouth, stretching to the edges of the frame.

'Jesus!' Charlotte screeched.

'Sorry, he's busy on another call.'

Saul sat in his chair and watched the small TV tucked under the front desk. The Leafs were losing again. The walkie-talkie was silent. Footsteps crunched over the snow outside, coming closer to the front door, striding with purpose. Saul did not like the sound of purposeful footsteps. It never brought anything good.

The footsteps tromped up the front steps and onto the porch. With a *bang*, the door slammed open. Snow and wind pushed two thuggish-looking men into the room.

Heavy wool coats flecked with white.

Short hair and trim moustaches flecked with ice.

They were regulars at the hotel, but not ones Saul liked.

'Detective Smith.' The older one flashed his badge and nodded over to his partner.

'Detective Jones.' Detective Jones nodded at Saul.

'Yes, officers. What can I do for you today?' Saul tried to sound cheery. He knew them. They knew him. And still they danced.

'So, how's business?' Detective Smith asked.

'Same as always. People rent rooms. I hand out keys for those rooms.'

'We're looking for two people. One is a missing person and the other is a person of interest.' Detective Smith held out two photos. Both were mug shots. One was Tatianna staring straight at the camera, chin down, eyes forward. She had long black hair and tired eyes. The red line behind her head indicated she was a little over five feet tall. The other photo was of Charlotte's current date. At five foot nine, he was a white Everyman: bland expression, average nose, oval face, some stubble, muddy blue eyes. Impossible to pick out from a police lineup except for the ridiculous purple hair.

Saul pointed at the picture of the woman. 'Tatianna? I kinda know her. Don't know her last name though. She's been here off and on the past year. Is she okay?'

Saul suspected the answer already but waited.

'She was reported missing a couple of weeks ago. We're trying to get on top of it, but, you know … her line of work makes it a challenge.'

Saul frowned. He liked Tatianna. She was nice. And she never gave him any grief.

'When was the last time you saw her?' Detective Smith asked.

'About a month-ish ago. Around American Thanksgiving. I remember there were a lot of Americans up in town for the holidays. Low Canadian dollar, I guess. Better exchange rate.'

'Yeah, more bang for your buck. I get it,' Detective Jones said.

Detective Smith sighed and gave a quick sideward glance to his partner. 'You might want to cap the trash talk. I don't want to do another session of sensitivity training.'

'Copy that.' Detective Jones nodded.

'So, this guy then?' Detective Smith pocketed the photo of Tatianna and held up the mug shot of Charlotte's date. 'Any thoughts? Quite the piece of shit. He's fleeced a lot of old ladies.'

'Him and Tatianna came here quite a bit before…. Did you say fleeced?'

'Yeah, the guy's got a bit of a skin fetish. Cuts 'em right down the middle, like a giant peel-and-eat shrimp.'

'Eww. I thought you meant the other kind of fleeced.'

'That too. Anything valuable and easily portable — gone. Money — gone.

Nothing's shown up at the local pawnshops. We figure he must have it stashed somewhere.'

Saul couldn't get the image of peel-and-eat shrimp out of his head.

Saul started, 'He sounds pretty dangerous. Any reward—like from Crime Stoppers or something—for his capture or information leading to his capture?'

'Not yet. We're working on it.'

Saul pursed his lips then asked, 'Does this guy have a name?'

Detective Smith nodded. 'He goes by a lot of aliases, most of them strangely sharing the same root: Chris-with-an-*h*, Cris-without-an-*h*, Christos, Christian, Christiano, and Christopoulos. Sometimes he substitutes the capital letter X for the C. He's not exactly a diabolical genius. He's just diabolical.'

Detective Smith turned and watched Peter walk through the propped-open fire door by the hallway. Peter stopped, backtracked, kicked the wedge of wood from under the propped-open fire door and waited for the door to shut.

'Hey buddy, seen this guy around?' Detective Smith held the mug shot of Cris towards Peter, who was still twenty feet away.

Peter squinted as he got closer. 'Well, maybe—'

Saul interrupted, 'He's a big-money fraudster.'

'Murdering fraudster,' Detective Jones interjected.

'Occasionally murdering, but always, always fraudstering.' Saul did his most subtle mad-dog stare. 'He's got lots of money stashed somewhere.'

Peter stopped. 'Haven't seen him for a while. Always gave me the creeps though—like he's some freak distillation of everything average.'

'Nice.' Detective Jones nodded. 'An insult without insulting any one target group. I could learn from that.'

Detective Smith stared at his partner for a few beats, then turned to Saul. 'Here's my card. Call me if anything comes to mind, 'cause you know, we could just keep coming back. I'm sure all your patrons would really enjoy the added security of having a couple of cops standing by your front desk.'

Saul nodded and watched the detectives leave. Their large wool coats flapped like wings as they pushed out into the cold.

'Jesus fuck!' Charlotte smacked one of her high heels against the side of the tub.

Her date was refusing to follow the script. His naked heel was jammed hard into the drain and his dick bobbed uselessly in the water. Blue lips puckered below the surface.

'You fuckin' piece of shit, motherfucker!' Charlotte added. She took her other high-heeled shoe off and threw it on the tiled floor.

With some effort, Charlotte pulled the man's jammed heel out of the drain and lifted it over the side of the tub. The water drained. Her date remained motionless. Charlotte stalked into the bedroom and shimmied on her clothes.

Peter and Saul stood outside Charlotte's door listening. They could hear someone pacing. Saul hoped it was Charlotte. He tapped lightly on the door as he looked down at the floor. The brass door numbers lay on the carpet with a few screws beside them. Saul looked at Peter. Peter shrugged.

'I had to do something that made it look like I was working,' Peter said. He added, 'And notice how the space left behind on the door looks like the letter B now instead of 13? How cool is that?'

'Charlotte! Are you okay?' Saul bellowed.

The pacing stopped. Slow deliberate steps towards the door.

Charlotte cracked the door open. Her eyes were red and puffy from crying. 'I'm fucked.'

'Great. The business arrangement has been transacted and you can leave with us for the debriefing.' Peter winked while making a cutting motion across his neck with one finger and pointing dramatically past Charlotte with another.

Charlotte stared blankly at him for a few moments then continued, 'No, I'm really fucked.'

Charlotte opened the door all the way and jerked her thumb towards the bathroom. Two feet dangled over the side of the tub, the rest of the body swallowed in the belly of the porcelain beast.

'Did he OD?' Saul asked.

'I don't know. He was supposed to be "pretend" dead, but it looks like he's real dead.'

'Maybe he's still pretending.' Holding the hammer in one hand and the multi-bit screwdriver in the other, Peter advanced towards the bathroom. Saul followed, holding out the walkie-talkie like a weapon — antenna first.

Cris's torso was flat and grey against the bottom of the tub like some large bony bottom-feeding fish. Saul studied Cris's face. It wasn't serene or peaceful. It was blank. Tabula rasa blank.

Peter leaned in and poked the body between the ribs with the screwdriver. A small line of blood bubbled up along the cut. 'Shit. I should have used the Robertson or Phillips head instead of the standard. I don't want the police to think I killed him.'

'That little cut is nothing. You're overreacting.'

'Thanks.'

'Indignity to a human body is what they'd charge you with.'

'Thanks.'

Saul looked over at a neatly folded white T-shirt and black jeans sitting on top of the toilet tank. The man's Blundstones were tucked in behind the door with the gel insoles pulled up like blue tongues. There were no socks.

'He didn't wear socks? It's winter for Pete's sake. That's nutso.' Saul poked around the jeans and shirt. 'Did this guy have a wallet?'

Charlotte came into the bathroom. 'No wallet. No socks. Told me he doesn't like the feeling. Too restrictive. We're all meant to be free.'

'That's crazy talk. Where does he keep his money then?'

'In his pockets. But I took my cut up front. Pay yourself first—that's what the experts say.' Charlotte reflexively touched the slight bulge at the side of her bustier. 'Why you so interested? Shouldn't we be figuring out what to do with the body? Are you gonna call the cops?'

'Eventually.' Saul picked up one of the Blundstones and tipped it upside down. The gel tongue fell out, along with a few hundred-dollar bills and a couple of fifties. Saul emptied the other shoe. A silver key and a slip of notepaper fell to the floor along with another blue tongue. Saul carefully picked up the key, paper, and most of the money. He left the two fifties.

'Gotta leave something or else the cops will think robbery and then they'll be looking for robbers,' Saul offered.

'Do you know where this guy lives, er—lived?' Peter asked.

Charlotte shrugged. 'Some shithole apartment above a store on Gerrard Street. Why?'

'He's a con artist and a murderer. We're interested in the con artist part,' Saul said.

Charlotte started pacing back and forth again, flapping her arms occasionally. 'I gotta get outta here. I got work you know.'

'Sure.' Saul stared at the body in the tub. Track marks pocked along both arms, with blue veins shooting out like chemtrails between each puncture point.

One tattoo.

Over the left breast.

A dream catcher, or a spiderweb with landing gear.

Ink fail.

'What was this guy into?' Saul asked.

'Fantasy stuff. Weird crazy stories where we'd have to dress up and be in character the whole time.'

'Interesting. Did he ever talk about money?' Saul asked.

'A little bit. He was obsessed with cryptocurrencies. Once he wanted me to pretend that I was a super-sexy auditor and he was a Bitcoin money launderer. I was supposed to seduce him into confessing which offshore account he was using, but I fell asleep during his speech on blockchain. We had anal instead.' Charlotte flopped down on the bed and rummaged through her purse. 'They're not gonna arrest us, are they?'

'Certainly not me.' Saul shook his head. 'I only came in *after* the fact and I did not stab the already dead body with a screwdriver — unlike some people. So, I'm good.'

'Okay. This is freaking me out.' Peter handed the hotel's master key to Saul. 'I've got fish to fry. Dreams to catch. And none of them involve going to prison.'

Saul handed the key back to Peter. 'And we will do all of that, and more.'

'Except the going-to-prison stuff.'

'Except the going-to-prison stuff.'

'So, what shall we do with the body?' Charlotte asked.

'Nothing,' Saul replied. 'We leave it as is. Call the police tomorrow morning. In the meantime, I'll go to his apartment and look for his stash.'

'I don't know,' Peter said. 'Kinda risky. What if someone shows up?'

'Who? The guy's a murderous junkie. The people who don't know that fact are probably dead — at his hands. The people who do know are going to keep away.' Saul ushered everyone out the door. 'Pete, you can run the place while I'm gone — a couple of hours tops. Charlotte, you come with me. I'll need a lookout.'

'He's got a cat. I like cats. I'll take the cat,' Charlotte said.

Saul nudged the brass door numbers on the carpet with his foot. 'Hey Pete, maybe put the thirteen back up. Otherwise it'll look like we've been up to something already.'

'Sure thing.'

Charlotte stared into her purse without focus for a few seconds. 'Shit. I think I left my lipstick somewhere.' She pushed past Saul and darted back into the room.

Saul understood. Ounce for ounce, that tiny bullet of colour was more expensive than a decent bottle of scotch.

Unfortunately, no matter how much goes on your face, you can't drink it.

Saul followed to make sure nothing incriminating had been left behind.

'Found it!' Charlotte called out. 'Rolled under the bed. No dust bunnies under there either.'

'As I said before, the room rarely gets used. No skin. No dust. No bunnies.'

Saul stared at the two feet hanging over the tub. One of the big toes seemed to twitch but Saul wasn't sure. He noticed the incandescent bulb above the sink had flickered a bit when they first walked in. A loose element could do that — play tricks on your eyes.

Dead bodies could play tricks too. Muscles contracted. Gas escaped. He had heard a story of a corpse that sat bolt upright on the autopsy table during the dissection.

Still.

Saul waited.

A large bony hand crawled to the lip of the bathtub and sat there, fingers pulsing like a hungry spider.

The fingers tapped rapidly.

A tarantella dance.

'Hey Petey!' Saul called out. 'We need a plan B.'

Standing on the ice-hardened sand, in the middle of Northridge dog park, Benjamin gnawed on a stale bagel and thought about his sorry life — divorced and downsized the same year he hit fifty-four. It was looking to be 'freedom fifty-five' soon, but not in the manner he had expected.

It had been rough.

He was raw.

Worse still, his hair had abandoned him as well.

All his gorgeous locks gone.

All those bad dye jobs and the questionable hair products of his youth.

All for naught.

All gone.

Hello, depression and anxiety.

Albert, a friend in the film business, had turned him on to micro-dosing with LSD. One-tenth of a tab of Blue Heaven diluted in a mug of water every third or fourth day seemed to take the edge off. It also opened his heart and mind.

He looked up at the night sky.

Gauzy grey clouds scudding across flat blackness. Some stars. Not many. A jaundiced sliver of moon smiling.

He opened himself really wide.

A jaundiced sliver of moon
kicking me in the balls
and laughing,
laughing,
laughing.

Benjamin turned his attention to one of the darker corners of the park. His dog—a shaggy, scruffy, buff-coloured Schnoodle named Nia—groused and whined as she scuttled over frozen leaves. It was the last full week of December, but there was very little snow. Benjamin liked the snow. It was the best part of winter, or so he liked to think. He imagined the millions of interlocking crystals that transformed the landscape into quiet brilliance. One could forget all the shit and mud underneath.

His dog preferred the shit and mud underneath. She pulled at something dark and lumpy stuck to the ground.

'Nia, no!' Benjamin barked at his dog.

Nia, like most dogs, ate all manner of disgusting things. There had been a few close calls with her ingesting god knows what, followed by massive vet bills; however, each time, after a few days of ground-up pills hidden in bowls of rice and chicken, Nia would bounce back to life—a four-legged Lazarus.

'Nia! Out! Out!'

Nia really belonged to his ex-wife, who had named the dog as an acronym for her favourite fitness class: Neurologically Integrated Activity. Benjamin attended the class once. It involved a lot of dramatic swooping, sighing, and silk-scarf swirling. It was oddly invigorating and emasculating at the same time.

Nia the dog kept Benjamin the human on a similar leash between opposites: calm and chaos, enjoyment and exasperation.

Thank god the ex-wife had kept the parrot. The parrot was chaos and exasperation only.

'Out!' Benjamin flapped his arms as he bent forward.

Nia scampered away, leaving behind a tufted grey mass of fur and flesh. Benjamin nudged it with his boot and grimaced. It was a dead, dried-out squirrel. Its bedraggled tail stuck up like a bent flagpole.

Behind Benjamin, the firm clank of the gate opening and closing.

Benjamin turned and watched the blur of a large grey Irish wolfhound gallop past.

A familiar voice, 'Hey darlin'.'

The voice, and the ungainly dog, belonged to Benjamin's neighbour, Crystal. She lived in the basement apartment next door to Benjamin's basement apartment. She owned her house but rented out the main floor for extra income.

Benjamin lived in the basement apartment because he did not own a house anymore.

Crystal laughed. 'Only us losers here tonight. I thought you'd be out painting the town. What with your new single status and all.' Crystal was wearing Kodiak winter boots and pink flannel pajama bottoms beneath a full-length Canada Goose parka. She had three new dogs with her.

'I *am* painting the town. It's just a really dull colour,' Benjamin said. He was surprised to see her out here on a Saturday night as well. She was vivacious and outgoing. She should have a fully booked social calendar.

Benjamin ventured, 'Haven't seen you around for a bit. Been away?'

'Oh, I was in Mexico.' Crystal snapped the leashes off the three new dogs—bruising Rottweilers. The dogs galloped over to the squirrel jerky.

'Sounds fun.' Benjamin was about to smile then realized he probably had poppy seeds stuck in his teeth.

'Fun all right.' Crystal stepped closer.

Crystal smelled of alcohol, cigarettes and perfume. Benjamin thought it was a promising combination. She was 'around his age' and had a wicked sense of humour—another promising combination.

'I was at one of them four-star all inclusives. It was fancy for sure. A last-minute deal, with the gals,' Crystal said.

'Sounds super-fun.'

'Super-fun, yeah, though we were too afraid to leave the resort, what with the drug wars raging in the streets. Some yahoos shot up a tour bus the day we arrived, so we missed a tour of a Mayan temple, and a local tequila factory. I was really bummed about missing the tequila factory.'

'That sounds bad,' Benjamin said, while thinking, *That sounds good ... a last-minute deal ... with the gals ... no guys.*

Crystal added, 'Yeah, it had its moments though—kind of like being on lockdown, but with free booze and dancing.'

'I'm glad you're back safe and sound.'

'Thank you, that's sweet.'

'What's with Cerberus?' Benjamin nodded towards the three Rottweilers. They stood guard over the squirrel carcass, their shoulders seemingly fused.

They growled whenever the Wolfhound or Schnoodle approached.

'Payback. They belong to a friend who looked after Molly while I was away.' Crystal's red hair tumbled out from her hood as she pushed it back and lit a cigarette. 'I gotta say, they're well behaved, but they give me the heebie-jeebies. I think they're reading my mind.'

'Dogs are like that. Your face is an open book to them.'

Benjamin exhaled. His breath frosted upwards and quickly dissipated. He thought about the sweeter fog of nicotine and ash.

'Want a smoke?' Crystal shook the package of Belmonts at him like it was a box of candy.

Benjamin studied the picture of a diseased lung on the cover for a split second. 'Sure … it was one of my resolutions to quit but … whatever.'

'So, how's the new digs? Settling in?'

'Great. Living in a basement is just great. Who needs natural light when you've got all the comforts of being buried alive.'

'Oh, you gotta know how to work the illusion — lots of lamps, fake plants, long curtains. All my casement windows got nice thick curtains that hang from the ceiling to the floor. You'd never know you were underground. Did I say lamps? Table lamps, floor lamps, ceiling lights, accent lights. The whole shebang. Light 'er up I say.'

Benjamin wanted to say: *I haven't got a pot light to piss in,* then follow that statement with a string of colourful analogies comparing his ex-wife to a soul-sucking demon, or a chest-crushing snake.

Instead Benjamin said, 'Yeah. Maybe the ex will lend me some lamps that I once owned from the house I once owned.'

Crystal's smiled tightened. 'The ex got a name. Never forget that.'

'Soph — Sophie — ' Benjamin spluttered.

Crystal could turn on a pin — like his ex. It must be the red hair. Benjamin felt aroused and crushed at the same time.

'Oh yeah, and all us women make out like bandits at divorce time, what with all the free houses, cars and stuff. That being said….' Crystal exhaled smoke slowly. 'I mostly only got a mortgage, and a car lease when I got the golden handshake. Oh, and a huge credit card bill — thanks to the ex. I guess I divorced wrong.'

Benjamin stared at the ground unsure of what to say next without digging himself in deeper.

'Yeah, Sophie *was* a good woman, I guess. She had trust issues from a previous relationship.'

'Oh, I guess the sun shone so brightly out of *your* ass she must've been blind to your innate goodness.'

Benjamin thought for a moment, trying to figure out whether that was a put-down or an aggressive compliment.

Benjamin replied, 'In my defence, I wasn't a postie like her old boyfriend who went … um … postal.'

Crystal nudged him. 'Jesus, you are a serious boy.'

'Oh, I thought you were being serious.'

'I joke with a knife — razor wit and all — but I wasn't intending to get at your jugulars.'

Benjamin moved his shoulders and stretched. Tension manifested across his back. It was the price of carrying the weight of the world, real and imagined. 'Yeah, it's a complicated story. Sophie was dating this other guy for a long time — from their university days. He proposed. She got cold feet. He choked out their parrot in revenge.'

'Oh dear!'

'Parrot survived,' Benjamin added without much enthusiasm. 'Anyway, the boyfriend took off. Never heard from again.'

'People who mistreat animals are pure evil. No wonder your ex had trust issues.'

'Yeah, they think the guy might've become a serial killer. Or maybe a victim of one. Apparently, the cops are pretty vague about communicating that kind of stuff. It always seems to be on a need-to-know basis and to them, you don't need to know.'

'Yikes, that's a story for another day. Let's be changing the channel — how's the job hunt going? You did accounting, right? They've got to be clamouring for bean counters. They all love counting their money out here in Toronto.'

'Yeah. It's slow right now. I'm mostly a forensic audit kind of guy … not very popular. Most people want to hide money, not have it discovered.'

'Right on that.' Crystal nodded. 'After Christmas is a lousy time to be looking anyway. Just enjoy the holiday while you're off. Doesn't matter if the glass is half-empty or half-full as long as it's got something in it.'

The Irish wolfhound galumphed past with the bent squirrel tail in its mouth. The other dogs followed.

After a few awkward seconds, Benjamin said, 'I'll drink to that?'

Crystal fiddled with her cigarette, flicking grey ash over the frozen mud.

Silence.

Crystal started again, 'Don't worry, you'll get something. I'd be worried if you actually did a real job. No offence. I mean, at the hospital the high-tech machines are more important than us nurses, and the doctors are always looking over their shoulders. That next big medical app may be a killer.'

'No offence taken,' Benjamin said, a beat too late, but glad to be part of the conversation again.

'Anyway, as I was saying, we're all being replaced by computers. They just need to teach 'em to like shopping and humanity is done for.'

'All hail our robot overlords.' Benjamin blew a giant smoke ring.

'Show-off,' Crystal said.

'It's all in the tongue … and breath.' Benjamin dragged on his cigarette and blew a series of smoke rings, each one floating through the one before. 'The only thing I learned in high school that I can still remember. The phys. ed. teacher showed us during health class.'

'In all my years, I've never been able to get that one down,' said Crystal.

'It's a marketable skill — blowing smoke.' Benjamin stopped and tapped his cigarette. 'In my old job I knew when others were blowing smoke, including my team leader. It probably cost me my job.'

'Yeah, I remember you telling me. I guess knowing that the bosses are cooking the books for a company whose job is to catch other bosses cooking the books is not good PR.'

Benjamin stared ahead. 'I should've kept my mouth shut or chosen my words much more carefully.'

'Words are like eels. A slippery bunch. Sometimes it's best not to let them out.'

Benjamin blew a few more smoke rings. He nodded.

Silence.

'Anyway, it's an awesome night sky,' Crystal said. 'Makes you wonder how we got here and where we're going to. Eh? That whole God thing.'

Benjamin stared off into space. He had been raised in a devout Christian home. Unfortunately, his parents belonged to competing brands. His mom was Catholic. His dad was a Jehovah's Witness. Benjamin didn't like Christianity. The God of the Old Testament was a sucking chest wound of jealousy and anger. The New Testament Jesus was a flesh-coloured bandage.

In the beginning, one of those triune bastards had blown smoke up Adam's ass, and now everyone was paying for it.

A spark from his cigarette arced through the air and glimmered into nothing.

Benjamin remembered that dreamers got laid. Cynics, not so much.

'I'm just a divine spark who has lost his way,' Benjamin said and he winked.

Crystal laughed. 'Oh, you are a smoothie.'

She nudged his elbow and changed tone. 'Listen, I'm having a few friends over to watch *Downton Abbey* at sevenish tomorrow. Come over and we'll drink out of fancy glasses, laugh at the chuckleheads and pretend we're the ones living on the up and up.'

'And not in the basement.'

'Amen to that.'

Nia whined at the gate.

'I'll bring treats from home,' Benjamin said. The words muffled into his scarf as he bent over to hook Nia back up to her leash.

Treats? I've been talking to my dog too much, thought Benjamin as he turned to go and waved to Crystal.

Crystal waved back.

Benjamin began the slow walk home, replaying the conversation in his head. He had scored some funny comments but whining about his ex-wife and ex-job had probably shaved a few points off the total score. He would be more upbeat and dynamic next time.

He thought a few moments. He would drink a cup of strong coffee *before* the party and then limit himself to one or two glasses of wine *at* the party. The acid should be out of his system by then as well.

At the corner of Benlamond and Trinity, Benjamin glimpsed something shiny under a bush. He stepped towards it.

Nia was having none of it. Benjamin had already mentioned 'treats' and 'home' in the same sentence.

Nia's small sinewy legs scrabbled forward on the cement. Her neck strained against the collar.

'Nia, stop!'

Nia redoubled her efforts.

Benjamin redoubled his volume.

'NIA, STOP!'

Nia stopped.

Yelling at his dog always made Benjamin feel like an idiot shouting at a moron. Benjamin had read somewhere that the average dog had the same vocabulary as a two-year-old child. Simple words worked well. Simple words shouted at the top of your lungs worked best.

Nia refused to move: front legs extended, back legs bent. Benjamin let the line out and walked the length without her.

Sticking out from the frozen mud, decayed leaves, and scatterings of frost was a toy space gun.

Benjamin whistled. 'Awesome.'

Benjamin's inner ten-year-old gushed: *Super-freakin' awesome.*

Benjamin reached down and pulled the toy out.

He brushed the dirt off.

He hefted it. It felt more substantial than a kid's toy. The cylindrical metal barrel was more gunmetal grey than shiny-tin silver. The red lights were hard and crystalline, not plastic.

This must be vintage or a movie prop. They're always filming in the neighbourhood. His friend Albert was always going on about how the area was so much like Connecticut but without the annoying Americans. Albert bragged about knowing which house they filmed Black Christmas *in years ago. The set decs purposely left the rocking chair behind in the attic when they struck the set. Apparently it was cursed. Props sometimes took on a life of their own.*

Benjamin pulled the trigger, expecting to hear an oscillating whir accompanied by flashing red lights.

Nothing.

Then...

The toy gun vibrated gently.

Tiny blue circles pulsed out from the nozzle and expanded into translucent, ephemeral smoke rings. They drifted towards his dog.

His dog looked at him, looked at the smoke rings, looked back at him. Her big brown eyes were saucer-like.

Benjamin felt a ripple of nausea.

Nia's ears flattened.

You moron.

A voice somewhere in the dark.

Benjamin scanned the street.

Empty.

The rings oscillated around his dog. Benjamin blinked as Nia blurred at the edges.

You stupid fucking moron.

That voice again, fading as Nia faded.

Nia was gone.

Benjamin walked the length of Nia's leash to the empty pink collar. His brain lit up, then collapsed into dull, flat blackness. His thoughts were grey scudding clouds. He looked down at his left hand. It was blue and melding into the gun.

Ring around the rosey. A pocket full of poesy.

Acid, acid. We all fall down.

Against his better judgement, or against any form of judgement, Benjamin returned to the dog park to see if Crystal could help him find Nia. As he hop/jogged along, the 'toy gun' broke from his hand and fell to the ground. He stooped to grab it, staring at his distorted reflection in the chrome barrel.

You are one helluva handsome devil — even with poppy seeds between your teeth.

Benjamin stumbled onward to the park gate.

Inside, the three Rottweilers rested on their haunches, guarding the dead squirrel.

'Crystal!' Benjamin called out, using his most melodious voice. It sounded a little creepy.

He scanned the rest of the park. Along the southern perimeter, a gaping black hole where a new condo was going in. No one had been sad to see the old building torn down. The St. Eliot motel had a lot of horrific stories associated with it, including a couple of murders.

To the north, the children's park: three swing sets, two teeter-totters, one enormous slide. Shadows everywhere. Metal glinting under the streetlamps.

It was all very magical, and very empty.

'Crystal!'

'Chill bro,' one of the Rottweilers interrupted. 'Crystal will be back. She had to take care of some business.'

Benjamin looked from one jowly, blunt face to the other. All three remained implacably Buddha-like. No lips moved.

And yet Benjamin could hear them.

'I think you got a chance. It's in her face,' one voice said.

'You gotta be more confident,' another voice said.

'A little vulnerability is okay, but don't overdo it,' a third voice said.

Benjamin was balancing on a tight-rope of conflicting advice … from dogs.

'Otherwise you're a wuss.' The third voice again.

'And a wuss don't get no puss.'

The three Rottweilers howled.

Benjamin didn't know why the dogs were talking with a Brooklyn accent.

More importantly, Benjamin didn't know why the dogs were talking.

'What do you suggest?' Benjamin asked.

The three dogs looked at each other.

'Tell her a story. Bitches love stories, even if they don't really believe them. It's how they fall in love.'

'Isn't "bitches" a little harsh and derogatory?' Benjamin asked. 'It is 2019, after all.'

'I am a bitch. The real deal. I own it.'

Benjamin couldn't argue with that logic.

'What about Nia?' Benjamin asked. 'Where is Nia?'

'Everywhere and nowhere. Dogs are like gods: helpful at times, a hindrance at others, destined to bite the hand that feeds them.'

Benjamin nodded. Sage words.

He would remember those sage words when it came time to explain to his ex-wife about the ex-dog.

Or not.

At the far end of the park, by the construction site, Crystal emerged from a porta-john. She untethered the Irish wolfhound from a nearby post and walked towards Benjamin.

She lit up a cigarette.

Benjamin looked up at the night sky. The clouds were clearing. Sirius, the dog star, was glimmering: blue, white, red-purple. People sometimes mistook Sirius for a UFO.

It was not a UFO.

It was a star.

A winking star.

'Where's your furry little friend?' Crystal nodded towards the dog leash clutched in Benjamin's fist.

'I don't know.'

'You don't know?'

'I don't know.' Benjamin held up the toy gun with his other hand, pinching the barrel between thumb and forefinger and angling the barrel away from himself and Crystal.

'I found this instead.'

'A stick?'

Benjamin looked down. He was holding a stick.

It was shaped like a Y.

A gnarly Y.

He was holding the business end of a dowsing rod.

The three Rottweilers clustered close to the gate and barked at the stick.

Drool and spittle flecked onto the frozen ground.

Benjamin noticed that each animal, along with its dog tag, had a crystal charm attached to its collar: amethyst, quartz, garnet.

The charms glinted like stars.

Crystal followed Benjamin's gaze. 'We're all stardust, just like the song says. Born in the belly of a supernova and ass-kicked across the universe with only a short story to tell. Not much sense. Just pure magic.'

'Did Joni Mitchell say all that?'

'Carl Sagan put his two cents in for sure.'

Benjamin looked around the park again: at the overwhelming darkness, at the pinpoints of starlight and the wash of streetlamp light, at the dogs, at the dead squirrel, at Crystal.

'What about Nia?' he asked.

Crystal ignored the question. 'I read in one of them fancy holy books during my university days something about acting without being attached to the outcome of your actions. Krishna said it—over and over again, to some dude who was about to go to war against family, friends, and strangers. My daddy put it a little more bluntly: shit happens, carry on.'

'Harsh.'

'Harsh ain't the least of it, but lookit, I get that you're a little freaked out. We all need a little something or someone to hold on to.' Crystal seemed to tower over Benjamin for a moment as she reached deep into a side pocket. Benjamin reflexively crouched.

The three Rottweilers growled.

Benjamin looked at them. He was on their level. Their jowly, blunt snouts pressed up against the fence, breathing into his face, growling, growling, growling.

Benjamin felt a noose wrap around his neck and tighten with a *click*.

A collar.

The leash extended upwards into the dark, into the hands of Crystal.

Crystal winked.

Benjamin felt safe.

This was the end and the beginning.

ACKNOWLEDGEMENTS

Whereas writing a story can be a solitary endeavour, writing and publishing a book is a communal effort. I would like to acknowledge and thank Tim and Elke Inkster of the Porcupine's Quill for saying yes when they could easily have said no. I would like to acknowledge and thank Stephanie Small, also of the Porcupine's Quill, who has provided wit, knowledge, and support as I navigate this new territory. Above all, I am indebted to editor Chandra Wohleber, who helped me craft this book and without whom it would not exist. I also thank mentors Will Ferguson, Paul Quarrington, and Antanas Sileika.

A special shout-out to David Moses and Mike Rueckert, who gave me advice about the story 'Ghost Note' and some of its Indigenous characters, and to Joel Wasnicky, who is a friend and not a serial killer.

A very sincere thanks to my co-workers and the people on my mail route. You brighten my day and illuminate the importance of community.

And remember: any resemblance to actual events or places or persons, living or dead, is entirely coincidental.

I dedicate this book to Nancy, Nate, and Lydia, whom I love and cherish always.

ABOUT THE AUTHOR

DANIEL BRYANT was born in Montreal and grew up in the small town of Aurora, Ontario. He graduated from York University with an Honours B.A. in English and received the Timothy Findley/William Whitehead Scholarship to attend the Humber School for Writers Correspondence Program. He has mentored with Paul Quarrington and Will Ferguson. *Rerouted* is his first collection of short stories. When not writing, Dan has worked many jobs: at a large printing company, a tannery, a tart factory, and on a film crew. He currently works for Canada Post as a letter carrier. He lives in Toronto with his wife, Nancy.